SWANN

by DAN SHERMAN

ARBOR HOUSE

NEW YORK

SWANN

Also by Dan Sherman

RIDDLE
THE MOLE

And the seven thin and ill favoured kine that came up after them are seven years; and the seven empty ears blasted with the east wind shall be seven years of famine.

GENESIS 41:27

SWANN

CHAPTER 1

ALLEN CASSIDY stood on the gleaming black and white tiles, a thin cigar hung in his fingers. "I'd say that when it's over you should take a bit of time off in Rio. Have you ever been there, John?"

"No, sir, but I've heard about it." John Donne was a short, stalky boy. Everyday he lifted weights, but what did one do with muscles in Mr. Cassidy's drawing room?

"Oh, I know what they say about leaving the country after a job, but make a nice, clean sweep of it, and I don't think there will be any harm in taking a few days off in the sun." Cassidy leaned on the marble mantel. His brandy went sloshing up the sides of his snifter. "And buy yourself a girl if you like."

Through the iron filigree on the frosted glass, past the boxwood shrubs, John looked down and saw a leashed black poodle squatting on the strip of lawn. "Yes, sir, I'll do that," John returned, and then dropped his eyes because maybe it wasn't right to talk about these things with Allen. After all, hadn't it been Allen who had known

1

straight off that John's mother had named him for a poet whom she had never understood? Even now John could remember the feel of Cassidy's arm around his shoulder and his breath in his ear as he chanted, *Go and catch a falling star . . . tell me where all the past years are, or who cleft the devil's foot.*

Cassidy tapped an ash into the crystal tray. He was a tall, lean man with deep lines in his face. He wore his clothing well, and now especially, an elbow posed on the marble cornice, the blanched light through the folded shutters, he may never have been more the definitive gentleman spy. For this final chat with his below-the-line agent, Allen chose his English tweed, while his shirt of pale blue silk gently accented a tie woven in stripes of a darker shade. "They tell me that there comes a time when a man in the field wants a girl."

John's own tie was choking him. The buttons of his shirt were straining. His polyester jacket was digging into his arm pits. "Yes," he mumbled, "sometimes you'll want a girl."

"And they're lovely in Rio. Get yourself some tawny lady. It's an experience you shouldn't miss." Cassidy sucked in his cheeks and blew out smoke. His lips were glossy and contented. Then he slowly shook his head and smiled, smiling perhaps into a vision of his own youth. They said that years ago, when Allen was operational in Europe he had been famous for his string of bedroom agents. Had the Russians with their pants down, and the Germans before them; that was what they said about Dancing Allen Cassidy.

"But I was wondering about one thing," John stuttered. His face was flushed. He had never dreamed that Dancing Allen would ever admit him to the inner sanctum of the CIA.

2

"Yes, what was that, John?" Cassidy's eyebrows raised, and his head cocked slightly to the side. Now he was the perfect father again, understanding and judicious, because in the trade a father and son relationship was held to be the strongest bond between agent and case officer. Only how could the erudite Allen Cassidy ever have sired such a rude pig as Donne?

"I was wondering about what I asked you the other day." Donne stared at his own thick wrists.

"What was that, John?"

"Well, it was about Josey Swann." On the shelf of a Hepplewhite bookcase, behind the small blue squares of glass, a tiny ballerina stood. John's eyes were fixed on the bone china arm flung carelessly above her head.

"What's this? Swann?" Cassidy blinked.

Donne felt very much the thick kid in his awkward suit. His ears were on fire. "But I thought maybe he could come down with me. You know, to run interference? He wouldn't be any trouble."

Cassidy clicked his tongue. "I realize that Josey is a friend of yours, but I'm afraid he's too unreliable."

Donne was staring at the rim of his own glass. He had hardly touched the brandy. He was a beer man. "But he could help me, you know? Josey's okay, really he is."

Then came Cassidy's secret smile, and he spun his snifter by its stem. "There are some men in whom the intelligence community has a great deal of faith. You're one of them, John." Cassidy's head was bowed to the chess board floor. "Josey, on the other hand, does not inspire such faith. Oh, he's fine for some of the more . . . how shall I say, coarser work? Yes, he's appropriate for that sort of thing. But here, I really don't think he'd be right. Now, don't misunderstand me. I personally like Josey. He's one of a kind. He's a very interesting boy, and, of course, he

3

can be exceptionally good. They tell me he has phenomenal timing. Fast as lightning and without the ensuing thunder, that's Josey Swann. But frankly, John, I think that Josey lacks the vision. You have the vision, but Josey, that's another matter. Yes, vision, John, do you understand what I mean by the word 'vision'?"

ALL THROUGH the weeks of preparation John Donne had been given visions. He was soothed with stories of printless white sand, warm, glittering sea, and dark-eyed native girls swaying to the samba. He was plied with nudges and winks which gave him the impression that he had finally been admitted to the fraternal community of gentlemen spies. He was wooed and coddled, humored and flattered. But in the end, he found that Cassidy had screwed him. Because when John reached Brazil, all that he found were the shadows.

Sao Paulo was an industrial city, mean and sultry. There were long blocks of blackened factories, and narrow streets where twisted iron balconies hung from the dead walls of sooty bricks. Even the better sections were oppressive. The boulevards ran between canyons of high-rises, and the rag-tag intensity of the traffic never stopped.

Now John stood in the shadows. These were cast by sandstone arches and white plaster eaves that walled him into the slum. In places, the tarmac had worn down revealing the older cobblestones of red clay. All around were the crumbling, baroque facades of colonial tenements.

To this street came the sounds of old Brazil. Someone was singing. The soft, Portuguese syllables were running together in sandpaper breaths. There was the syncopated clip of a steel drum and the haunting trill of wooden flute.

For three nights John stood on this street. Sometimes he took the north-east corner under a blue tiled stairway.

4

Other nights he hung in the gutter beneath the groin of an archway. Brackish water fell on his shoulder, drop by drop. Waiting was part of the run. Each night he saw the target drive past in a red Volkswagen, back from his office in the heart of the city. At one point John had even considered making the hit here, among the rat-trap dwellings of Sao Paulo's working class. But he junked that plan in favor of a wide open ambush along the final stretch of the target's route.

It was half past. The street lamps were sputtering. John heard the agony of the grinding gears. He checked his wristwatch as the Volkswagen rattled by. Now all preparations had come to an end. Tomorrow, he thought, you go. The courting was over. Tomorrow night, same time, he would be waiting in the grass by the edge of the highway to kill the man.

But twenty-four hours was a long time for a blown agent to drag himself through the field. Not that John was sure he was blown, but the signs were there. Earlier that day he had caught the glimpse of a tall, thin man walking behind. In the rippling glass of a storefront window he had seen the watery reflection of two women floating at his rear. Even the bellboy in the lobby of his hotel had given him a bit too much of the eye, although no one was supposed to have used bellboys anymore.

But now on the dark, ugly street he felt fairly alone. That did not mean that he was alone, not if they were any good. Half way down the block a ragged gang of mulattos were jiving to the clap of their hands and a small steel drum. Their shadows were jittering against the stone and graffiti. John crossed the street, which was what any good tourist would have done. What was the point of traveling if you ignored the local color?

5

He passed dank factories that smelled of oil and burned meat. Once he thought he heard the slap of a leather sole behind him, but when he turned there was nothing but the unreal vision of an empty street dipping into the gloom.

He was wandering. A rank, brick alley let out into one of the larger boulevards, and he moved into the crowds of night shoppers. There were mobs of people dressed in dacrons and doubleknits. They converged at corners, waited, and then surged out between the lines of cars and buses. A whiff of music snaked up from a basement club and then became lost in the squeal of brakes and whining horns.

Outside of his hotel he saw the makings of what might very well have been a classic formation. There were two men in wrinkled suits chatting on the steps. Across the way a woman was staring into the glass of a jewelry store. These three would have been the forward team. He had no idea where the others might have been. But then, maybe there were no others, which meant that he had been dreaming from the start.

Into the revolving doors of his hotel, John was horribly conscious of his soggy arm pits and clammy back. The two men on the steps hadn't so much as looked up when John passed, but that proved nothing. The best spotters never looked directly at you.

John flinched. There was a hand clutching his elbow. He spun and turned into the sly grin of the bellboy. "How about that action?" The bellboy was leaning into John's ear, cap falling over one eye. "You want some action, maybe?"

John couldn't tear himself away. The bellboy was clinging. "No, not tonight, thanks," Donne muttered.

"Okay, but I got something for you. Mmmmmm! She's nice. You sure you don't want it?" Then the bellboy's sleepy eyes were suddenly wide. "Oh, maybe you want to go the other way, okay? Maybe you want a nice little boy. I can get you a nice little boy. Hey, is that it?"

"No, really, I'm fine, all right?" John pulled his arm away and picked up his pace.

"But you let me know when, okay?" the bellboy called after him.

"Will do," John smiled, and the corners of his mouth were twitching.

Chances were John's room had not been searched, not at least by any dumb shit Brazilian team. The Brazilians, like all the spics, were just not that good. And they would have had to have been good to make a clean search of John's room. First there were the heads of matches stuck in the jamb. Everyone used some sort of wedge, but for John they were only first line. Guy comes in, sees the match heads and thinks he's clear. All he's got to do is replace them on the way out. But John had another trick. Before he left a room he always ran his hand across the carpet, ruffled up the shag so that it would retain any footprint. However, both match heads and carpet were just as he had left them. So either the room had not been touched, or else he was up against some very professional talent. No third world counter intelligence group was on to Johnny Donne. If you're being followed, he told himself, then this is the major leagues.

The rest of the night went badly. He made a mess of a meal they brought him on a silver trolley. Some agents ate when they were scared, John never could. Around midnight he fell into bed, tossed in the sheets for an hour, and finally dropped away to a patchy sleep. Sometime later he awoke and heard tangled voices murmuring in the hall outside the door. A quick hit of fear sent him scrambling to the window. Then naked, drenched in perspiration, he

7

slowly drew the curtains back. But there was no one lingering in the streets below, no flickering shadow under the cone of dirty yellow light, no telltale van with blacked out windows and too much antenna.

Cold, aching, he dragged himself back to bed and dozed until dawn when he rose with the fragments of a dream still simmering in his head. There had been something about a cat. He had seen the creature flattened against the gutter, licking at a lump of rancid meat. Then the cat had turned into Josey Swann so that John awoke with his friend's name on his lips.

ARMING IN the field: Langley teachers said it was the worst way to go, especially when the dealer was one of Cassidy's shiftier stringers. Donne met Cassidy's man in a bar, three blocks from the police station. The place was dark and muggy, and filled with lots of local talent. They were mostly off-duty cops, but word was that for a price they would do anything.

The dealer's name was Dante Mescal. He was a short, wiry mulatto with two gold teeth up front. He made a point of telling Donne that he had lost the teeth when a woman hit him in the mouth with a bottle. For some reason John thought the man was lying, probably lost his teeth in a fight.

There were nudie pinups on the wall, and a television blaring above the bar. Donne bought Mescal a drink, although had this been a first class run it would have been the other way around. They took a booth and began shuffling into business, shuffle because Langley instructors said shuffle when you weren't sure, so John was talking in circles.

"We have a mutual friend," Donne said.

"Sure, I know all about it," Mescal grinned. His eyes

were flitting all over the bar.

"He told me to contact you because you might be able to supply me with something that I need."

"Sure," Mescal tossed out the word. "You're Allen Cassidy's boy."

"Yeah," Donne said. "I'm his friend."

"Oh hell, everyone is Allen's friend."

"So can you?"

"Can I what?"

"You know, supply me with what I need." John was rattling the ice in his glass, rattling like broken teeth. "See, Allen said I could pick something up from you."

Mescal began drumming his fingers on the table. "Buy, friend, not pick up. You got to buy."

"Yeah, well I got the bread."

Mescal stuck his pinky in his nose. "What kind of bread? What's the color, you know?"

"American, small bills."

The Brazilian squinted and shook his head. "Sure, but I like local money, you know? Easier to deal with local money. Don't you have any local stuff?"

John opened his hands for a small appeal. "I haven't had time to get the money changed. I've been busy."

"I'm sure you have, friend, but I like local money, okay?" Mescal softly whistled through the gap in his teeth.

"But I've got to pick up the goods today. I don't have time to change the money." John was speaking to his glass.

"All right, friend, but I'm doing you a favor, okay?"

John nodded. "Thanks. I appreciate this." The Langley teachers were right, this was definitely the worst way to go.

"Okay, you got a car?"

"Yeah," Donne said. He had a red Pinto. He had rented

9

it that morning. The girl behind the Hertz counter had given him a hard time.

"Okay, we ride to my warehouse." Then Mescal downed his drink like the hardcore boozer that he probably was.

Ten minutes later they stood in the thick heat of Mescal's garage. There were cardboard boxes piled in the corners. Packing confetti was littered on the concrete floor. Mescal pulled at the flaps of a sealed box he had dragged out. Then, with a spray of newspaper shredding, he lifted a rifle out of the box.

"Not this," Donne said. He wouldn't even touch the thing. "I want something fully automatic."

Mescal ran his hand along the barrel. "Ah no, this is a fine piece. This is much cleaner than any machine gun. Come on, just hold this in your hands."

But John shook his head. "Automatic. I want an automatic weapon."

"Okay, tough guy." Mescal dropped the rifle back into the box. "I've got an automatic for the tough guy. You just take a look at what I got here." He scampered up a pyramid of boxes and returned with an M16. "How about this, tough guy? It's never been fired. See, it's still in the original grease."

John held the weapon in his arms. He pressed his cheek against the smooth, warm metal, and sighted into a wedge of dusty light, streaming through the window slats. "Yes," he whispered. "This will do just fine," and finally smiled at last.

"Yeah, you like this one, tough guy? Uh?" Mescal slapped his thighs and spat. "Uh? You tell me now. Is that the gun for a tough guy or isn't it?"

10

TOUGH GUY: if John could only believe in that person, but he didn't feel tough, not in the fetid heat of the afternoon. The pavement might have been melting, the windows of the storefronts steaming away. He drove fast and made erratic turns at the oddest corners, because that was the only method he knew to lose tails. Not that his tail was any more tangible now, but knowing that an unregistered M16 was buried in the trunk made him hustle.

The rest of the day he spent in his room. For a while he tried to sleep, but the sheets grew alive with his sweat and tried to strangle him. So he began to pace, glancing out the window, listening at the door. It had never been this bad.

It was fully dark when he reached the highway. He drove until he came to a clean stretch of road that gave him an open line. On either side of the pavement high grass afforded good cover. There was also the crucial bend which meant that the target would have to slow down. By anyone's book the spot was a classic.

John's wait was also classic. He was the Langley man in the grass, watching for lights on the highway, watching the second hand sweep round the luminous dial. If only he were as good at the wait as Josey. Now there was a guy who knew how to move in the night. Invisible—that was Josey Swann.

But John wasn't looking too bad himself, not when that red Volkswagen came slowing through the curve. He took one long breath, and began to squeeze. He didn't just squeeze the trigger. He squeezed his whole hand, just like they had taught him years and years ago. Then the M16 was kicking in the crook of his arm, fire flashing from the muzzle. The first burst tore off the wheel and sent the Volkswagen into a skid. Sparks flew out. Silver shards of

11

glass glinted and sprayed off into the dark. He fired again. The car screamed into the shoulder, bucked and finally settled on its side.

Close, but no cigar. That was what they used to say in Vietnam when the bodies were still twitching. Then some poor joker had to go out and kick the heads one by one. John had always hated cleanup work, but it had to be done. So he rose from the grass, brushed the mud from his knees and walked to the wreck of the car.

One look and he moaned, pressed his hand to his mouth and turned away. The man inside the twisted car was still alive. A bullet had severed his arm at the elbow, but the eyes, glazed and questioning, were still staring up through the shattered glass. John moved back, gagging. His fingers were fumbling to reload. Before he emptied this second clip into the wreck, he caught one quick vision of blood coming up from the dying man's lips.

JOHN WOULD have had the night swallow him, suck him up into some safe neutral void. Instead, he felt very out of touch with the rhythm of the run. Every run had its rhythm. It was just a question of getting into the groove. But now John's only groove was the straight, black road which led to the city. The road followed the drift of the hills and the lay of the land. John might have been traveling on a midnight sea, for all the comfort that highway gave him. The vague mountains that humped in the distance were like the swell of waves about to toss him into oblivion.

He drove fast until he saw the city. Sao Paulo was adrift with lights, purple and red. John drifted with them. Sometimes ruts in the road twisted and pulled at the tires. Once he hit an oil slick and nearly lost control. He was moving through the valley of slum tenements and cheap shops filled with the dusty junk that no one ever bought.

His hotel seemed to have changed on him. He had gone out, killed a man, and now the damn hotel was trying to turn his head around. Small details looked different. That potted plant in the lobby had never seemed so big. The thing was nearly spreading across the ceiling. And what about the walls? Now they had a sickening yellow pall to them.

At the door to his room, John dropped to one knee and ran his fingers along the jamb. The heads of the matches were still in place, thank God. But the key wouldn't fit the lock. Maybe he had the wrong room, and he actually glanced up at the number before it hit him. How could he have had the wrong room if he had just felt the match heads? Unless the place was filled with . . . *pull yourself together.*

The key turned with a double click. How many nights have you dreamed you heard that sound and then sprang out of bed and reached for your gun? The door swung open, and John reached for the lightswitch. The lamps flooded on. He paused in the threshold. Then he saw the footprint on the patch of rucked-up shag. Someone had been there, he thought, and saw the flicker of a shadow in the bathroom.

John was already turning, stretching out his hand to the wall to swing himself back to the hall. But the figure emerged from the bathroom, bent and lowered a revolver. There was a muffled thump from a silenced barrel. The force and shock spun John around, but he didn't go down. He scrambled back down the hall, reached the stairs and stumbled down two flights to the lobby. Heads turned as he reeled by, holding his chest, doubled over in the frantic neon. Then he was crashing back through those revolving doors, staggering down the pavement, struggling for the keys to his car.

He drove aimlessly, punching the accelerator and riding the brakes. He drove down twisted streets until he came to a jerking stop beneath a shriveled tree. The gutter was flooded from a backed-up drain.

Where he sat now there were no people, no moon and no lights. The sky above was an unbroken, dark blue sheet. The night was complete. He dabbed at the wound with the torn off tail of his shirt. There was not much pain. Nor was the bleeding as bad as all that, or at least he had been through worse. Yeah, keep telling yourself that, chummy. Keep telling yourself that you've been through worse, but if you sit like this for another few hours, sure as hell you're going to bleed to death.

He had no options, none at all. There was Cassidy's punk at the embassy, and no one else. His passport was blown. There was a bullet in his chest, and Josey was two thousand miles away. But if Josey were only here now. You could believe in Josey. Whatever the assholes like Cassidy said about him was bullshit. Josey Swann had it together. John was sure of that. After all, John had actually seen Swann's moves in the night.

CHAPTER 2

SINCE TIME had collapsed on the wreck that was Josey's life it seemed that the memories of war would never settle. They leapt out at him. They tried to drag him down. Everywhere he looked there was something to remind him.

Sometimes when the blob of the sun swung low in the evenings, Josey had to tell himself that the war was over. It was the sunlight gouging through the tops of the buildings that might have been the hills of the jungle. It was backed-up filth in the atmosphere glowing orange and red. Columns of burning napalm had looked the same. But the war *was* over. Everyone said it was over. So, then, why did it keep on raging inside the head of Josey Swann?

At some point during the war Josey had an interesting cognition. He realized that he was dead. He was not dead like Hunter Jack was dead, splattered all over the elephant grass by mortar shell. (They found his dog tags hanging in the branches of a tree.) Nor was he dead like Happy Dick, who had been stabbed in the spine and would be numb and cold for the rest of his miserable life. They were the obvious dead. Swann's death was subtler. It was an equivocal death, a death that particularly snickered at life. The soul was dead, and what a strange manner of being dead was that!

Anyone might have said that he was alive. "Well, I'm not," he used to tell Kim. "You can't understand because you're alive, and life is the mirror. But I know. I'm the original: dead."

"All right," she would laugh. "So you're dead," and that proved that she did not understand. Only the others like himself understood. And there were a lot of them. Josey had seen hundreds in the Nam. Most had been young, eighteen, nineteen years old. However, their lives had backed up on them so that whole decades were smeared into their faces. The landscape behind their eyes was as ragged and desolate as the face of the moon. Many had difficulty speaking, and most, like Josey, could not sleep without Valium, although they were tired all the time.

Josey got into drugs after he saw his first death. It had been in Saigon, the start of it all. There was good killing going on along the horizon. The muffled thump of mortar fire was rolling in from two hundred miles away. The edge of the sky had been glowing red for three days.

There were four known Vietcong sapper units in the Saigon-Cohlon area. The week Josey arrived two kids from the boonies were beheaded. A tiger lady succubus rode the streets on a Vespa, blowing away grunts with a silver .45. (She had stolen the piece from a general.) An M.P. finally stopped her by pinning her against a wall with his jeep. Josey watched as the M.P. popped the clutch again and again until the woman was pulverized into the bricks.

16

Drinks all around.

But drinks made nothing acceptable, so Josey began to do dope. They were handing it out like candy anyway. Medics recommended Dexedrine for the night, and then Quaaludes to smooth out the trail. Guys were dropping them by the fistful.

"They give you the range for the jungle," an old grunt once told Swann. But the man's tongue had been like a snake, snapping and striking against his teeth. He couldn't stop talking. Even alone he muttered to himself, "Hail Mary . . . Pray for war."

In the end, Josey, too, began to pray for war. He had no conscious prayer, but he was lapping up the wasted horror better than any of them. He was probably the only one who knew that it was an Irish poet who said, "God give us war in our time," the only one who had studied Goya's prints of the French atrocities. Yet he also knew that literature and history were no substitute for experience. So Josey became a LURP.

LURPs—Long-range recon patrolers. They had their own war, and like vampires, they fought it all at night. When the sun plunged behind the shaggy tangles of hills, Josey would paint his face with night-fighter cosmetic, and slide out into the jungle. This, then, was how he killed; being one with the shadows, as faceless and quiet as a dead branch. Vines snaked around his legs, receiving him as part of the jungle that he hated. When Charlie came he took them down silently, knifing them to the rotten bed of leaves from whence the forest sprang.

By the last few days of the war Josey was shattered. He could not sleep without barbiturates. Food appeared gray and insipid. Once in Saigon he bought a girl. Later in her shabby room he walked to the dresser. There were mosquitoes floating in the porcelain bowl. Her head on the pillow was a greasy, black lump. He had not been able to make love. He had only gone through the motions. He gazed into the mirror above the dresser. Then he whispered, "I'm dead," and finally saw the vacant ghost that was he, hovering behind the membrane of his eyes.

When the war was over, Josey was something of a hero. In certain quarters they even called him a legend. They gave him medals. He brought the medals home with him, and put them away. He had forgotten exactly where. He never showed them to any of his neighbors in his apartment building. He never took them down to the local bar where he was occasionally known to drink. In fact, Josey rarely spoke to anyone. Those that lived on the borders of his life had no idea that Josey had brought home the medals, just as they had no idea that he had brought home the war.

That was what it was called; bringing the war back home. For most who had been over there and had every ounce of humanity sucked out of them it was just a state of mind. Josey, however, took things one step further. He went to work for the Central Intelligence Agency, the Company as it was called, and he fought the war for real.

It was all just one war. They would send him out to spike some target and it was really no different than it had been in Nam nailing the enemy to the rice paddy walls. It didn't matter where he was—Paris, Hong Kong, Berlin, Madrid—it was all the same. He had never left the jungle, probably never would.

On the first impression Josey did not look like a killer. He was a handsome man with delicate features. He had blond hair that fell with an easy curl over his collar. But then there were his eyes. His eyes told the whole story, because looking into Josey's eyes was like looking into forty fathoms of clear water to a dead, sandy bottom.

It was fairly common knowledge among the other Company stringers that Swann was out of his mind. But like everything else about Josey, he was only quietly mad. You could miss the madness if you didn't look too closely. But then don't let him catch you looking too closely, they would say. You can never tell what Josey Swann will do.

Which was precisely what Lyle Severson was wondering as he climbed the steps to Josey's apartment.

Swann lived in a flat, gray building. It was one in a block of many. Further south were the slums, but where Josey lived they called it the borderline. The street may not have been littered and devastated by the wasted droppings of impoverished lives, but it was bad enough. The facade of the building was molded plaster, chipped in places, peeling in others. Garbage was piled in an adjoining alley. There were broken toys, a plastic chair, a crapped-out sofa; all the cheap and nasty junk that was gone before a season.

Lyle could not understand why Josey chose to live where he did. It wasn't as if Josey could not have afforded better. Severson knew what the Company paid the boy. But, then, perhaps Josey somehow needed a place like this, a place as ragged and desolate as the landscape in his eyes.

There was no door to the building, just a concrete entrance with trash on the step. The stairs moaned as Severson climbed. There were whiskey voices coming from the walls, the throb of rhythm and blues. Josey lived in room nineteen.

The door to his room was sour green, half glazed, and one of the numerals was missing. Lyle knocked once, then twice, then over and over. Finally the door pulled back, and there was Josey slouched and scowling in the threshold.

"I couldn't hear you, man," he mumbled, and then ran a dirty hand across his face. He wore blue jeans and a

19

stained white shirt. The tails were out, and the cuffs undone. He hadn't shaved, and his eyes, heavy and dull from not enough sleep or too much dope, were nailing Severson to the floor.

Lyle had no doubt, that in his way, Josey hated him. It was nothing personal. Josey hated all the old line Company men. They didn't know shit about the jungle, Swann had once said, and Lyle had to admit that it was true. Unless one said that the CIA was a kind of jungle, what with the next man's loyalty as tangled as any jungle vines. But still, the gap between Lyle and the ones like Swann was immense. Severson was tall and thin. He had a respectable head of even gray hair. He dressed with care. He looked very out of place in the doorway of Swann's apartment.

"May I come in?" Severson asked. The question might have startled Josey.

"Yeah," Swann sighed. "Come in." He led the way into the horrid, little room. There was clumsy, flowered furniture that bulged at the sides and sagged in the seats. The armchair was riddled with cigarette burns. Bits of gray stuffing were blistering out between the seams. It was oppressively hot. The flimsy, yellow curtains hung in the dead, still air.

Josey cleared away a stack of yellowed newspaper that he had never read, and gave the man a seat on the sofa. "I've got something in the oven. I've got to turn it off," Swann muttered.

"Sure, Josey. But if you're about to have lunch, if this is a bad time . . ."

But Josey's lunch was a wretched frozen thing in a silver foil package. More than likely he would have pried the cardboard lid off, taken one look at the bubbling mess and thrown it out anyway.

"So, how have you been, Josey?" Severson always played this game with Swann, as if he believed that the boy lived a normal life.

"Yeah, I've been fine." Josey grunted from the kitchen. Then there was an awful clang as Josey slammed the oven door shut. When he returned to the armchair he was sucking the palm of his hand.

"What happened? Did you burn yourself?"

"It's nothing," Swann mumbled.

Severson nodded. He was sitting well forward with his legs apart and his hands clasped between his knees. "So then, how's the girl you were seeing?"

"Kim?" Josey looked blank.

"Yes, Kim."

"She's gone," Josey said, and it was obvious that he meant from his life.

"That's too bad. Are you seeing anyone else?"

Josey bit his lower lip. "Uh, I've been sort of tuned out recently, you know?"

"Sure, I understand," Lyle said quickly. He was picking nervously at the frayed ends of the sofa. Then he glanced up suddenly. "I suppose you have guessed that I didn't come for a social visit."

"Yeah," Josey sighed, and to prove that he wasn't the poor, dumb grunt that they thought he was, "I don't usually entertain on Mondays." Except that it was Tuesday.

"I came to talk to you about John Donne," Lyle continued. "I understand that he's a friend of yours."

Josey was pulling at the tufts of stuffing on the arm of his chair. "Yeah, John and I have known each other for a while." And suddenly Swann was lost in an image of John and himself sitting in a cheap Saigon apartment. John's hands were trembling over a joint. The Zig-zags

21

were sticking to his fingers. Grass was scattered on the purple shag.

"Josey," Severson called to bring the boy back from the nasty, quick vision. "Listen to me now. John is in trouble."

Swann shrugged. "So what else is new?"

"I'm serious, Jose. I got a call last night from one of our people . . . Tell me, may we have a little music?"

Josey nodded, and struggled up from his chair. He shuffled over to the kitchen table where there was an old portable radio. He turned it on, and the thing began buzzing with the morbid strains of rock 'n' roll.

Lyle continued when Swann sat back down. "I said that one of our people in Sao Paulo called me last night. That is Sao Paulo, Brazil. It seems that John wandered into the consulate with a bullet in his chest. He's alive, but from what I understand it's serious."

Swann began drilling his thumb into the arm of the chair. "Go on."

"Apparently, John claims that Allen Cassidy sent him down for a certain job."

"What sort of job?"

"To kill a man, Josey," Lyle said softly. "The target was the Brazilian Minister of Agriculture. His name was Daniel Miguez."

Swann smiled absently. "So, Johnny's got himself a big job. No nickel and dime hits for Johnny."

"The minister was an important man. There were all sorts of ramifications."

Swann tossed his head to the side. "So did John fuck it up?"

"No. The minister is dead, but later John was shot. He claims that Allen set him up."

Josey tore a strip of fabric off the chair. He was shred-

ding it in his hands. "Yeah, well isn't that a surprise."
Lyle ignored him. "John wants you to go down there
and bail him out. He needs interference, and he needs a
passport."

"Me?" Josey looked up. "Why me?"

"He trusts you."

"Yeah, well I don't know if I'm right for the gig. You
know what I'm saying? I got to take it easy for a while.
I haven't been well. They told me I was a little off the mark
just now." They also told him he was crazy, which was
exactly the word Kim had used the night she ran off with
some prick in a silver Mercedes.

Lyle began rubbing the palm of his hand. "I thought
John was a friend, Josey." The old man's eyes were milky.

"Why can't you send one of the regulars down? Get
John out through the soft route. Why all this under-the-
table stuff?"

"Because I'm afraid we have an under-the-table situation. You see, no one knows that John has been sent down.
It's a very curious problem. If, indeed, Allen sent John on
that run, then Allen is very likely operating on his own."

"Or maybe you've just been put out to feed with me,
Lyle."

"I haven't," Severson snapped. "I've checked, dis-
creetly, of course, but I've checked just the same. So there
you are. Nobody knows about the death of Daniel Miguez.
It's all very strange."

"So why don't you put Cassidy through the wringer?
They could sweat him in a day. Hell, I'll do it for nothing."

"I was hoping you would be able to help me, Josey.
Now, if I was wrong . . ."

"Don't play with me, Lyle. I'll go. You know I'll go."

"Yes," Severson breathed. "I know."

23

"So what's the schedule?"

"I'll need to have the passports made up, but I can do that tonight. So we should meet tomorrow at the airport. Say eleven in the morning?"

"Oh yeah, eleven."

"There's a coffee shop at the Pan Am terminal. You'll see me. If I'm ordering tea then the meeting is go. You walk up to the roof of the terminal. If I'm having anything else, then fall back here. Do you have that?"

"Yeah, but what if they don't have any tea?"

Severson ignored it. "Also, Josey, I want you to know that Allen Cassidy is a friend of mine. I'm not out for blood. If he's overstepped himself, then all right, but I don't want any vengeance here. I've come to you because John asked for you, because he's your friend."

"Got you, Lyle," and Swann held up a jaunty thumb. His smile was sardonic. "Meanwhile, Johnny is in some flop house dying, right?"

Severson shook his head slowly. "Josey, I can depend on you, can't I?"

"Sure."

"I'm serious, Josey. This is important. You will consider all the elements? I mean to say, I *can* depend on you, can't I?"

Josey smiled. Shrugged.

DESCENDING AGAIN the warped, narrow steps of Josey's vile quarters, Lyle Severson could not recall when the Company had been reduced to such extremes. Even with the Germans, he might have complained, we were able to manage without the likes of a Swann.

But no longer. Today the world was demonstrably Josey Swann's. Thousands of reminders made this clear to Lyle. Simply standing in the doorway at the foot of the stairs, and wincing at the sharp reflection of light off a line of windshields, he was expressly conscious of his age.

He looked right as far as he could, then to his left, and still he had no real certainty that his trail was clean. My tradecraft, he sometimes thought, all those daily precautions which hemmed in his life; why it's nothing more than an old spy's indulgence.

Not that Lyle had lost his touch exactly. Oh, he still knew the tricks. It was merely that things had passed him by. You could try and dismiss a Josey Swann as no real threat because all the boy had was speed and strength. "Swann is a silent killer," Allen had once said, "and he's as dumb as a hammerhead shark." But there you had Allen's vanity, because the truth was that Josey Swann was very clever indeed.

Sometimes Lyle saw himself as Eliot's figure in "Gerontion." Yes, he was an old man, dry in the mouth, and true enough, he had been blistered in Antwerp, although not by any metaphysical sun. Lyle had been burned by the very real strain of a spy's war.

During the war he had loved a frail Jewish girl named Maro. They had never gone to bed because Lyle was loyal to Jenny. But one night not long before her death he laid himself down by Maro's side. The sheets, he remembered, were as rough as canvas. No amount of washing had been able to cleanse the odor. Her hair was damp from fever. In the corner of the yellowed stone room a flame burned beneath the icon. The rug on the floor was red. He distinctly recalled the white mandala that the natives had woven in for luck.

"When you're old, Costaki," she had told him, using his work name of the day, "when you're old, you must stop this activity."

"I'll never grow old," he replied, and had been speaking

25

advisedly . . . the Germans were rolling up one network after another. . . .

But you are old, he told himself now, old enough to have fathered even a thin and clever killer like Swann.

In the hallways and offices of the CIA complex in Langley, Lyle was not quite as conscious of his age as he had been in that squalid room of Josey's.

He had driven through the main gates and the guard had checked his card and nodded with respect. In the elevator, onward to the fifth floor, he saw Noel Polly, and on the next stop they were pushed backward by two gold runners—messenger boys with high security clearance. For a moment they all stood silently. Then Polly coughed. "Missed you the other day, old boy."

"Come again?"

"At Gordy's. They said you would come, so we waited until nine." Polly was fumbling with his key chain. Sometimes when he spoke he pressed his hands against desks and walls to build up the strength in his arms.

"Oh, Lord, I meant to call. I hope—"

"Not to be upset," Polly said, and then he winked. "You know how it is at Gordy's. They served a roast, and the wine was only a cut above the jug."

"Yes," Lyle smiled, thinking, as if you could taste the difference, Noel.

"Oh, and I saw your Allen Cassidy," Polly continued.

"Allen?" Lyle's stomach knotted.

"Looking very dapper, too."

"Yes, that's Allen."

"Got to keep an eye on him, Lyle. How does the myth go? Chronos castrates his father for the throne, or something? Yes, I think that's it," and they both chuckled a bit, although Lyle believed that old men did not laugh, they wheezed.

In Lyle's outer office, prim Penny was typing. She might have been any of the new-school girls, fresh from Vassar, or even from one of the lesser publics. They came in droves to be intelligence officers, but ended up merely servicing the spies. It so happened, however, that Penny had roots to the old days by way of her father. He had been an unlovable boxer, now dead, and Lyle had spent some time with him in Vienna where they ran a catch and carry job against a Polish radio link. For two weeks they had shared everything, and now, Lyle thought, I have his daughter.

"How did it go with the dimwits?" she asked. Dimwits was their pun on unwittings. Whenever Lyle went down to the streets to meet with a stringer, they said he was meeting with a dimwit. But Penny's idea of a Severson stringer was a bashed-in newspaper man, a nervous consular clerk with acne and debts, or maybe some frightened professor with a girl to support on the side. In her wildest dreams she would not have imagined a creature like Josey Swann.

"Nothing for the memoirs today," Lyle grinned, and took one more step to his office door. Then pausing, as if something had just come to mind, he turned to her again. "Oh, Penny, I wonder if you would run a little errand for me, pick up a few files in archives?"

Age notwithstanding, Lyle thought he played it very well. He bent over her desk and jotted down the list of files. "I believe they'll all be in the current operational sections. If they give you any trouble, tell them to give me a call. Although I can't imagine why they should give you any problem."

"What's this then?" she smiled, taking up the list. "Curling up for an afternoon read?"

Lyle laughed, and then came the truly brilliant touch. "Run along, dear," he said, "and don't bother father Lyle

27

with any more questions." A man with nothing to hide did not explain himself.

She brought six files in all. They were bound in green plastic, which meant that the security rating was nominal. Of the six, five were smoke. There was a yearly roundup of Mexican military advances. The file on Peru dealt with above the board intelligence sources. The others he did not even bother to glance at. What Lyle was after lay in Brazil.

So in his rosewood chair, by the dormer window, Lyle began the hunt. By five the sun had fallen and the glass had darkened. No real leads came to him that evening, but it was enough to have begun. Like other hunts, this one was to be a family affair, discreet, compassionate. He was mainly concerned that Allen be protected from the ones like Polly, not to mention, of course, Josey Swann.

CHAPTER 3

IN ROGER'S dream he saw the dying streets of India. He saw them quite vividly. There was the smell of hot dust and authentic death. He dreamed that the wooden carts were creaking over the cobbled streets and he saw the bodies piled high upon them. The carts were drawn by animals, their bones sliding and rippling as they clopped along. The bodies on the cart were skeletal. The faces were gaunt, the stomachs bloated with gas. Sometimes when the bodies were laid, one on top of another, the gas was pressed out and there were terrible moans breaking from the lips of the dead. The wooden carts came at first light. The Indians have learned through experience that those on the edge of starvation usually die in the night.

The open country around the dying streets was flat and dry. The sun was hot. The dust was brown. There were gray skeletons of trees. The leaves had been stripped by the starving. The bark had been eaten and then spit up. Above, the sky was a vast blue dome with no clouds and no promises.

Whenever Roger dreamed of India he saw the land and the sky. He saw a silent land filled with dry brush and open secrets. He saw a sky that was limitless and white from horizon to horizon. In one form or another he always saw the starving and the dying.

Roger had come to believe that these dreams in which he saw distant places so vividly were somehow connected with his overall feel for his work. He had never given his special touch much thought, but in his dreams he often saw the humping clouds or the sheets of silver rain. Just as he sometimes sensed the chill of cold air, or the blast of strong wind thousands of miles away. He did not understand these visions. He could be at his desk, maybe plotting a low pressure front, or graphing humidity scales, and then suddenly, in his mind, he was there. He was right there with the wind and the rain.

Once Roger had read a passage from the diary of a Christian mystic who described how his soul rose up, and blew with the trade winds for thousands of miles. Roger was not sure if the mystic's experience was commensurate with his own visions, but Roger knew that he sensed things. There was not much else to say. He saw the weather in his mind, and that was that.

Except that there were some who did not hold with visions—Ed Allen, an acne-pitted vulture of a man, foremost among them. He stalked the gray laboratory, calling, "Where's Dennerstein? Up in the clouds again?" While on his angry days, Allen could even be more vicious. "Dennerstein is a Jew," he once whispered. "He's just a typical Jew."

But even Roger's most vocal critics could not deny that he was very good at what he did. His track record was just too impressive. So call it some vague "sense." Call it some mysterious intuition. The fact remained that Roger had

30

put together some mighty impressive long-range weather forecasts since he had come to work for the Carrage Grain Company.

Like anyone who traded in commodities grown in the earth—wheat and rye, cotton and soybeans—Carrage had a vested interest in the weather. When the year was good but not too overbearing, the sun sufficient but not too strong, then the harvest was plentiful and the prices low. But if the weather turned contrary, the air too cold or the rainfall low, then portions of the crop would be ruined and the prices would be subsequently high. There were other factors which determined the prices and, in turn, determined if the farmers, the processers and the middlemen like Carrage made profits or losses, but weather was certainly as important as any.

Carrage was the largest grain brokering house in the world. They bought more, sold more and made more than anyone. But even for Carrage, a giant multi-national with more than one hundred branch offices world-wide, dealing in grain could be tricky. The idea was to buy at a low price and sell at a higher one. However, everyone who traded in commodities played this game. So no sooner would the price of, say, wheat, drop to a profitable buying point, or rise to a profitable selling point than the word would be out and a reverse trend would begin, leaving somebody holding the short end of the stick.

And so entered the Carrage long-range weather forecasters. These men were by no means the sole indicators of trading practices, but when they were successful, when they made that forecast nine months in advance that proved to be dead accurate, Carrage achieved an advantage.

Carrage was one of the few commodity traders with enough money—some said, vision, because it was a maverick field—to hire their own weathermen. Even the Department of Agriculture did not invest as much in long-range weather forecasting as Carrage. But then the people at the USDA didn't hold with this long-range mumbo jumbo. Oh, they paid a little lip service to the long-range techniques, but only Carrage was willing to put in the big money.

Or throw it away as the hardcore, straight-as-the-ruler element of the weather community claimed. But one could not really blame these critics. After all, long-range forecasting was a mistrusted "science." Whereas the conventional weatherman depended on "the mechanistic method"—by which climatic events were extended a few hours through computer models, the long-range boys used statistics all the way. They might take a mid-Atlantic sea temperature drop in the spring, put that together with a dozen other signs and then confidently forecast a mild winter. It was done with statistics, they would say—cause and effect, just a matter of knowing the cause and forecasting the effect.

Terrific, said their critics, but don't ask us to ride those statistics to the bank.

However, the Carrage Grain Company was hoping to do just that—take their long-range weathermen's results to the bank.

As for specific results of forecasts, these were secret. What was the point of forecasting an event which tipped off a trader when to sell or when to buy if everyone had the data? So each night the weathermen locked their work in safes set into the wall in one corner of the lab. The finished forecasts were carried in sealed packets to the Carrage headquarters in Boston, and the weathermen were bound to silence on pain of enormous fines.

Word had it within Carrage circles that Roger had

made an awful stink about the secrecy clause. He didn't want to sign it, they said. "Probably can't keep his big mouth shut," added Ed Allen. But Billy "The Kidd" Watterman, who believed that one should know one's enemies, had other ideas about this Dennerstein character. The Kidd was a small man, smaller than Allen by a head, smaller even than Roger, and so perhaps he was suited for stealth. Who wouldn't trust the Kidd's chubby round face and curly red hair. Certainly not the upstairs boys who reportedly told the Kidd the truth about Roger Dennerstein. Then down came the Kidd, sly and breathless. Roger had not wanted to sign the secrecy clause, Billy explained, because he believed that the forecasts should be used for the common good. "He's got a thing about the starving millions," the Kidd said.

"Bullshit," countered Allen. "Dennerstein's a Jew. He can keep his own secrets, but he can't keep other's."

And what of Roger's secrets? There were several theories circulating around the lab to account for Roger's phenomenal success at predicting climatic trends. "Sheer luck," said Allen one grim and rainy day as they all sat in the lounge.

Billy shook his head and swallowed a mouthful of coffee. "There's more to it than luck, Ed. You've got to admit it. Dennerstein has a unique data base."

"Probably stole it." Allen laughed, and then frowned at the dregs of his own coffee.

But Billy would not write off the Dennerstein approach to forecasting so easily. Indeed, the Kidd had made something of a study. He had learned, for example, that Roger was the master of correlation. Here was a weatherman who truly understood sea temperature anomalies and their jet stream correlations. Which was to say that if the temperature of a large stretch of sea was the given, one could

33

reasonably calculate the temperature of certain high winds. Why and how was not entirely known, but that did not matter. Long-range weather forecasting was based on statistics of cause and effect. A certain weather condition occurring during one period of the year, said the long-range weatherman's bible, could be counted on to affect the weather later in the year. Roger, the Kidd had decided, held a lot of stock in the temperature patterns of great sea patches and their corresponding wind temperature. It was not a new approach. Catholic, Roger had called his technique, and Billy used this word now.

While Allen crushed a styrofoam cup. "What do you mean by 'Catholic?' The guy's Jewish. Dennerstein, Roger Dennerstein. If that's not a Jewish name . . ."

"No, Ed. It's not Catholic as in religion. It's catholic as in selective."

Allen may have had more to say but he was stopped by Michael Mullen strolling in, licking the remains of a candy bar from his fingers. "Roger's secret," he announced, "is that he sold his soul to the devil for the gift of vision, and he picked up his wife in the deal."

One did not laugh at Mullen's jokes. He was a slow, heavy man with manicured nails and razor cut hair. There had been a time when he was Allen's foe, but Allen proved to be no match for Mullen's wit, so he conceded defeat, the better part of an ass. "Dennerstein has made some unclean pact. Does that get you, Ed? We've got a warlock in our midst."

The truth, however, was that Roger's approach to forecasting was no different from that of the others. Well, not fundamentally different. He began with the initial postulate, "the veritable foundation of our so-called science," as Mullen might have put it. Weather events, said that postulate, relate to cyclic patterns, and are not random and

34

independent. With that it was merely a matter of measuring known trends and relating them to climatic phenomena.

If one wanted examples, and Billy had catalogued them all, then the Russian drought of '72 served nicely, even for Ed Allen. (Yes, they all knew that Allen was a rapacious bastard with his brains in his butt, but he had seniority so what could you do?)

The Russian drought was classic, maintained Billy. "If you saw the events from Dennerstein's viewpoint, you could have forecast that baby at least ten months in advance. Maybe more."

Ed Allen, however, had been meanly skeptical all afternoon. He had been eating a slice of pizza, watching the Kidd from the corner of his eyes. "Hindsight, Billy. You're giving me nothing more than hindsight."

But Billy was determined to explain, not so much in the interest of laboratory harmony but the technique was important. Roger had become an obsession.

It was Billy's theory that Roger could have forecast the Russian drought by noting the initial climatic indicators and then, using a standard timetable, sometimes called a "model," calculated their eventual effects.

"A rabid dog bites your leg, Ed," added Mullen. "One can certainly give odds that in the weeks to come you'll go out of your mind." Mullen's jokes tended to cut both ways.

But Billy had a directed mind, a mind that did not stray beyond the science. When Billy spoke of the Russian drought, he spoke only of that strong and persistent ridge of air that had hung above the northern hemisphere in both summer and the following winter. "This ridge may have been caused by—"

"*May* have been," Allen cut in. "You can't know anything for sure." It probably should be noted that Allen had been having difficulty with his wife.

"All right," Billy conceded. "May have been, but let's just say that this ridge may have been caused by a strong trough in the mid-Atlantic. From there it's just a question of graphing the thing and computing the odds based on past statistical facts."

"But—" Mullen said, one finger raised in the air for attention. "But, indeed," and he went on to remind the others that the mere digitized measurements were no real barometer. Yes, one could fill the right side of the grid with facts, but what of the left? The grid was the map of their projections. There was the known on the right, progressing to the unknown on the left. So, once again, yes, you could fill the right with known data, but as one tried to plot the future the bridge became more and more shaky. "There would eventually come a point when the figures dissolved completely, and one would then truly be at the proverbial crossroads. Amen. Do the temperature anomalies come from air-sea heat exchange, or from a horizontal transport of air from the pole to the equator? Answer me that, gentlemen."

None could, and so it seemed that Roger's—and how they hated the word—genius lay in his ability to successfully leap the gap from the known to the unknown. Science as alchemy, said some. Science as art, admitted others. But no matter what else was said about Roger, no one could seriously deny that he was very good indeed at what he did.

Once, when Roger had made a particularly adroit forecast based upon nothing that the others could see as tangible, there was a move to uncover the secrets. To hell with laboratory propriety, they were going to find out how he did it.

Ed Allen was elected inquisitor because of his rank. Billy, Mullen and John Haas all cornered Roger in the lounge by the coffee machine. They sat him on the vinyl couch, greased him with a candy bar, set him up with easy smiles, and then, "How did you do it, Rog? What made you include that northern ridge in the data base?" All of them were fingering their styrofoam cups of luke warm coffee.

On Friday nights, loose with beer at McGruffy's bar, Roger's answer was still good for a few hard laughs. John Haas, a fairly smooth number who dressed like a model, did the best imitation, puckering his lips. "You sort of feel it, you know?" Haas would say hesitantly. "I mean you sort of see it in your mind," he would say, and they would all start laughing into their beers, ears red, hot around the collars. Yes, there were times when they really were afraid of that Dennerstein character.

There were other times, however, when Roger was something less than a joke, or more, depending on how much you let him get under your skin. That Roger truly hated the Carrage Grain Company was fairly evident. Why, just look at him, they would say, and maybe nod to the window, where three stories below he was walking across the vast black parking lot. He was like some sad and furious boy. He was short, built like a fighter, but if Roger were a fighter he would have been the mad undisciplined kind, the sort that attacked with squinting eyes and flailing arms. He had large dark eyes and black hair. His nose . . . a beak nose they called it, but he was not a bad looking guy. Some claimed that he even looked a bit like Dustin Hoffman. Only you hardly knew what to make of him, marching across the jet-black pavement, head jammed down, a ratty briefcase shoved angrily beneath his arm, one hand bunched in the pocket of his corduroy jacket, the fingers undoubtedly clenched in a fist.

Then there was that second Roger, and here was the one that the others really did not understand. They had all seen him at the window, mooning up at the heaving clouds, or staring past the Carrage grounds to the hills and distant chaparral. Probably this was the Roger that most disturbed the others, because, after all, what *was* he thinking about for minutes on end as he stood gazing into the chilled white sky? It gave you the creeps. Maybe he was having a fit or something? Occasionally he looked so shattered one could feel sorry for him.

Roger, however, was not as bad off as he appeared. A few months after he had joined the Carrage stable came the surprise of surprises. Roger was married. "Not only that," exclaimed Billy, "but his wife is a fox."

There were some, particularly Allen, who refused to believe the Kidd. Then came the company picnic, and sure enough, Roger drove up with a honey-blonde girl who wore a telltale gold band on her finger. She was quite easily the most beautiful woman there. Remember, if you will, Billy might have told himself, how every man under sixty began to drool over her pert little ass. During the soft-ball game Julie Dennerstein played catcher, and nobody had been able to keep his eye on the ball.

So there was Roger, fierce and accusing. Billy especially knew how his glances sliced them all, laying bare their small lives. Or there was Roger distant and mute, entranced by the window. And if all that were not enough to set the others against him, there was finally his mysterious withdrawal.

The withdrawal developed in stages. The first ones were subtle . . . Roger never spoke much anyway. After a while, however, it became clear that something was definitely happening with him. They had all seen him lingering in the hall at the end of the day, watching, waiting for them to leave so that he could have the lab to himself. They had all seen his Pinto, first to arrive in the morning. They had all gotten the cold shoulder whenever they had asked him what he was working on. They all had their own theories as to why Roger had withdrawn.

There were some, notably Miss Hall from the typing pool, who said that Roger's withdrawal had been brought on by the others' cruelty. "They've simply bullied the poor dear too much," she said. "It's the straw that broke the camel's back. No wonder he won't speak to anyone. Poor dear, they've hurt his feelings."

But those closer to Roger, those like Allen and Mike Mullen who actually worked in the lab with the man, saw the reasons for this retreat as much more disturbing. Dennerstein is working on something, they said. It was something new and very complex. "Probably a big one, too," said Allen. "Sure as shit, the weed has got himself a biggie."

Conformation of the secret project theory came when Ed Allen tried to force the issue with upstairs management. His complaint was that Roger had differentiated from the group, a real crime. "We're a team," went the weathermen's code. "Act as a team and no one can be hit for the mistakes."

Three weeks after the beginning of Roger's withdrawal Ed Allen stripped off his white coat, straightened his tie and ran upstairs to rat on the weed. Allen met with Jerry Moss who held the title of Research and Development Officer. That meant that Moss sat on the fence between the weathermen and Boston, goading the former for results, and placating the latter when there were no results. Moss was a company toff who usually wore his shirtsleeves rolled to show that he was just one of the lab boys at heart.

But the morning that Allen saw him, Moss was all management heavy. "You're not to question Dennerstein. You're not to interfere with anything he's working on, and that's the word."

Obviously Roger was being covered from above.

Then, purely by chance, John Haas uncovered the first clue as to what the weed was working on. The clue came in the form of a small section of a computerized program that Roger had neglected to stow away for the night. Haas retrieved the tape from a pile of other scraps and stuffed it in his shirt. With others throwing up interferences, he spent the afternoon processing the data. When the job was done he met with Ed Allen and Billy in the men's room.

"It's only a piece, mind you," Haas explained. He was leaning on the basin with his hands on the shiny chrome taps. Allen and the Kidd stood before them. Somehow the thrill of conspiracy was a dim light and fading. Billy especially seemed nervous.

"But you've got to have found something." Allen was desperate. He was playing with his keychain. "It's got to point to something."

"Yeah," Haas nodded. "It points to something all right." He shifted his thigh on the porcelain bowl. "It's just that it's hard to explain."

"Well, try. Go on and give it a try," Allen said.

Haas coughed. "It seems that Dennerstein's trying to find some sort of statistical base for shortages."

"What sort of shortages?" Billy had his hands crammed into his pockets. "Precipitation? Temperature? What?"

"No." Haas screwed up his mouth to form the words. "Protein shortages. That is, it's my guess that he's looking at some kind of climatic twist that would result in a rock bottom grain shortage."

"How do you mean rock bottom?" Allen asked.

Haas threw up his arms. "Just that. Famine. Starvation level."

STARVATION: ROGER had once heard an instructor remark that it wasn't all that bad a way to die. After a week or so the discomfort ends and one simply wastes away. "An excellent method of suicide," the instructor had said. "If things begin to look up you can always start eating again."

But then came that day in Bengal when an official from the Indian Ministry gave Roger a tour of the famine stricken countryside. They came upon a mudcracked hut. The door was barred shut, and the official had to kick it in. Roger remembered the rectangle of light on the brown earth floor. Rats scurried away from the blast of the sun, and burrowed in the straw. There was a moment when he was actually relieved because here was just another deserted hut. The family had pushed on, perhaps to forage for food in the neighboring state. But then Roger stepped across the threshold. Initially, all he saw were the thin shadows reflected on the furthermost wall. But those shadows had been cast by bodies that hung from the ropes tied round the hut's central beam. There was the father and mother and seven small children, and they were all strung up like meat in a slaughter house.

"We must assume that this is preferable to a slow starvation," the official told him, and Roger ran out and vomited.

Odd, what aspect of that vision remained with him. He never recalled the pinched, dried faces with the lips drawn up over the long, yellow teeth. It was the shadows that Roger recalled, those seven parallel shadows on the wall. Sometimes in his dreams he would see himself approaching the door. Then the door would fly open. The straw would be rustling as the rats dove from the light, and there on the wall were the shadows, dead still and suggestive.

Those shadows became the dominant theme in Roger's life for more than five years. Under the banner of the United Nations Roger rode out to save the world from starvation, or at least give it a run for the money. But that was the problem. There was no money. To hell with a salary, Roger couldn't even get the equipment. Then if he got the equipment he couldn't get the technicians to run it. There was one time, however, in Delhi when he managed to get all three, except when he plugged in the IBM it blew the lights in the whole neighborhood because the rats had gnawed through the insulation. And there was Roger Dennerstein, pantomiming to three dumbstruck Indians in a flyblown office with half a million dollars of useless hardware.

But Roger loved it, and why not? He was actually doing something. In '74 he predicted a light monsoon four months in advance, which gave them plenty of time to prepare, buy reserves, increase planting, seek aid.

Only, as things turned out, he did not love it as much as he loved Julie.

She had been eighteen at the time they met, and too beautiful to be true. (Still was for that matter.) And after all those years of dreaming of a girl, he just couldn't let her go. So in the end it all came down to Roger's most personal equation: To hell with the weather, he was in love.

Roger went to work for the Carrage Grain Company shortly after his wedding. Sure it was the ultimate sell-out, but Julie wasn't about to live in Delhi or Bengal or any front line tank town in the war against starvation. She wanted to live in Los Angeles, which worked out well enough because Carrage maintained their research division there.

Roger's work at Carrage was really no different from the work he had done for the United Nations. It was still a question of assessing general long-range weather conditions. If anything, his work was more accurate, simply because of the sheer resources at his disposal. There were close to a hundred weather stations across the globe at his fingertips. The equipment was great, the help fantastic. Only the ends bothered Roger, for the ends were money.

Most of the time Roger could forget what Carrage used his forecasts for. All right, so you've sold out, he would tell himself, but in the evening when he pulled in the driveway there would be Julie bent over the roses, one thigh in the twilight where she hiked up her skirt, her arms reaching down to the dark tangle of flowers. Yes, it was easy enough to forget about those shadows in the Bengal hut.

But not now, not tonight, not as he lay twisted in the sweaty sheets of his bed. Because that dream which began in the dying streets ended in that hut.

For a long time Roger had not had the dream in which he saw the hut. There had been months when he hardly even thought of India. But lately he had been thinking about it a lot. And the dreams too, hardly a week went by when he didn't have that dream.

The dreams had started about six weeks ago. That was when he had finished the forecast. He remembered the night distinctly. He had been alone, sitting on a high stool in the gulch of dead computer banks. The console ran from wall to wall and nearly touched the ceiling. Earlier that evening he had climbed on top of that swivel stool and had written "fuck Carrage" in the dust of an IBM. Funny

43

how they never cleaned the tops of computers. Which was just about all he had been thinking about when the first reams of print-out had come snaking on to his lap. Then on to the floor, because Roger had dropped it. He didn't want to see it. The tape could bury him for all he cared.

He had been right. All those months of guessing and in the end the conclusion was statistically undeniable. There was going to be a famine. It was strange, however, how he had reacted. There he had been stunned and shattered, because when he knew for sure the shock was terrible. Then he let the ribbon slip from his fingers and coil around on the floor. There was a knackwurst on rye with extra mustard on his desk. He reached for it. That must have been the point when he ruined his shirt. Julie had never been able to get the stain out. It was still there. But reaching for the sandwich like that, it had somehow been symbolic.

Finish your meatloaf, Roger. Don't you know there's people starving?

Yeah, Ma. I know all about starvation. Roger turned on his side and kicked off the covers. Julie stirred and moaned. "Are you up?" she asked, and rubbed her palms in her eyes.

"I'm all right," he whispered. A wind had come up since the night fell. Outside their bedroom window the trunks and branches of a sycamore tree were scraping at the shingles. "I couldn't sleep," he finally admitted.

"Do you want me to make you something? Some hot chocolate, or something like that?" The leaves were slashing against the window. Julie's face was glazed in the moonlight.

"No thanks. I'm okay."

She was fully awake and ready to help. They had been through this before. "Did you have another dream, Rog?"

44

"I'm all right." His legs were drawn up to his chest. His arms were laced around his knees.

"Well, dreams can't hurt you," she said blankly. "That's what mother used to tell me. Dreams can't hurt you." Then she laughed a little, and a terrible gust was beating the leaves against the glass. "Oh, will you listen to that."

What is that? Roger wondered. High pressure over the Joshua flats whistling into the low off the sea? Then he spoke again. "It's not just the dream. It's the forecast, I can't get it out of my head."

Julie whipped the sheet back from her throat and Roger saw the perfect outline of her breasts. "Oh God, we're not going to start that again, are we?" Her jaw went tight waiting for an answer.

"I'm concerned, that's all. There's going to be trouble. I'm sure of it. The rainfall this year, it's going to be very low in certain areas."

Julie propped herself up on an elbow. "I wish I had made a tape of the first time you told me all this. Then I could just play it back. I mean, really, it's not like I haven't heard any of this before." Her hair just now was a soft, blond storm. Outside tiny gales were wrestling with the tops of the trees.

"There's no one else that cares," Roger said softly. "Carrage won't care, they won't care at all."

"Oh, Roger, you don't know that. It's only been a few weeks since you sent the forecast off."

"But they still won't care. I mean, why would they? All they care about is the money. Do you know how much they have to deal with? Three hundred million. Profit, loss, that's all they care about, Julie. Carrage doesn't have a conscience. They have their own freighter line, their own train line. They even have a trucking company. They're too big to care about a famine. In fact, they might even like famines. They can make a lot of money out of a famine. I mean if we make a mistake the roof falls in. But they're covered for anything. If they can't go short, they go long and look for profits on the processing end. You know they process grain, too."

Julie sighed, and ran a hand through her hair. "But what's the point, Roger?"

He was staring out through the blackened panes of glass. "This drought," he said vacantly, "it's going to be very bad in places. I don't know how they'll manage to flood the rice paddies in Asia."

Julie lay back down and stretched. "You can't be sure, can you?"

"I'm sure," he said in a low blank voice. "There are certain signs that can't be ignored. There's the temperature drop in the Atlantic, the jet stream pattern over . . . look, I'm telling you there's going to be a drought."

Julie's mouth shriveled into a knot. "Well, there's nothing that can be done," she said curtly.

"No," Roger whispered, "nothing." He rolled over to face her. "There is nothing."

He had given up trying to convert her years ago. Once he had had a dream of the two of them marching off to India for the sake of the starving millions. There they would have been, Roger with his knobby knees in khaki shorts, and Julie looking very smart in a field jacket and bush hat. They would have been dedicated and with-the-people, but Julie hadn't bought it. Obviously she had her own dreams of Roger, and not as the stalky crusader either. She probably thought ideals were a bit much. She was far more entranced with that trace of innocence in him. Yes, that was it. Vague Roger, she could control him even if she did not understand him. Here I am, she may have decided in breathless white at the altar. Here I am, the bitch goddess with my hopeless genius husband. Now, however, she was his mother. "It's only that I worry about you, Roger." Her eyes were soft. "I care about the things you care about. You know that."

There had been a time when her eyes had been enough to wash him clean of any nightmare, but tonight the vision was too real, too intense. "Something is happening," he murmured. "This is important. Something bad is happening."

"Stop it!" Julie's voice cracked. "I'm tired of this. Nothing's happening. Everything's okay."

He had been known to open windows and sit facing gales, but he had never been able to deal with her fury, so he turned on his side and drew the sheets across his shoulder.

She reached out and took his hand. "Hey, I'm on your side." Now their fingers were interlaced. Her lips began to inch along his back. "I love you, Roger. You know that."

Yes, he knew, or at least he knew that she sometimes loved him. "I love you too," he mumbled.

"So no more bad dreams?" She kissed the nape of his neck, and ran her tongue along his collar bone.

"I promise," he told her, but Roger might as well have promised to keep the wind from blowing or the rain from falling. That night he had the dream again. He dreamed that he was with the cold in the north. He saw great sheets of ice and ran his finger along their slippery surface. Under the sea, icebergs were moaning and jostling one another. Then the sheet of ice became a dais. Sitting high above him were Allen and Mullen and the Carrage board of directors. He had come to plead his case, to tell them about the drought. But they didn't care. Allen and Mullen were talking about graphs. They wanted to see the graphs. Well, you could show them the graphs of declining humidity rates, or the graphs of the rainfall estimates, but there was death, squatting like a rat on the shelf of an empty larder, smirking, "Try and graph me, weatherman."

CHAPTER 4

THE FINAL form of the Dennerstein forecast was a fifty-five page brief with accompanying diagrams and graphs. The papers were bound between buff cardboard. To the uninitiated the material was abstruse, even incomprehensible. The title was inexplicit.

The main body of the forecast dealt with sea temperature anomalies. The forecast drew upon certain correlations between oceanic and atmospheric trends in which wind patterns were statistically associated with sea-surface temperature patterns. It was not a new approach. The brilliance lay in Dennerstein's sensitivity. To those privy to the science, the man's forecast was an extraordinary piece of work. It was more than a demonstrable set of conclusions. It was a startling walk through the dark, arcane streets of a gifted man's mind. At times the road became tortuous, but the logic was never faulty. And the power of its message was no less frightening than the power of the tradewinds or great slabs of shifting ice to which the forecast alluded.

49

Among other things, the forecast maintained that, "as in the 1972 Russian drought, we are once again seeing a strong mid-Atlantic ridge that will result in sinking air masses. As the air masses continue to sink, their relative humidity will decrease and cloud formation will be inhibited."

Dennerstein went on to cite the "even more ominous" shifting of the westerlies to lower latitudes. Such shifts, he calculated, "may very well produce widespread North African drought, and more importantly, will mean that the mid-latitude jet flow will remain south of the Himalaya Mountains from six to nine days longer than normal. This delayed seasonal migration of the jet may, in turn, lead to a delay of monsoonal rains in Asia. A delay in the onset of the monsoons usually produces poor distribution of seasonal rains throughout Asia and the Asian subcontinent." Furthermore, there were lengthy correlations between a monsoonal delay and a delay of spring rains over the Russian grass lands. Reduced to its raw numerical form, the Dennerstein forecast was even more explicit, even more alarming.

The papers arrived in Boston on a Tuesday. Adrian Riggs, one of the earliest analysts to read the forecast became so disturbed that he ordered his entire department sealed off. "War Rules," he called it. The document was awarded a "Top Secret" stamp and Riggs prepared the most exclusive subscription list of his career. There was no end of jealousy.

Rumors began on the second floor. Here were the rooms where the hard young brokers sat at banks of black telephones and tickertapes. They knew something was happening, but no one seemed to know exactly what. However, working their jaws, grinding their teeth, they all felt the ripple of secrecy run through the Chateau walls.

On the third floor, in the offices of the Carrage hierarchy, the rumors became more defined. There were Bobby Jameson, Mike Gaddas, Henry Doris and George Bandy, and they all knew that a forecast had come in. Furthermore, they knew it was big, because Adrian Riggs had, as they said, freaked out. But even to these number one men, each an executive director of some aspect of the Carrage field, Howard Sax was not talking. Weeks passed, and still their president gave no word. But knowing Howard Sax, the first line people were not surprised.

Sax had always been tight-lipped about his weathermen, perhaps because the others didn't hold with this long-range shit. So when the Dennerstein forecast came in, Sax went mum. They had all seen him moving through the halls with Riggs, *sotto voce* to whispering. They had all noticed his absence from the Chateau for days at a time. He was meeting up in Washington, the word went. But meeting with whom? And about what? Sax wasn't saying. Even the regular monthly wrap-up session was postponed, and then delayed again, until now, two weeks into the new month, Sax had finally called them together.

Bandy, Jameson, Gaddis and Doris, they all sat at the long table. Some were absolutely still. Others shuffled papers, while George Bandy traced the arabesque around the table's edge with his thin, white fingers. Only Sax stood. He pressed his palms against the arms of the Hepplewhite and waited.

"For us to ask?" Jameson said. Always depend on Jameson to break the ice. The man was a climber, but clever.

"You can ask," smiled Sax. "But I'm not going to tell you, not yet."

They said that Howard Sax was a hawk for opportunity. But then you had to be when dealing with commodities, because, as they liked to say, one man's "grain was another man's loss."

"You can give us a hint," joked Bandy. Perhaps he hated Sax the most, but he still respected the man. You had to. Bandy could count the guys on one hand that had gone as high as Howard Sax, and survived, putting their head to the muzzle day after day, spinning the chamber and pulling the trigger. No wonder he was scared to talk.

"I'm not afraid to talk," Sax said. "It's just that I'd rather not get anyone's hopes up."

Henry Doris laughed. "Oh, I don't think you have to worry about that." Doris was a computer man. He had been the one that pushed for the team of computer gunslingers who packed all kinds of mathematical schemes to shave points and psyche out the trading trends. The idea was that a good computer man could reduce the variables to a quick, cold equation, but Sax didn't like computers. He liked his weathermen.

"We're not opposed to waiting," Mike Gaddas put in. "But if we're sitting on a time bomb, we'd like to know." Gaddas was the wheat trader, and the word was that he was heading for a fall. Although he was probably too dumb to know it.

"I think Mike means that you can trust us," Bandy added, and the others could have whistled for the nerve of it. They were waiting for Sax to swoop.

But Sax merely tightened his lips. "If I knew what to say, I'd tell you. Right now it's too vague. I think the weathermen may have finally given us the ball. But I'd rather not huddle until I know which direction to run."

They had all heard that line of shit before. Sax was famous for his hedging. But George Bandy knew why. He had been at the top once, and he knew what it was like, waking up at three in the morning, shivering in the icy sheets, listening to those voices in your head, taunting, *it's fallen again. That makes thirteen points today, and now your number is up.*

"But we can take it, then," said Bandy, "that this particular forecast is different from, say, the one last June?"

Last June, the weathermen had predicted an early spring and a Canadian bumper crop. The prices naturally fell, Carrage sold short and went into the big chips. But still, Bandy and the others were not convinced about the weatherman's worth. There was money floating on every commodity, they maintained, and you didn't need a weatherman to tell which way the wind blows.

"No," Sax said. "This forecast is different."

"How is it different?" Jameson asked. "Good? Bad? What?"

Sax shook his head. "It's just different."

"All right, we can take the hint. You don't want to talk," Doris grinned.

"It's not a question of me not wanting to talk," Sax responded. "It's just that I'd rather not say anything until I know for certain where we stand. Fair enough?"

It was not fair at all, Bandy thought, but at least Sax wasn't as mad as some. Bandy had personally known guys that were so freaked out by the day to day pressure that they went right over the edge. There were traders who claimed to hear voices from beyond telling them when to buy and when to sell. There were others who forecast the market with the stars. By those standards, Sax's weathermen were not all that radical. But still, Bandy always had wondered if they were worth the cost. The weathermen were expensive, expensive and nutty.

"So, then, it's business as usual?" Jameson asked.

"If you gentlemen don't mind," Sax returned. "I should think you're all just burning to pitch. So who wants to go first?"

Somebody laughed and Bandy shook his head. Then came Sax's predictable, "Don't everyone speak at once."

Sometimes these meetings were jocular free-for-alls. Ideally, however, each man was to report on his particular section. Henry Doris, for example, handled corn and other domestic grains. Jameson was essentially the European and Middle Eastern man, buying from the latter and selling to the former. Doris was strictly wheat.

Sax believed in wheat, wheat was his staple. Come revolution or high water, no one could do without wheat. It was just a question of whom you screwed—the growers or the consumers. "And so where's my wheat, Mike?"

Gaddas reddened. "Oh, it's growing," he offered as a poor joke, but there were no takers.

"How much?" Sax asked.

"Well, the USDA reports haven't come out yet," Gaddas was stalling and everyone knew it. Sax wouldn't have asked if the Department of Agriculture had released their crop estimates.

"But what do the farmers say?" Sax continued.

"What do the weathermen say?" Gaddas countered.

Mike, all felt, had really gone too far this time.

But when Sax slit throats he did it in private. Now he only smiled. "I'm not singling you out, Mike. I'm just asking, okay?"

"Okay," and Gaddas sucked his lips in. "The farmers aren't saying much. You know how the farmers are." Gaddas might have been a farmer himself with his big hands and his rough weathered face.

Sax was the opposite. He was wiry and smooth. They said he used to streak his hair gray at the sides for that right touch of sagacious authority. "Well, I'd like to see you get something a little more firm on that point, Mike. You know what I'm talking about?"

"I'll try," Gaddas replied. He was still sulking.

Doris was next, and they all enjoyed seeing the jerk shuffle through the rounds. "I got corn," he spouted. "I got plenty of good, yellow corn."

"How much?" Sax asked.

"Oh, hell, I can't give you figures, but my boys tell me that they've been planting."

"Well, maybe you can pin down a figure for me, too. What do you say about that, Hank?" Sax always humored the stupid ones.

"Sure," Doris shrugged. "I can do."

Bandy would have been smirking with the others, but Sax was watching him. "South of the border, George, what's happening south of the border?"

Bandy cleared his throat. "I prepared a general brief of all the market areas." He flipped through the pages of a yellow pad. Actually the pages were blank, but you had to make points with Sax. "I was going to read it to you, but something has occurred down there, and now I don't know what to say. I may have mentioned this to some of you. Bobby?"

Jameson nodded. "If you're going to say what I think you're going to say, then you certainly did, George."

"All right, then. I haven't really had a chance to kick this around much, but let me just throw it out and get some feedback from you. Ah, Daniel Miguez."

Sax nodded. "Brazil? Minister of Agriculture?"

"That's right," Bundy sighed. "It seems that Danny Miguez was murdered Friday night, some sort of terrorist action."

"Jesus," Sax said. "But why wasn't I told sooner?"

"We just found out," Bandy said. "It's taken them this long to find the body. His . . . wife reported him missing, but apparently the man was machine gunned as he drove home. His car ran off the road and was hidden by the high grass on the shoulder. Some kids found the wreck this morning."

"I thought cars burst into flames," Doris muttered. The others ignored him.

Sax swore again. "So where do we stand now?"

"Difficult to say, really," Bandy continued. "Could be bad for coffee prices. Miguez always protected his people against us. Now the coffee growers aren't saying much. I think they're waiting like everyone else—"

"Waiting for what?" Doris cut in. He liked to think he knew a little about everything.

"The new man is a guy called Jorge Alvera," said Bandy. "Frankly, I don't know much about him one way or another. He was the second man on the ladder next to Danny Miguez, but he's young. He's always kept a low profile."

"So?" Sax was fingering a Waterford tumbler.

"So, I don't know what this Jorge Alvera is going to do. Now, Danny Miguez, whatever else you could say about the guy, he was at least honest. He was a nationalist. He didn't much like us, but I could work with him. He had a hard line on soybeans, though, which you probably should know after last year. Remember? He wouldn't sell us the beans, or rather would sell but we had to throw in our first born. Danny was so intent on building up Brazilian beef, it was a real bitch getting the soybeans out of that country because he needed the stuff for animal feed. But coffee, he was always fair with coffee."

Sax was still toying with the crystal tumbler. Now and again his eyes darted up to Bandy's, pierced the man and

56

then darted away. "Do you think he'll hike up an export tariff?"

"Don't know," Bandy replied. He was tapping the table with his gold-rimmed glasses. "Brazil, right now, is a funny place. Ah, if I can take a minute."

"Yes, go ahead, George," Sax mumbled.

"Brazil has always been the hard line down there against the Communists. They were the first to adopt the U.S. position regarding Castro. Am I wasting time?"

"No, go on."

"All right. Brazil has been run by the military for years. Geisel has been in since '64."

"Who's Geisel?" Doris asked.

Bandy shook his head. "He's the president, Hank. He was a general like all the other presidents they've had for the last ten years."

Doris laughed it off. "Okay, I've never been big on my geography."

"Anyway," Bandy continued, "until recently Geisel has been a strong U.S. supporter. He's hard as nails on the reds, loves hot dogs, you know, that sort of thing. The guy's a fascist. However, recently, there's been some strained relations. It seems that Geisel asked Jimmy Carter for fifty million in aid, and that was military aid, I should add. Okay, Jimmy gives him the money. But you know how Jimmy is, he's out to make a name for himself. So he wraps up the bills in a critique of Brazilian strong arm methods. They're a bunch of real animals down there, or at least they can be when the fire is up. The Brazilians have had this group called the Death Squad. No kidding, that's what it was called. It was a group of vigilantes, mostly off-duty cops. These guys would go around and nail anyone who spoke out against the government. On top of that, the prisons were filled with political enemies, and torture was not uncommon. Typical south of the border bullshit, got the picture? Anyway, Jimmy Crusader Carter decides that he's not going to give the spics any money for guns unless they clean up their act. So he sends them down this report which says what bad boys they've been."

"Carter may have only been following his convictions, George," Doris said, because he knew that Mr. Sax quite liked Jimmy Carter.

"Yeah, okay," Bandy shrugged. "Where was I? Oh, so Geisel takes one look at the Carter report and tears it up."

"Which means that he refused the fifty mil," Sax said.

"Yeah. Not only that, but Geisel also tore up a twenty-five year old military agreement with the United States. Okay, so now it seems that Brazil is in the lurch, right? Not so. Geisel goes to the French and West Germans and they give him all he needs. Now there was a time when I could go down to Brazil with my Mickey Mouse watch, sing a few bars of 'America the Beautiful,' wave the flag about, and I could get anything I needed in the way of soybeans or coffee or what have you. But lately things have been different. As I said, Danny Miguez was of the new breed. He wasn't about to take any shit from us. I mean, you all remember what happened with the coffee prices. What did they say was the reason for the price increase? Frost killed the beans? Well, that was the biggest crock I ever heard. Frost, nothing, they just thought they could get more money. Okay, Miss American housewife proved them wrong. When the prices of coffee got too high, she just stopped buying the stuff. But soybeans are a different matter. People have got to get those beans. So if this boy Alvera is intending to follow the same track as Miguez then I'm afraid we can't expect too much in the way of soybeans."

Sax was staring above the heads of the others. They all watched his tongue rooting around in his mouth. "This murder, George, what's the reason?"

"I don't think anyone knows. The official government line is that it was the Communists, but then they always say that. Frankly, I can't see why the reds would have wanted to kill Miguez. He was part of the reform movement, if you can call the handful of concessions that the people have been given reform. But anyway, Miguez was concerned about protecting domestic industry. He was never one to let us screw him, or buy him off. He was always afraid of selling me stuff too cheaply. You know the problems I've had with the man."

"Yeah," Sax said, and his mouth became a thin, tight line again.

"On the other hand, maybe some sort of terrorist group did bump him off. I mean we're talking about Brazil, right? All kinds of weird shit goes on down there. If that's the case, maybe there's going to be some strong arm moves against the growers. If that's the case then we could be in real trouble. I'm looking at the possibility that someone down there could be trying to move in on the action. Right now everything is controlled by the government, that means Alvera now, and the co-operatives. Those are the big farmers banded together for clout. But sometimes there are little wars that take place between the various factions. Sometimes you'll have one farmer fighting it out with another. So maybe someone down there is trying to move in and swallow everything so he can really dictate prices. Or maybe the government is trying to push the farmers into a corner and they hit back by killing Danny. I don't know. It could go a number of different ways."

"A sort of food mafia," Doris laughed.

"It's not funny, Hank. It can happen, and then you try

going down there and buying product."

Sax pulled at the folds of his chin. "So what have you been doing about it, George?"

"Doing?" He tossed up a hand. "I sent Danny's family some flowers and charged it to you."

There was general laughter, and then Jameson with an imaginary telephone to his ear, said, "Hellow, Jimmah. Der maybee some trouble down in this here place called Braazil, and I'm wonderin' if me and some other good old boys could borrow them marines."

THOSE WHO study power, George Bandy believed, generally have a better sense of it than those who exercise power. For example, George himself had no real power, nor did Jameson, nor did Gaddis, nor did any of them. Sax was the mother hawk with all the eggs beneath his rump. Yet George was fairly sure that Howard Sax had no perspective on himself. He was a man who merely reacted to the market. He hovered over the globe, spying, swooping down on Midwestern corn, South American coffee, oriental rice and the rest of it. Sax was the quintessential mercantilist, a man whose conscious loyalties were not determined by his affections. Yes, George liked that description of Sax, for despite that ridiculous futuristic rhetoric, Howard Sax had an eighteenth century mind.

It was pathetic when you thought about it. Howard Sax actually believed the myth of the multi-international— what's good for Carrage is good for the world. It wasn't that George was a reformer, but if we're going to sell them down the river, he would have said, let's not pretend that we're anything more than pimps.

Now Howard Sax was again the rational man. Like the eighteenth century encyclopedist, thought Bandy, Sax's religion this afternoon is his rationalism. "A word with

60

you," Sax had said, one very white hand placed on Bandy's elbow. Then Sax was carefully leading George down the long corridor. There was subdued light breaking through the small rose windows.

They paused in the melancholy foyer. Once this room must have served as a pantry, and there was still the smell of cold moist earth. "I thought we might talk in the garden," Sax mumbled as he turned the brass knob. Bandy glanced back to catch the last view of the hall and a painting of muted fruit in oil.

When the door drew back, light burst into the foyer. Then the two men descended the damp, stone stairs. Here was the smell of moss and rotting grass. Their shoes were scraping over the flagstone path. Wet leaves of ivy brushed their trousers legs. "I like this end of the grounds," Sax called over his shoulder. They were moving still deeper into the tangle of trees and shrubs. "It reminds me of something." He had picked up a supple stick along the path and was stripping off the last few leaves to make a whip. "It's a real garden here." He breathed deeply and slashed at the leaves above his head.

They had reached the leafy grotto. Falling drops from where the gardeners had watered were sounding all around them. "This doesn't mean anything," Sax began. He was gently probing the face of a rose with his stick. "Haven't we met here before?"

Bandy toed a crack in the flagstones. "We used to come here during the Maddy investigations."

Sax speared the rose and several petals fell to the mud. The Maddy investigation had been his first quick flirt with Washington's moral backlash. At the time Ed Maddy had been a green muckraker from Kansas who had leaped into office with a private pledge to bust the big grain traders. For a few months, led by Maddy, the senate had come

61

down hard. They wanted the lists of the Carrage payroll, and not regular company either. Maddy had his eye on the entertainment slush fund from which too many USDA grain regulators seemed to be enjoying Christmas. Bandy remembered quite vividly standing here beneath the trees while Sax defended himself to the branches.

"But this is not that sort of thing at all," Sax finally returned.

"To be sure," Bandy said, and wondered whatever became of Ed Maddy.

"We're here now, George, because of this Brazil business." Sax had found himself another rose to prod with the point of his stick. He would prod this issue just as gingerly.

"The death of Danny Miguez?" Bandy asked.

"Well, indirectly, yes."

He's afraid to talk about it, Bandy thought. He stood at Sax's profile. Both men seemed intent on the mutilation of the rose. Petals began to litter the path.

"I thought the situation might put us in a sort of limbo," Sax continued. "We can't really act effectively, can we? I mean not until we know which way the wind blows."

"By wind, do you mean Alvera?" Bandy loved to nail an ambiguity, to pin it down and watch it wriggle, just as Sax did. Only George was proud of his subtlety.

Leaves began to shudder in the wake of an actual gust. "What I mean to say," Sax continued, "is that this seems to be a good time for you to look into something for me."

So the knife was for me all along, Bandy thought. He's taken me out here to murder me. "You want me to keep away from Brazil. Is that it?" At least he would die on his feet.

"That's not really the point, George. That's not my intention at all," and Sax cut at the nearest flower and sent the petals flying. "I'm just wondering if you might not hop off to San Francisco and see if you can't strengthen our position with the shipping line. That is, just until we're sure which end is up as regards Brazil."

Bandy turned his back on the man. He was ripping the leaves off a thread of vine. "How long?"

Sax dug a heel into the mud. "Hey, it's not like I'm sending you off to exile." There was still wind, but the garden may have been quivering with tension. "No one is going to move in on you, George. It's just that I don't see any reason why you should have a free ride."

"There are other markets south of the border," Bandy said to the black earth. He was coiling the vine around his finger.

"Of course there are other markets, George, but I think your man can handle them for a few days."

"My man?" Bandy was spitting the compliment back in Sax's face. "Do you mean Janus?"

"Yes, Paul Janus," Sax said, and it was true that Janus was Bandy's aide, being groomed perhaps to one day fill his shoes, but that was years away. They both knew that. "So, you can speak to him, George?"

Bandy let the length of vine drop to the ground, and there it lay uncoiling like a worm. "You'll have to fill me in on the San Francisco situation."

"Sure, George, first thing. I thought you could leave tomorrow or the day after."

"I can leave tomorrow," said Bandy coldly. "Tomorrow will be fine."

"I'm sorry you still see it this way, George," Sax said after a moment.

But all that Bandy really saw was that Sax conclusively wanted him out of the way, and then to himself; this is how the gentlemen kill. In the eighteenth century Sax would have been the sort who kept a bone-handled pistol beneath his handkerchiefs. "I'm leaving, and that's enough," Bandy finally said.

Sax stood spearing the fallen petals. He was driving them into the mud. "You can take a few days off if you like. San Francisco's a nice town. This time of year there's a fog, of course, but then I like the fog. Atmosphere. Do you know what I mean by the word 'atmosphere'?"

Very funny, thought Bandy.

FOURTH FLOOR lackeys to Howard Sax were kings on the third floor. This was one more unwritten code in the Carrage Chateau, and more than one dumb joker had lost his job for not observing such propriety.

Sax believed in propriety, just as he believed in his mission: world peace through world trade, or some such. But on the third floor there was no pretense. Everyone knew which end was up—the fourth floor, and you made it there any way you could. Which was why George Bandy sometimes liked to go slumming down a flight. The third floor was real. The young dogs tore at one another's throats and nobody made any bones about it.

The third floor hall was brighter, but not as opulent. The Byzantine busts in the niches were fakes. The landscapes of New England countryside were the works of lesser artists. However, only George Bandy noticed the flaws this afternoon, stopping from time to time to rock back casually on his heels as he made his way down the hall. Once he even took the chance to pause before a gilt-edged mirror, but it was hard to see yourself reflected on this floor, he thought. There was too much youth.

George was a trim, tall man. Only his temples were gray. Still, forty-eight was a dangerous age on the third floor. Your back could not support the weight of all those scrambling feet.

Paul Janus was working, or more likely scheming, Bandy decided, as he came sauntering into his office. He slouched against the door jamb, because it was the most youthful pose he knew. "What's the word, Paul?"

Janus was startled and several pages slipped from his fingers. "Mr. Bandy," was all he said.

"Trying hard to save my neck, are you?" This was their joke. Janus often wrote the Bandy briefs, at least all those that George could not be bothered with. "Or are you sharpening the knife for my slaughter?"

Janus smiled. "I'm not doing anything that you haven't taught me."

"That's what I'm afraid of." Bandy laughed, and then the lines set around his mouth. "I'll be in San Francisco for a few days, Paul. Do you think you can watch the store?"

Janus dropped his eyes and began to finger the edges of his papers. "Is there some sort of problem? I mean, it's the start of the buying season."

"No problem, Paul. I'm just going to fart around with some shipper in San Fran, okay?"

Janus began nodding a bit too emphatically. Then he stopped suddenly. "Does this have anything to do with the Daniel Miguez thing?"

Bandy might have just been shot. His eyes went wide. "How did you know about that?"

"Telex this morning from Cy Vanderoff."

Bandy shook his head and swore. "I told that son of a bitch—" He broke off suddenly.

Paul filled in the silence. "It's just a matter of hours

anyway. You can't keep something like that secret for long."

But Bandy was not listening. He was gazing past the desk, through the window and beyond to the trees of the grounds. There were long shadows on the gentle slopes of the lawn. "When?" He was able to manage that much.

"Sir?"

"When did the telex come in?"

"I told you, it came in this morning."

"Yes, but what time? What time exactly?"

"Uh, nine, nine-thirty. Why?"

George spoke to the vision of this dark afternoon. "Where is it?"

"Where's what, sir?"

"The *telex*. Where's the damn telex?"

"Mr. Sax took it."

"Sax?"

"Yes, he picked it up just as it came in."

"Before the meeting? Is that right? Think, Paul. Did Sax see the telex before the meeting?"

The boy's hands were nervous. "Yeah, he saw it before the meeting."

George walked slowly to the glass. "I knew it," he said to himself. "I knew it at the meeting, and I knew it in the garden. Sax had known all along."

"Known what, sir? About Miguez?"

Bandy made a fist as if to break the glass, but only pressed his knuckles against the surface. "Not a word, Paul."

"Not a word about what?"

"Any of this. Everything that was just said in this room did not happen, okay?"

"But why?"

"*Okay?*"

"Yeah, sure."

Then softly, mostly to himself, "There's something damn peculiar going on . . . I don't know what the hell it is, but I'm going to find out. . . ."

THEY WERE strange hours, these hours before a job. In Vietnam the time had been the same before a battle. Those on the edge of madness usually went around the bend before a battle.

Swann spent the better part of the day prowling about his room. For a long time he lay on his bed and watched the shadows from the venetian blinds inch across the ceiling. Finally hunger drove him to the streets.

Supermarkets were the worst. There were all those natty housewives who glared and frowned at your canned beans and frozen dinners. Once, one of them even had tried to lecture him on nutrition. He would have liked to hit her. Except you're not supposed to do that sort of thing. They put you away, don't they?

So tonight he stayed clear of the supermarkets. He bought a package of macaroni and a carton of milk from a grocery store. Only, he was a few cents short and the clerk made him sign an IOU. The clerk laughed. "It's not the money, son, but this way I know you'll come back."

"Yeah. Now I'll come back." He jammed the package under his arm and banged out through the door. . . .

At midnight he made a frantic stab at packing. He pulled a warped suitcase from beneath the mattress. He tore through a tangle of socks and shorts. He found one clean suit and emptied a drawer of razor blades, deodorant and a mauled tube of Gleem. But the packing broke down when the half darkness in which he worked became an inescapable dome. In the fuzz of light his furniture seemed to be drooping more than ever. Cats began screeching in the alley below. Outside the night was rocking back and forth. Swann squashed his nose against the window glass, and above the city he saw mounds of intestinal clouds uncoiling. . . .

Later, just before dawn, time seemed to stop completely. Memories backed up. The minutes became elastic. Swann lay on the bed, sweating and smoking. He thought about Kim, and remembered her now as he had known her the best; a pretty thing, dressing, calling to him from behind the bathroom door. "I found something of yours, darling," she had said on that particular October evening. "I meant to show it to you."

Her apartment had been done with a working girl's budget. There were copies of Picassos on the wall, and one particularly beautiful if morbid Modigliani. Swann had been sitting in the white rattan chair, staring into the lugubrious eyes.

"I said I found something of yours," she called again. "When I was cleaning up your apartment."

"Yes," he said, but why had he ever let her see his place?

"Did they give you this in the war?" The door opened and her hand slipped through for an instant. His medal was dangling from her fingers.

"Yeah. They gave me that." He had forgotten about the thing.

"So what did you win it for?"

As if Kim hadn't known what he had done in the war. "They gave it to me. They just gave it to me, that's all."

"But you must have done something specific." The water in the bathroom had been running. Kim had been sluicing her face under the tap. "I said they must have given it to you for some specific thing."

Specific . . . horrific . . . "No, they give them out. They just give them out. I don't remember what it was for."

"It's not the purple heart, though, is it?"

"No."

"They give the purple hearts to the men that get wounded, don't they?"

"Yes."

"And you were never wounded, were you?"

And then the most honest answer he had ever given her.

"Not so you'd notice."

On the night that Kim had left him she had done the crying. Crazy. She'd left him, hadn't she? Hadn't she? . . .

As always, there came a point when the professional clicked into place. This time it was at dawn. No dramatics. But he had finally grooved into the run.

He left his room at ten in the morning. He banged down the stairs, passed two Puerto Rican girls and nodded. Outside in the streets the light was scorching off the pavement. He walked past the black grills and saw the brown faces of children flickering in the doorways. On the corner he had a bit of luck and got a cab. The driver was a wiseass kid who smirked when Swann told him to circle the block. For the rest of the trip to the airport Swann sat twisted in the back seat. He was concerned about the stationary vans with smoked windows. He saw cars that pulled out from behind. He didn't like the faces that turned as they drove by. Not that you didn't trust Father Lyle, but Lyle was old school and everything about old school cut both ways. Whatever he'd become, Swann thought, those for whom he worked were no better. . . .

Not since the war had Lyle Severson felt so alone. True, there had been that run in Prague, and Gustav who'd said, "You are the last man on earth" (they had hanged three agents the day before, and Gustav had been running for his life). But even in Prague he had not been completely alone. Switzerland had been watching, and for that matter, Langley too. Now there was no one.

Last night, to add to the misgivings, he had had to confront John Eustace. Mad John, they called him, although in his day he had been a first rate forger. Now he was only a patchy, grubby little man, obsessed with the Nazis and generally said to be over the hill. But one took what one could get, so he met with John Eustace in a dirty room off Beacon Street.

"I've done good work here," Eustace was saying. "Take a look at these." He wore a sleeveless undershirt and cheap baggy pants. His belly hung over his belt. On a crooked card table lay the passports: Swann's and John Donne's. "It's the little touch that counts. Well-thumbed ones. I always say the well-thumbed ones do the best."

"Oh yes, of course." Lyle was bent into the weak light of a gooseneck lamp. He was flipping through the pages, but he couldn't get his hands to stop shaking. "Yes, well, these will do. No doubt about it."

"They took me a long time to do. I want you to know that, Lyle." The man's fingers were twisting in his pockets. "That's what I wanted to remember to say. It took me a long time to do them right, Lyle."

"I'm sure it did, John." Lyle was still squinting at the binding on the passports.

"So if I could, uh, get the payment. I mean I wouldn't just ask, but they took me so long. That's because I know you like good work."

"Cash suit you?"

Eustace couldn't help smiling now. "Cash would suit me fine."

Before Lyle left, Eustace insisted that he see his collection. In a glass case filled with dust and flakes of paint there were several German combat helmets. There was an

Iron Cross and a dagger taken from the body of an officer. "I never tire of them, you know." He was clutching the dagger. The blade slowly turned in the feeble light. "The war, that's when we were most alive. No one likes to admit it, but it's true. I'm going to do a book about it. I've got some things to say, you know."

Then there was that awkward moment at the door. Eustace had tried to put his arm around Lyle, because of what they had been through, the years, the war and the rest of it. But Lyle had flinched. He couldn't bear the man's smell. So there they both stood. Eustace's eyes had begun to water. His smile was stillborn. . . . The coffee shop was fairly crowded. A plane from the coast had been delayed and the mood was restless and angry. Lyle had to wait for a table while Swann sat in the corner hunched over his eggs that he had drenched in ketchup. He wore a beige cotton suit. He had no tie and his shoes were canvas. When Lyle was finally seated he ordered only tea, which meant that the meeting was on.

As per their arrangement, Swann left first. He made his way up the stairs to the roof of the terminal. Lyle met him by the railing ten minutes later. There were a few others there—a young couple, arm in arm; a group of children.

Lyle made no pretense of meeting. There was no need. This far, he knew they were clean. So he simply strolled to the railing, and now they stood side by side. Below, and in the distance, there were the long stretches of criss-crossed runway. Everywhere the jets of aircraft were whistling.

"You look tired," Lyle said. "Didn't you sleep well?"

Swann shook his head.

"I remember what it was like," Lyle said, and he did too. He remembered how the fear ate at his guts.

Suddenly there was the cyclone of roaring as a descend-

71

ing jet floated over them. The railing was shuttering. Severson's knuckles went white on the gray metal bar. When the plane had passed he had to speak to get his bearings. "I have these for you, Josey," and he handed Swann a buff envelope that contained the passports. "There's some money there as well. I'm sorry it couldn't have been more."

Swann took the envelope and dropped it in his pocket. "Thank you," he muttered, but still had not turned his head. He was blinking out at the space of the runway.

Lyle had never imagined that Josey could seem so fragile. "I wish there was more I could do for you," he said, and he honestly did . . . Or maybe it's just me, he thought. Maybe I can't stand to send them out anymore. Everything seemed uncertain now. Even the runway was shimmering and unreal in the exhaust of the jets.

"I'll be all right," Swann said softly. His lips were dry. He was sniffing at the kerosene air.

"When you arrive," Lyle continued, "contact our man. His name is Nugent. There's a telephone number in the envelope.

"Nugent," Swann repeated. His voice sounded dead to him. "I'll call him first thing."

"Not that I know him." Lyle's head bobbed. "I mean that I've never actually met this man, but I understand he's rather good."

"Yes. I'll call him."

"And then there's the possibility that John will not be well enough to travel. We've got to look at that, Josey."

"I have."

"In that case you may want to wait it out. Either way, at least the poor man will have safe transport out." Then Lyle saw that Swann actually touched the envelope for a moment. "Josey, are you sure you're all right?"

Swann did not answer. His eyes were vague. The finger that had gone to the envelope now brushed the corner of his mouth.

"Josey?"

"Yes, Lyle, I'm okay. Fine."

"Because it's important to me that you *want* to go. Do you understand what I mean?"

"Yes, Lyle. I'm okay."

Again the trembling clamor from overhead rose until their space was shattered. In the wake that followed both men were silent, still gazing into the vast flat landscape. Finally, Lyle spoke. He desperately needed reality now. "This is my area," he said. "I mean to say that it's my job to follow these situations to their end. However, you . . . what I mean to say is that if you—"

"It's okay, Lyle. Everything is going to be okay."

"All right, Josey. Then I'll see you in a few days."

"Yes."

Swann did not turn around when Lyle backed off. There was no last word from him. There was only the hissing jets. But ten feet from the railing Severson stopped. He turned suddenly and called out. "Josey!" He had not been able to stop himself. Swann had also turned, and for a moment their eyes met.

Days later Lyle would remember this last etched vision of Swann. He had been standing straight against the railing. The fabric of his clothing had been flapping in the breeze. One hand had been raised as though to wave goodby, and hadn't there been a suggestion of a smile?

Who would ever have expected such a thing of Josey Swann?

73

CHAPTER 5

QUITE POSSIBLY there were those who noticed that Roger had withdrawn further into himself. His all-consuming forecast complete, one would have thought that even Roger would return from the cold depth of a North Atlantic dream. But this was not the case. He became even more aloof, more reticent.

Yet it was just as possible that Roger was fairly forgotten, because it was not long after his forecast of drought had been submitted that the lab itself was chilled by a soft and disturbing wind.

Never, for example, had the Global Atmospheric Research Program's annual report met with such an apathetic response in the lab. Ed Allen, in particular, who always had a snide remark for the GARP report, seemed listless and despondent.

"I read it," he told the Kidd. "So what?" Allen was hanging on the coffee machine, gazing into the black, plastic facing.

"Well, what did you think about the fact they failed to

identify most of the cloud lines?"

"Cloud lines? Anyone can screw up," he said. "You, me, anyone."

For two weeks running, Allen's absence was noted at McGruffy's Bar. "He's suffering in the wake of another matrimonial defeat," Mike Mullen ventured.

But Billy had seen other signs. There had been Allen's enormous Chevy pick-up first in the lot when Billy arrived in the morning, and Allen had never been one to come in early. Then there had been Allen quietly slipping out of the lab at odd hours in the day for what Billy guessed were hasty meetings with the upstairs people. And, finally, there had been Allen in one corner of the lab. His desk was always piled with graphs and reams of print-out, his hands quick to cover the pages from prying eyes.

So Allen was working on something, Billy concluded. Sure as shit, this time they've got Allen.

Then, too, John Haas developed the hunted look. Word was that John had been brought up on a security breach. "A trifling matter," said some. Questioned, Haas shrugged it off, but Billy soon realized that the jokes were gone.

As for Roger, Billy was fairly sure that he was faking it. He had seen Rog studying figures from the grids laid out on his desk, then adding up the inconsequential figures and running them through the computer. But more often than not, at the end of the day, Roger's wastebasket was filled with shredded coils of paper.

Gone were Roger's outbursts where he clenched his fists and turned away from the banter, muttering like the furious boy that he sometimes was. Gone, too, were his spells of serious innocence when he desperately tried to explain himself and then, failing, would shrug, spit out some vague insult and pad off to his own grounds.

Even more curious to Billy's mind was that Roger had taken to arriving late and leaving early. No one from above reprimanded him but Billy was quite sure that Roger, in his present state, would not have given a damn if they had. Were Roger older, say, a once great figure now on the eve of his career, one might have called his behavior a decline. As it were, however, Billy decided that Roger had finally come to the end of his rope as regarded the Carrage Grain Company.

Which made the arrival of the Carrage heavy all the more surprising. Bandy—first name was John or George, nobody seemed to know for sure. He arrived on a dark day in the late afternoon. A Tuesday, it was, and he came in a long, black Mercedes Limo. Then John or George Bandy, this bona fide Chateau executive, scuttled out of the back seat and tramped up to the topmost office. What does he want? they all asked, peering through the venetian blinds down to the sleek car obstinately parked on the lawn. You could see the swirling clouds reflected on the hood.

Then came the most intriguing twist of all. Bandy's leather soles were heard slapping back down the concrete steps, and who should be on his heel? None other than their own Roger Dennerstein. There were stranger things beneath heaven and earth, Mike Mullen was heard to remark, while the others merely shook their heads.

DUSK HAD fallen, and the promise of a darker night hung in the clouds. They drove along a broad, straight highway. Here and there were fields filled with dry weeds and the rusting heaps of abandoned cars. There were also factories, long, low brick buildings with familiar signs; Sunkist,

Ford, Pacific Telephone. At one point, Roger turned around to see the setting sun, orange in the bank of smog that ringed Los Angeles.

"This won't take but an hour," Bandy had said at the outset. He had desperately felt the need to explain himself to this weatherman. On the flight down from San Francisco, George had actually seen himself as the Carrage hammer. He would have thrown his weight around if necessary, but Dennerstein was too unsettling. So now they sat in their awkward company, each one groping for a handle on the other.

"If you want to call your wife?" Bandy pointed to a telephone set into the back seat.

"There's no need," Roger replied. "I mean if it's only going to take an hour."

"Yes, just an hour. I thought we might stop for a drink. I remember a place down the road." He leaned forward to ask the driver. "Jack, do you recall that place? Could you just pull . . . thank you, yes, I'm sure we can get a drink here."

Bandy's security measure was a roadside café. In the mornings this valley grease palace serviced truckers from all points north, while after dark, women danced naked in steel cages suspended from the rafters. But there were no naked women dancing now. Only a dour barmaid, looking much too tough for her twenty-one years. She wore Levi's with rhinestones along the seams and a halter top made from a red bandanna. In the rear-end gloom three or four locals shot pool. Above the bar was the head of a wolf; the animal's teeth were yellow.

Bandy and the weatherman took a plastic booth. "I thought we might feel less inhibited here," said George. It was his show. He was buying.

The hard, blonde girl slouched forward to take their

orders. She had had her eyes on Bandy from the start, but only because of the limousine outside. Bandy asked for a scotch, both for his nerves which were hanging all over, and to set an example for the weatherman. But Roger took a beer, and all the while sat fumbling with the salt shaker.

"I've wanted to meet you for some time," said Bandy when the girl had gone. "The Dennerstein forecast, it's made quite a mark at the Chateau."

Roger shrugged, but his face was so still and wooden that he might have been holding his breath. He mumbled, "Thank you."

Then Bandy thought of smiling, but only glanced around the room. A bearded drunk in a tie-dyed tank-top was watching them. "It's too bad that Carrage is such that two of her employees like us have never met before." *Her,* he thought, and could have cringed. I shouldn't have used that pronoun.

Roger did not notice. He filled up the silence with anything. "Well, it's a big company."

"Too big?" Bandy bit his lower lip. "I've always had this theory, you see. That is, I've thought the companies such as Carrage are oddly archaic. Do you know what I mean? The company mind, if there is such a thing, is so much like the rationalist mind. This big corporate mind sees itself as stamping out myth and superstition. White man's burden, that sort of thing. Follow me?"

Roger nodded and George began to grin uncomfortably, thinking: why am I on this line? Except there had been the weatherman's file which conclusively marked him as a rebel. Well, show him that you're no company jock yourself, George had told himself.

"I sometimes think," he continued, now unable to stop, "that these companies are trying to build the modern incarnation of Adam Smith's invisible hand. Only this big company mind can be so . . . naive. Don't you think so? And then, laughing nervously, "Defang the nationalist monster, so to speak."

Roger also laughed. What the hell else should he do? Then the kissing was over, and Bandy began to move in. You've warmed the ice, he thought, now break it. "So I was in San Francisco, as I've mentioned," he said. "It's such a short hop, and I thought I might as well take advantage of the situation to meet you, to ask you some questions that have . . . well, been on my mind."

Roger gazed over the rim of his glass. "If I can help, well, certainly . . ."

"Yes, because it's regarding your forecast. A remarkable piece of work. Did I tell you how enthused we all were? Good, all right then, but there was an area which I've been wondering about. Of course, I've been briefed by Adrian Riggs. We all have. And do you know Adrian? Yes, well he's very good. You'd get on well with him. But as I was saying, although Adrian wrote a wonderful brief for us, I still wanted to ask you a few questions. That is, there are still a few points I would like to clear up.

"Yes?" Roger's hands were in his lap, intent and waiting.

But Bandy began to waver. You've bullshitted yourself right into the wall, he thought, and took another long sip from his scotch. "Uh, Brazil," he finally said, praying that no bomb went off.

"Brazil?" Roger asked.

"Yes, I'm wondering about the correlations, or connections actually, involving Brazil."

"I'm sorry. I don't follow."

"Of course you don't." Bandy laughed and mopped sweat from his forehead. "What I mean is, what I really mean is this . . . how would an area like Brazil fit into the overall scheme of things?"

"What scheme?"

Bundy could have cursed the little bastard for not helping more. "Of your forecast."

Roger dropped his head. He was wedging the salt into neat little piles. "I never thought about Brazil, not in such specific terms," he said. "I mean that it's hard to pin down such a small geographic area. To say you've got a chance of rain, or no rain, or what have you, in an area like Brazil is extremely risky. I really can't—"

"I only ask because I do a lot of business in Brazil, buying, and . . . well, I thought maybe I could get some sort of edge on this coming year. If I knew, even roughly, where we stood . . ."

Last night, alone in a posh but sterile room, nothing had seemed impossible to George. He had stood before an open window and seen the lights of the city flashing out until they reached the dark bay. Yes, anything had seemed possible last night, even an inside peek at the Dennerstein forecast.

"You see," Roger was saying, "anything I tell you now regarding, uh, Brazil would only be the wildest guess. Off the top of my head. However, I suppose I could say that Brazil, as would all the South American areas, should remain largely unaffected. I say this because the situation at hand is caused in part by a polar ridge . . . that's a bank or wall of air around the north pole. It's the cold air which inhibits the cloud cover and so sets off, uh, the chain reaction."

"I see," Bandy nodded, and Janus could have the stinking job.

"But of course the situation would mostly affect Asia,

because of the monsoonal delay, although North America and the Soviet Union would also suffer."

"Suffer?"

"Of course, suffer. What do you think this is, Mr. Bandy?" Roger's knuckles whitened around his glass. "This is the most important part. It's extremely important that you people at the Chateau grasp it. You have no idea, but . . . well, I've seen what these situations mean to the peasants. There's the crops . . . I've seen it, sir."

"Seen what, Roger?" Bandy's elbows lay on the table, the intensity set in the edges of his mouth.

"Drought, Mr. Bandy. I don't know what Adrian Riggs wrote up in his brief, but I'm afraid, sir, that there's going to be a drought."

"Yes," Bandy breathed. "I understand entirely." Then he remembered Sax again, standing on the garden path, bent over the roses, the petals in the mud, his shoulders dappled with milky light. That bastard Howard Sax.

ROGER LAY on the sheepskin rug. His eye quite naturally followed the lines of Julie's hardwood floor. She had had that floor pegged and grooved. Like George Bandy pegged and grooved me? Roger wondered.

Most of the house had been furnished according to Julie's taste. There were all those ferns, potted in rough stone bowls. There were other rugs, Belgian copies of the Chinese. There were etchings, generally abstract, framed with simplicity, signed by artists that Roger had never heard of. He did not disapprove of what she had done, only maybe there were times when the house did not feel like his. Maybe this was someone else's house, he sometimes had the urge to say, just as Julie, extraordinarily beautiful, occasionally seemed like someone else's woman.

I have the house, Julie had told him time and time again. *I have the house, because you have your work.*

Oh, yes, Roger had his work, and there was a consummate nightmare for you, particularly now, tonight, when he could not get George Bandy's face out of his mind. Roger had been over that meeting a dozen times since he had stepped out of the limousine two hours earlier, and still he could not quite pull it together. That Bandy had been lying seemed fairly evident in retrospect. But lying for what reason? *I should have pinned him down,* Roger decided, *should have come right out and said it.* Now, of course, it was too late. You couldn't exactly call the man up on the by-the-way. Still, by hook or by crook he would know. *This is important,* he had known that much from the start. *It's important. Whatever is going on in Brazil is important.*

Julie had never really understood. One could give her the facts, but sometimes the facts were not enough. There were four hundred and sixty million people living under the constant threat of starvation, he had told her. Someone died of starvation every 8.6 seconds. Every minute there were seven deaths. That was four hundred and fifty deaths an hour, ten thousand every day. Until Julie screamed, "All right, I care! I honestly care, Roger, but I can't spend my whole life in mourning."

But, honey, would you also care if I told you that Carrage is cutting off my balls? Very often Roger saw that his manhood—not soul—was the real issue. And it was at these times when he deeply hated the company.

From where he sat now with his legs tucked under him, he saw one clear image of his body thrown back from a tiny mirror at the end of the room. He looked leaner now, certainly not hungry and mean, but at least less dumpy, less the comical goony bird with ruffled feathers. And more the man that Julie had married? (Working at Carrage had taken its toll.)

Roger rose from the sheepskin rug. One eye was slightly narrowed. He ran his hands through his fine, black hair, not thinning really, but stay at Carrage and you'll be gray before your time.

Scattered about the room were mementoes of four years of marriage and a life of determined normality. Roger hefted a crystal ball up from the marble mantel. He had bought this mysterious thing from a wall-eyed untouchable in the streets of Delhi. "See the future," the little brown man had said. "See the future for only eight rupees." So he gave the fist-sized opaque rock to his wife and here it sat on the mantelpiece. Above the ball hung a passionless oil of storm clouds over a white-capped sea. This had been her gift to him, "because you have to understand that there's also beauty in the weather," she had told him.

There were other relics here. Roger tapped a finger on the gilt plaque that Carrage had given him for what they called "outstanding service." He remembered there had been an awful moment at the presentation dinner because the engraver had spelled his name wrong. Across the room there was Julie's watercolor—horses in a north Virginia pasture. This was her only testament to her fling with painting. When Roger began to earn the big bucks from Carrage, Julie started to collect.

But of all these odds and ends, there was nothing that bespoke the essential Roger. That part of him had been lugged up to the attic years ago.

The attic was properly Roger's study. It had been a phase for Julie, like painting. She had decided that her man—her genius—needed a place where he could go and work, and think, and maybe even accomplish great things. She had workmen in who hid the visceral plumbing and oxblood brick with panels of sanded pine. She covered the floor with bright thick rugs from South America. She even destroyed a wall so that Roger could have his window to the sky.

Now Roger lay on the gray divan in his study. An hour had passed since he had climbed the stairs. Twenty minutes since he had lain himself down. He had not moved his hand. His head was supported by a wad of cushions at just the right angle to see the sky.

There were times when Roger came to his study only for the view. Then he would sink down on the cushions and stare at the sky for hours. But this time he had not come with such a defined purpose in mind. He had drifted up those stairs, running a hand on the pine banister, slowly, pensively, seeing and not seeing. Or, perhaps, he had been drawn up those stairs, drawn, as it were, by the file.

It was not really a file, just an old Shasta box. The clippings from the magazines and journals, the occasional newspaper article were in no particular order. The stuff had simply been thrown together. There were papers from graduate days, and a lot from the time he had spent with the United Nations. All of the material was from a period before Julie, but then that was understandable. Julie would not have wanted him to keep such a file as this.

The first clipping that Roger found told the story of a group of parents in Central Africa who implored a United Nations relief official not to send drugs when diphtheria broke out. The land had been seared by eight years of drought, so it was kinder, the parents argued, to let the children die rather than suffer more hunger. Then there was an article on the Indian famine victims who had drowned themselves to end the slow starvation. He found a chart he had compiled when still in college that showed that Asian drought might increase from year to year as the climate seemed to be following a cooling trend. The theory had put him at loggerheads with his instructors. They claimed that Roger was predicting another ice age, which was a little farfetched. Even now, of course, not enough time had passed to prove him right or wrong. But there were others who had seen similar signs. The great Reid Bryson, for one. There was a figure for you, Director of the Institute of Environmental Studies at the University of Wisconsin, no less. *Science News* called him the "scariest man in America" because he predicted something like a billion people starving in the next decade or two.

Next there were the photographs. Maybe they were not clinical studies that could be graphed and digitized, but they tore at your heart more than any of it. Roger laid them out on the bright red rug. There were some happy snaps of him and his colleagues, arm in arm on the steps of the Bombay agency. They were all wearing khaki shorts, and one of them was clowning with a pith helmet. There was a shot of Roger, posing by the jeep with the skin of a cobra wrapped around his head like a turban. There were also shots of the famine.

He saw gaunt faces and the brown husks of starving bodies. There were long dry landscapes where the soil had been ruined by a year of no rain. Farmers dug through yards of sandy earth only to squeeze out a few drops of water from the muddy clay. Finally there was a shot of blind, white-eyed children with bloated bellies and open sores.

How does one interpret these images? Roger could have asked himself. Six or a million years ago there had been an idealistic Roger, a Roger who believed that the world was honestly trying to save itself. But no more.

He raised his arm and stretched it above his head. Now he saw the moon framed in the web of his fingers. Two hours ago Roger had virtually cursed himself for impotence. I should have given the facts to Bundy, he had told himself. I should have hammered the man with the facts of a hard-core famine. Instead, he thought, I sat like a chicken, bobbing and pecking on command. Yet, now, Roger was glad that he had not made waves, because the time had come to play it cool. There would be no more soap box orations on the plight of the starving millions. The time had come to go for blood.

It was nearly eight in the evening when Julie returned. She came in the door calling his name. Her hair was in disarray. Her shoes were dangling from her hand. Roger made them both a drink, and they dined on last night's meat loaf. Afterward they sat on the rug, that same sheepskin rug, and chatted about meaningless things. She said that she had seen a pair of shoes she had nearly bought. "But they were really too much. I don't mean too much money. I mean too much, you know?"

Roger was tweaking a button on his shirt. Julie bought his shirts, nice ones, really, but the buttons never stayed on.

"Because you pull at them when you're nervous, Roger. If you didn't pull at them they would stay on." Then she puffed a bit of hair from her face and smiled. "Am I nagging? I don't mean to nag." She leaned over and rubbed her knuckle across his cheek. Sometimes she called him her darling leopard, although he rarely felt like a leopard.

"But you could have bought those shoes if you really wanted them," he told her, and then began to glance about the room.

"Oh, to hell with those shoes." She pulled at the cuffs of his trousers with her toes.

Here was the Julie that you married, he thought, and then he pulled her down so that she lay in the crook of his arm. "Listen, love, I may have to work late again this week. Something has come up again at the lab."

"Ugh, the lab," and she wrinkled up her nose. The actual details of his work bored her, or perhaps even frightened her, such was the power of those colliding blasts of wind. What Julie liked about what Roger did was the possibility of recognition. She often dreamed of him on the lecture circuit. Of course, there was also the money.

"It's just a possibility," he added. "I'm not sure I'll have to work late, it's just if things continue . . ."

"Well, if you have to work late, then you have to work late, but Thursday we're supposed to go to the Fastbinders' for dinner." She started to feel the bones of his chest. Her fingers were bouncing over them. "You like the Fastbinders."

He didn't really. They were Julie's friends, but Roger could not complain because he had no friends of his own. There had been a time when he had dragged her to the parties given by his U.N. colleagues. At first she had been excited by the prospect of a radical chic fundraiser. However, instead of the Beverly Hills socialites, all she found were some born again liberals, a few beatnik survivors and a fair amount of campus types in tattersalls and sandals with white socks. Julie, Roger remembered, had once been chastized for bringing California wine. "Don't you realize what they're doing to the farm workers?" They made a ceremony of pouring it down the drain.

"So you don't think you can make it Thursday? I don't want to pressure you, but I've already accepted."

"I'm sure Thursday will be all right."

"They're certainly using you for a lot of work, though, aren't they?" She began to toy with the cuff of his shirt. "It makes me proud, it really does," and to prove it she gently bit his palm.

He did not doubt that she was proud of him. She had always said that she liked a man who used his mind. When they had first met she had been working as a waitress, broke and hungry, for a man who would buy her things. Roger had gotten by with a cute face and a string of jokes until he could truly afford her. But even now he did not feel safe, because there was that other side of Julie, the side that may have secretly longed for some muscle-bound joe who could really protect her, right on down to the brass tacks.

By eleven, however, she was safely asleep in his arms. They had both run out of things to say, so he turned on the news but kept the volume low. A ridiculous weatherman spoke of a storm. There were reports of low pressure along the coast, and the weatherman stuck cardboard arrows on a map to make his point.

But when Roger closed his eyes he saw great mushrooms of cumulous forms, pure white in the upper billows, while closer to the face of the sea, the clouds were gray and finally black.

CHAPTER 6

JOSEY WAS stoned. He was plastered into a green lea-
therette chair in the waiting lounge of the airline terminal.
His eyes were reduced to red slits. A woman with a hungry, stiff smile had given him a glossy brochure of Brazil.
Now he was thumbing through the pages and glancing at
the photographs. He saw pictures of the cities. There were
great, white slabs of sculptured concrete, flanked by
smooth lawns and silver ponds. He saw scenes of lean,
young girls lying by the sea on the scalloped sand. The
Tourist Board called their nation "a young and cosmopol-
itan country." But later during the flight, the plane
dropped through the lip of clouds, banked into a long,
slow turn and far below Swann saw the miles of tangled,
green jungle as vast and devouring as any he had seen in
Vietnam.

He landed in the night. Nugent, the consulate man that
Severson had sworn by, was predictably not at the airport
to meet him. But Swann didn't care. He would get a hotel
room and then ring the bastard up. He would shake him

out of bed if necessary, maybe even scare him. At least it would be something to do.

But when Josey finally got to his hotel room and called, Nugent was out. He tried the consulate and the night watch knew nothing. He tried the man at home again, but all he got was that nasty ring over and over. So Josey slammed down the receiver and settled in for the night. He would suffer the wait, just as he suffered the disgusting, brown shag carpet and the cheap, ceramic lamps with their checked plastic shades. He would suffer the wait until morning, just as Johnny was suffering in some rat-hole safe-house with his chest all torn to shit.

But if Josey was practiced at waiting, tonight was worse than usual. He couldn't sleep, which was nothing new, but for some reason the old war was kicking up hard. The nausea, too, because the war and the nausea were one and the same. As far back as he could remember into the war there had been the nausea. Drugs occasionally helped him live with it, but it was always there. He would walk into a restaurant. A waitress would shove food in front of him. He wouldn't want it. He wouldn't be able to eat it. If he managed to force it, close his eyes and bolt it down, then the stuff filled nothing. It became an alien lump in the pit of his stomach, and the nausea threatened to spit it up at any moment.

Josey struggled out of the damp mess he had made with the sheets and went into the bathroom. Then hunched over the sink, he began downing handfuls of pills with tepid water. The front of his shirt was soaked to the skin. There were puddles of water all over the floor. But once the dope took, peace passed over his body, and he sat for hours by the window loading bullets into the clip of his .45 and then popping them out again one by one.

After what seemed like only a minute the sun came

blasting through the window and burned him out of sleep. Swann moaned and coughed up phlegm. The mattress was soggy from his sweat. There were traces of blood from where he had cut his fingers the night before, although he could not remember how.

He dressed in a beige cotton suit and blue leather track shoes. Then he called Nugent. "Oh, yes, I was expecting you," Nugent beamed. "Had a good flight, did you? All settled in now?"

They agreed to meet in an hour, which gave Josey time for breakfast, although breakfast was a joke. He went down to the coffee shop in the lobby, ordered two eggs that he couldn't eat, and made a mess of a stack of greasy toast. All that he could really manage were the half a dozen cigarettes and the bloody mary. It was a rank morning, and the only thing that got him through it in the end was the little hit of methedrine that he popped in the men's room before he left the lobby.

Because Nugent was scared, scared of Josey, scared of the whole bad dream he was in with John Donne, they did not meet at the consulate. They met in a park by the side of the fountain. A marble fish shot jets of water into a pond. The light was defracted in the windy spray, and rainbows formed in the mist. Josey and Nugent sat side by side on the marble edge. Swann was angry, mean as a crab. Nugent, a small, young man in a neat brown suit, was merely frightened that they would be seen together.

"It's a pretty bad scene," Nugent said. He was pulling at his elastic socks.

"Just tell me what happened." There was a cigarette bobbing in Josey's mouth.

"Uh, let's see, three days ago. The story goes like this. Donne had just come back from, you know, killing that guy Miguez. Donne goes up to his hotel room and a guy

93

is waiting for him. There was a struggle or something and Donne winds up with a bullet in his chest. Then he makes it to the consulate and demands to see the local resident, me. The night watch lays him on the couch, and I come running with a doctor. Caspar, know him?"

"No," Swann said. "I don't know him. Is he a Company man?"

"No, but he's witting. Anyway, Caspar operates right there on the sofa, made a mess, but he got the bullet out. Now I've got Donne tucked away in a little place at the edge of the city."

Josey threw his cigarette butt into the pond and swore.

"Well, I couldn't very well keep him at the consulate, could I? The place is too straight. The man's passport is completely blown. The army could very well be combing the streets for him."

Across a stretch of spiked lawn there was a row of daisies. Already the morning heat was withering the petals. The flowers were drooping like the heads of strangled birds.

Nugent pulled at his lips. "Anyway, he wouldn't go to a hospital, and he's got a gun. He won't part with it."

Josey ran his fingers along the scum that was caked on the tiles of the pond. He liked the feel of the stuff wedged up in his nails. "Is John well enough to travel?"

"I'm not sure. He says yes, the doctor says no." Nugent clutched his ribs. "Apparently there's some internal bleeding."

Nugent hiked up the sleeve of his coat and studied his watch. It was an elegant piece of gold junk with a black dial and an alligator band. Josey had a sudden urge to tear it off the man's wrist and toss it into the water. "You have to go somewhere?" Josey began.

"I'm expected back at the consulate."

"But first you're taking me to John, right?"

"Yeah, sure. I'll take you to John." Nugent glanced back over his shoulder. "But you know it's not safe here, no one's safe anymore."

Josey sniffed. He felt ready to retch in the heat. He felt as dry as old death. "Yeah," he slurred, "so what else is new?"

But as Swann had expected there was nothing new, nothing he hadn't seen before. Not the sagging staircase that ran from the cramped slum street through a narrow, dark corridor to the door of Johnny's room. Not the fly-blown room itself where Johnny lay on a dirty mattress. Not Caspar, the gray flunky doctor who sat nervously in the only chair by the window. "You're late," Caspar snapped when Swann walked in. "He was expecting you last night." The doctor rose and began pacing the room. There was blood on his shirt, and blood on his striped flannel trousers. In the corner of the room there were wads of brown gauze. An empty penicillin bottle lay shattered on the bare wood floor.

"Just get the fuck out of here," Josey said. "Wait outside, and don't listen at the door. If you do, I'll know, and then I'll tear your fucking ears off."

Donne was up on one elbow, laughing. "Hey, Jose, he's all right. You've got to be nice to the good doctor. He's okay."

Josey knelt on the edge of the mattress. "How are you doing, man?"

Donne coughed. "Oh, they fucked me, Jose, they really fucked me good."

"Yeah, well I can see that, asshole. But how are you doing?"

"Been better, man. I've been a whole lot better." Donne's smile was starting to fade.

95

"I've come to get you out of here. You know that?"

"Yeah, sure you are, Jose." John's fingers clutched at the brown, wool blanket until his knuckles were white.

"I've got a couple of passports. I've got some money. We'll make it." Josey was toying with the buttons on Donne's bloody shirt.

"Listen, I got to tell you something, Josey. I've got to tell you." John may have only been living for this moment. Already his eyes were growing soft.

"Yeah, I'm listening. I can hear you, Johnny."

Donne wiped his mouth with the end of his blanket. "I was blown, man. I didn't fuck it up. I was blown, blown right out of the fucking water."

"What are you saying?"

"I was blown. I don't know why, but I do know that somebody set me up, right? Cassidy sends me down here, and as soon as I make the hit, I get it."

"Cassidy, uh?"

John shook his head. "I'm not saying that Cassidy was the one for sure. I'm not saying that he was the one that blew me. Maybe he was working through a cutout. Maybe he was just doing the job for someone else. But I was blown, man. That's why I had Nugent call Lyle to get you down here. I don't want anything to do with Cassidy, not until I'm ready. Know what I mean? There's something weird going on down here. This isn't no regular Company gig. There's someone else dealing the cards. I don't know, but it feels that way."

John had taken Josey's hand. His fingers were digging into the flesh. "We'll get this straightened out, Johnny. We'll get you back and then we'll find out what's happening."

Donne's jaw went limp and his lips stretched to a crazy

smile. "Yeah," he drawled. "You're fucking right about that, man. See, I'm going to just lay here and bleed for a little while, okay? Then we'll get up. But you're going to stay with me, aren't you?"

Josey nodded. "Sure. I'm not going anywhere, John. I'm going to stay right here."

"Ah, that's good, Jose, 'cause I'm just going to get up and get on that plane, and we'll go back and sweat Cassidy. If he's not the cocksucker who set me up, then we'll find out who is. And we'll stick it to them, Josey. Okay?"

"Yeah, we'll do it."

Donne's mouth was twitching with the words. "Yeah," he smiled. He might have been staring out beyond the walls, out to the sky above Brazil. "We'll stick it to him, Josey. We'll stick it to him, stick it to him . . ."

There was no electricity, so when night fell Josey lit candles. Now the walls were alive with the flickering shadows. The doctor had left. He had said there was nothing more he could do. Then he left. He gave Swann a telephone number and told him about the phone booth in the hall. "If he makes it until morning," the doctor had said, "he'll have a good chance."

But Josey knew what kind of chances the losers like John Donne and himself were given. At best you died quietly with a friend in your room, and your veins filled with morphine. By that standard, John was about to hit the jackpot.

For a long time John slept. Then he woke and called Swann over to his side. It was some indefinable hour past midnight. Josey had placed the candles around the bed and now the wavering sheets of light were mesmerizing them. "I dreamed you were dead," Donne said.

97

"No, John. I'm not dead." The two men's words were also dream words.

"Yeah, and you're looking good, Jose. You're looking real good."

Swann's face was very close to Donne's. Their breath was mingling. Once or twice their fingers touched. "How are you doing, man?" Josey asked.

"Okay," John groaned. "Okay." A moment passed when neither spoke. Donne was staring into the candle's flame. "Hey, man, are you still seeing that chick?"

Josey shook his head.

"That's too bad. She was great. What about anyone else? You seeing anyone? I mean do you have a girlfriend, Josey?"

"No, John. I don't."

Donne reached out and placed his hands on Josey's knee. "I got a girlfriend. I mean I used to. Her name was Nancy. She was incredible. Really beautiful, you know?"

Swann bowed his head. His eyes were locked onto the spray of light.

"She was a cheerleader, and homecoming queen. No kidding. We went together all through high school. We were even going to get married. I mean, she wanted to, you know? I remember that she didn't want me to go to Nam. She cried, but I gave her the usual bullshit. I don't remember too much of it, because it was a long time ago. But I know that she cried for me. Can you dig that? She cried, and said the war was stupid. I couldn't fucking believe that. Nancy said the war was stupid."

Josey smiled a little, but only because Donne was smiling, smiling into a memory of sweet knees and pompons.

"Once I went back to see her. It was just after the war. I went back home, and I saw my folks, and I saw all my old friends, and I saw Nance. But you know how it was, man. I just couldn't cut it. At first everyone was real glad to see me. They were asking me all these questions and shit, but then it got real clear to them where I stood. It was like I was from a different planet or something, or maybe they were from a different planet. Nancy sort of got freaked out. I guess I didn't play it too cool. I tried, I really fucking tried, but I just couldn't hack it. Nancy was going to college then, and she was into the sorority scene. All the guys she knew were into fraternities. It was real rah-rah college. We'd go to a party, and maybe start drinking a little beer and just bullshitting. Then maybe some guy would ask me what it was like over in Nam, and shit . . . that's when I'd start staring into this fucking jungle that's growing inside my head. You know what I mean? Next to Nancy, I was really something weird. I just couldn't keep it together. All the guys that I saw . . . I was . . . Fuck me, I was ready to start wasting people. If I had my gun it would have been bad. Even though I really loved that chick, I just couldn't keep it together, couldn't make it right. That's why I joined the Company, man. I just couldn't keep that jungle from growing. You know?"

Swann knew. Their hands were clasped. "You're all right, John. You're going to be fine. Everything is going to be all right."

"You're not bullshitting me, are you, man?"

"No, you're fine, man. Everything's cool."

"Yeah," John slurred, "and I'm looking fine, too. I'm looking real fine." Except that his mouth was cracked in a silly smile and his face was tracked with tears.

Across the room the dripping wax was sputtering in the flame. Shadows lashed at the ceiling. Moths wheeled at the light. "Ah, Jesus," Donne got out. "Why the fuck is this happening?" Then his fist crashed down on the mattress and he died, shuddering.

99

SWANN ROSE and left the room. He made his way slowly down the stairs. Night was down on the city like black gauze. Teenagers in sunglasses to look mean veered their bicycles from Josey's path. Barefoot children with sandbagged eyes looked out from basement windows. No one approached Josey. No one wanted to be caught watching him. He was as spectral and dangerous as he had ever been in the jungle.

Half a mile into the center of the city he found a cab. He gave the address to Nugent's home and arrived there a few minutes later. Nugent lived in clean suburbia. His house was surrounded by a high stone wall. The other consulate boys probably lived in small, neat apartments, but the CIA flim-flam man earned enough to buy a house.

Tonight, however, the flim-flam man was too destroyed to shuck and jive. He was not used to death, even an animal's like Donne's. He let Swann in the door with a naked, sleepy grimace, and pulled his bathrobe tighter at the waist. "Would you like some coffee?"

Swann nodded. He was rooting about the living room, laying his hands on the edges of the chrome furniture, taking in this contempo bachelor's pad. Finally, he settled into a Naugahyde easy chair. The ash from his cigarette exploded on the rug.

"He died, didn't he?" Nugent's voice was cracking, although he tried his best to stay cool, shuffling forward with two mugs of black coffee.

"Yeah, he died," Josey said. He was still looking about the room. There were potted plants in the bay window, and a leather bench with splayed lion's paws carved into the dark stone legs.

"Look, I'm sorry about that. I mean if he was a friend of yours." Nugent perched himself on the edge of his couch. He was rubbing his feet nervously on the rug.

"I want to know a few things," Swann told him. "I'm going to ask you a few questions, and I want you to answer, okay?"

"Hey, anything." Nugent could run faster than he could be pushed.

Swann suddenly felt he could have killed the man, done it just for the hell of it. "What's Allen Cassidy got going down here?"

Nugent sipped at his coffee. "Not much. He's mostly got the peanut circuit. He's got a few agents in the local police, maybe a few government people, nothing heavy." He winced as the coffee burned his tongue. "If you want to know why your friend Donne was so scared of Cassidy, I can't help you. All I know is that Donne tells me to call Lyle Severson and not Cassidy. That's all I know about that end of things."

"Do you think Cassidy sent John down here to make the hit on Miguez?"

"I don't know. I couldn't imagine why. It's an unprecedented move. I mean there hasn't been that kind of action down here in a long time."

Josey was dipping his finger into a ring of coffee on the glass top table. "Who do you think set John up?"

"I don't even know if he was set up."

Swann frowned. "All right, let's take it like this. Who would Cassidy use down here if he were going to run a job like this?"

Nugent was pulling at the draw string of his robe. "Cassidy has a two-bit stringer named Dante Mescal. He's an arms dealer by trade, although he does all kinds of other stuff."

"Did he supply John with the M16?"

"Probably. He picked a lot of those things up after the war, so, yeah, I'd have to say that Mescal probably sold him the rifle."

"How would the exchange be arranged?"

"Cash and carry. Mescal isn't under a Company contract. He's freelance. Everybody owns him."

"Who's everybody?"

"The French, the West Germans, the British. Basically he's straight, but he's not above the take when the price is right."

Swann wet his lips. "How does Cassidy service his stable?"

"I do a little, and the local resident does a little."

"Who's that?"

Nugent threw up his hands. "Come on, Swann."

Then Josey began gulping into the silence. He could have pushed the prick, but it didn't matter. "How about lately, any action?"

"Not really. Like I said, it's the peanut circuit."

"Oh, yeah?" Josey's eyes were locking on. "Fucking Minister of Agriculture gets hit and you tell me there was no action?"

"Okay, so I heard some rumors." Nugent's cheek was lumped. His head turned to the side.

"What sort of rumors, Tony," and Swann drew out the name, "Toneee."

"Look, I just heard bits and pieces."

"Yeah, what did you hear?" Josey wanted to shake him, rub him right into the shag.

"Word is that Mescal has been receiving and delivering big money, but not necessarily from Cassidy. The money could have been from anyone."

"How big?"

"Well, I heard about fifteen grand, but that's not too accurate."

"Did you ever ask Cassidy about it?"

Nugent reached for his coffee now that he felt the heat was off. "Might as well ask the man in the moon. Cassidy said he didn't know a thing about it. The only link that Cassidy has to this whole affair is your friend's word that Cassidy sent him down. Now, I'm not saying that Donne was lying, okay? I'm just saying that there isn't any other connection between what has been going on down here and Cassidy."

Swann tapped a finger on the glass. "Go fuck yourself, man."

Nugent pulled the ends of his robe over his knee. "I'm just trying to help. I'm just saying that it doesn't look to me like Cassidy. Cassidy doesn't have the clout to make a move like hitting Miguez. He couldn't get the money, and there has been some big money floating around. So if it didn't come from Cassidy, then who did it come from?"

"This Mescal, where can I find him?"

Nugent rose without a word and left the room. He returned a moment later with a slip of paper. "This is the guy's address, but I don't know if he'll be there."

Swann nodded and stood. By the time he reached the door, Nugent had fully recovered. He was that flim-flam man again, covering his ass from every angle, more than happy to help the winners. "If there's anything else I can do. Maybe you'd like to wire Severson or something. I can let you into the consulate."

"No," Josey said. He was halfway into the night.

"Well, do you want me to send a message up the line?"

"Just take care of the body. Have Johnny sent home, will you?"

"Anywhere in particular? I mean if I send it to Operations in Langley, there will be a better chance that wife and family can get a pension. Operations can make it official. Killed in the field, know what I mean?"

"Yeah, send it there." Josey remembered that John had a mother someplace. She used to send him socks for Christmas. She believed her son worked for a travel agency. She also drank a lot.

"And, remember, if there's anything I can do, anything at all." Nugent was holding the door. He couldn't wait to get the maniac out of his house.

"Yeah," Josey said, pointing with his finger to his temple. "I'll bear it in mind." Then he moved out of the light and into the darkness.

SWANN WALKED through the half-deserted streets. The restless night had died. There was no movement from the blank tenement windows. Streaks of pallid light danced on the oil-slick surface of stagnant gutter pools. Josey was following the shred of paper, fluttering in his hand.

Dante Mescal might have been the resident slum landlord of these desolate blocks on the bad side of Sao Paulo. His apartment was aloft, high above the others. Swann climbed thirteen flights of concrete steps until he stood before the door. He began rapping on the wood, first gently, then harder and harder. A voice broke from inside, three drowsy words, but Swann kept beating at the door.

His first vision of Dante Mescal grew as the door drew back. Here was the night's own ghoul. Mescal stood scowling, running his fingers through his black, jagged curls. He wore a purple velvet bathrobe, and the one hand jammed in the pocket probably clutched a pistol. "So, who are you, uh?" Mescal's eyes were bloodshot, and the lids swollen.

104

"I'm a friend," Swann whispered. He was holding his ribs, like the frantic agent that he had suddenly become. "I'm one of Cassidy's men. Allen Cassidy, you know?"

Mescal shifted the pistol. "So what does Allen want this time?"

"I've come to finish the job."

"What job?" Mescal yawned and his gold teeth winked.

"You know, Donne. The guy that hit Miguez." Swann was so locked into the role that he could not even keep from shivering. Cover is not believing, cover is knowing. "I can't find the target."

Mescal nearly laughed. "Okay, come in," and he swaggered back from the door.

The apartment had been done with a tinsel elegance. The drapes were dreamy blue, the carpet thick and darker. The ends of the sofa were tucked and rolled. There were portraits of naked women on the walls.

Mescal flicked his eyes the length of Swann. "Okay, friend, you tell me your secrets and I'll tell you mine." Then he grinned, and his lips were glossy. "At three in the damn morning, you come knocking at my door."

"It's important, Dante." Josey sank to the couch and crossed his legs. A clean-cut Company killer, loyal to the cause, fired up with visions of an American Jesus. "I've got to finish the job," he announced.

"Sure, I know how it is, friend." Mescal was only too willing to play the flippant intelligence whore. "But you got to tell me the score."

"Donne, we've heard he's still alive."

"No, I had my man shoot him, okay? I think he's crawled off in a hole and died."

"But Cassidy is worried. I got to make sure the job is finished."

Mescal was rubbing his skinny shins together. "Oh that

Cassidy . . . Oh, that Dancing Allen Cassidy, what's he got to worry about? I take all the risks. I'm the one who has to put his neck in the lion's mouth. I'm the one who gets woken up in the morning by the kid. No offense, kid." Then Mescal's mouth puckered. "Me, I got a cold. I got to take care of myself." Mescal stooped at a cabinet. When he rose, a bottle of pale whiskey was swinging by its greasy neck from his hand.

"No thanks," Josey smiled. Tonight he was the sort that didn't touch a drop until the job was done. Then he clapped his hands together. "So, can you help me?"

Mescal sucked at the bottle, swallowed and belched. "Okay, boy, it goes like this. I meet Donne the other day, and I sell him a gun. Then I go to some guy I know and arrange the hit. So my friend muffs it. Donne is hit, but he doesn't go down. He doesn't fall dead, okay? He's a tough guy. He runs out of the hotel, jumps in his car, and that's all that Dante knows." Mescal scratched his neck. "So I muffed the job, so sue me." Then he was massaging the soles of his feet on the rug, and his eyes rolled back in ecstasy.

Josey stood, because he was the agitated spy, too nervous to sit. He took a step, and the step became his move. Transformation, Josey went low, cocked his fist at his thigh and slammed it into Mescal's groin.

Mescal grunted. His knees buckled and he dropped face down to the carpet. Swann knelt over him, his .45 jammed into the neck. "This is how it's going to go, cunt. Some things I know, but I'm going to be asking you to see if you're straight, okay? *Okay?*"

Mescal groaned. His nose was bleeding, his face pressed into the carpet. "I'll play, okay? I'll play."

"Who set Donne up?" Swann smashed his hand into the back of Mescal's head, just to set a precedent.

106

"Cassidy," Mescal cried. "That's all I know, friend."

Swann had a handful of Mescal's hair. The thick, black coils were disgusting. "Sequence, give me sequence."

Mescal gagged into the rug. "What do you mean, this sequence?"

"What happened, step by step," and Swann pulled up the head, ready to throw it back down again.

"Okay, Cassidy said there's this soldier coming down. Donne, right? Cassidy says he's going to hit the minister. Oh, man, that's a big job. Okay, Cassidy tells me to sell him a gun, help him and then when he makes the hit, I'm supposed to have him blown away. Okay, that's what I do."

"How did you talk with Cassidy?"

"No talk, it was all on the one-time pads."

"Who did you use to hit Donne?"

"A local guy. He's a cop. He doesn't know anything."

"How did you pay him? How did you work the money?"

Mescal was sweating furiously now. His hair was coiling round Josey's fingers. "I don't know too much about the money. The money comes into a post office box. Maybe there were four or five deposits, okay? Then I take what's left and dead-drop it."

"Details."

"Okay, I take it to the university. There's an old water tower near the field. Beneath the tower there is this pipe. I drop it in the pipe. I take the money, I wrap it up good and then I drop it in the pipe. There's a section of the pipe that's been cut, okay? Dead-drop, and that's all I know. I don't know who gets it or anything."

"And you paid the cop out of that money, right?"

"Sure, where else?"

"How much money has come in?"

"Lots, about twenty thousand dollars."

"When did it start?"

"About a month ago. I don't keep no notes or anything. I just do it like Cassidy tells me. I don't skim off the top. I don't talk to anyone."

Swann's thumb replaced the catch on the .45. "How many drops did you make?"

"I don't know. Maybe I made five. For a little while it was twice a week. Then it stopped. And that's all I know. Mother of God, that's all I know."

Josey pulled his fingers out of Mescal's hair. "Sure, Dante. I believe you, sure." But Josey's arm was slipping down, snaking past the collar bone, moving into the neck. "I believe you, man. So everything's fine." His arm was gripped by his one free hand so that now the vice was complete.

"What are you doing?" Mescal gagged, and Swann pulled his arms in tight and broke the man's neck with an audible snap.

WHAT WAS left of the night Swann spent in a bar down the street from his hotel. There, slouched on the lavender stool, chain smoking, drinking cool gin, he was once again the perfect effigy of himself. On a tiny stage, lit with orange lights, a woman in sequins and feathers was swaying to the samba. A few locals slouched at the rickety tables. Some were softly murmuring the words to the Sergio Mendez song. Others merely nodded with thick lids into their drinks. The two or three tourists were lost and frightened in this pre-dawn sleeze. A young black girl in a low, red shift was crying in the corner. No one seemed to care.

CHAPTER 7

ROGER'S RECOVERY was so swift, so complete that certainly George Bandy had to have brought him more than the best of luck from the Carrage hierarchy. Such was the general consensus.

Several ideas circulated.

"They're moving him out East," said Billy. East meant the Chateau, and the Chateau meant the really big money. "Imagine Dennerstein running the show!"

But no one could. Roger was too quirky to qualify as a Carrage heavy, so on second thought the Kidd came up with a more modest proposal. Roger was in for a raise, or at very least a bonus.

Yes, it had to be money. A pat on the back, even from a Mr. George Bandy would not have been enough to account for the change, because the change, when you thought about it, was pretty dramatic.

One day Roger is the angry young man, serious, sullen, throwing his papers about his desk, and the next he is the cheerful imp. He walks in the door, gives them all a shy smile and a little wave. "What's happening?" Billy asks. Roger makes a little joke about some television weatherman, and then throws Ed Allen a Mars Bar.

Ed Allen! What does one make of that?

Or two days later Roger actually offers to give Allen a hand graphing a strong ridge in the mid-Atlantic with an anomalous sea surface temperature pattern.

There the two of them stood, sharing a bag of potato chips, slashing at the plastic chart with bright red crayons. "What do you make of this?" Allen asked.

"Strong wind," Roger laughed. "A wind like that could carry for, oh, quite easily ten thousand miles."

Five o'clock came around, sneaked up on them really because they were having such an intense go at it. Allen was in a hurry to make a tennis match, and so what do you know, Roger even offers to lock up for the night. "Just leave your safe open and I'll put this stuff away," he told Allen. "I'd like to take another look at that wind anyway."

"Good enough, Roger," Allen replied, then bent down, opened his safe, and he was out the door, calling, "I think you're right about that wind. It's going to be as strong as hell."

YES, ROGER thought, a wind like that could tear the roof right off the Carrage Chateau.

Never had the lab seemed so imposing. He stood between the banks of computers. Someone was whistling in the corridor beyond the double doors. Below in the parking lot someone was revving an engine. A woman's high-heels went clacking past the door. Go, Roger told himself. For once in your life do something.

The safes were nothing more than padlocked cupboards set into the wall at the far end of the lab. Allen's was the first in the line. Then came John Haas's, then Billy's, then

110

his own, but the green metal doors were not marked. If anyone comes in, Roger had to remind himself, just play it cool. No one will know this is not your safe. He was sweating.

Hunched over, peering into Allen's safe, Roger could hardly see the gummed labels fixed to the sides of the computer tape canisters. He found a box of ballpoint pens that Allen had swiped from the supply bin. There was also a bottle of rank after-shave and a can of Right Guard deodorant.

The canisters were piled in no particular order, and Roger began rifling through them. "Convective Systems," read one label. "Relative Humidity Scale Diversion," read another, and words went sputtering off Roger's lips. His mouth was dry. His hands were shaking, and in the throe of cold sweat he realized that it was hopeless. There were just too many tapes. Allen could have been working on anything.

A canister began to slip from his fingers. Roger stretched for a better grasp, and they all went clattering to the floor. It's over, he cursed. You've blown it.

"Everything all right in there?"

Roger turned and saw the guard's head poking through the door. "Ah, just fine, Frankie. I'll be staying on a little, so if you'll leave the door unlocked . . ." (and don't come in for a social chat).

"Good enough, Mr. Dennerstein," the guard returned, and continued down the hall.

Roger was down on both knees now, piling the canisters back into the safe. It's over, he told himself, just put them back and get out.

Then it came to him. Don't look at the labels, look for the dates. Allen was working on something toward the end of last week, so what was that? The tenth? No, the eighth?

111

And then he had it. "Synchronous Meteorological Correlations," read the tiny label. That could have meant anything, and so he would have to run the tape through.

His foot had gone to sleep, and he nearly stumbled when he got up. Then thank God that you didn't forget and lock the safe behind you.

He was shaking by the time he reached the computer, shaking so badly that he had difficulty threading the tape through the plastic catch. But once the program began running back, he was cooler. You're good at this, you're clicking, and a moment later the print-out pulled him into its trance of numbers.

Even before the first complete digital groupings emerged, Roger could see that Allen had been working with his own model. And so it was true, something important was being concealed.

But why use Allen to follow up my forecast?

The answer was obvious. Carrage was spreading the work among many so that no one would have all the facts.

And what were the facts?

Facts were that one dead, balmy afternoon when a hot wind came winding down through the badlands, Jerry Moss put Roger to work on the forecast. "Your initial notes have caused quite a stir back East. Do you think you could put together a more complete picture for us?"

Facts were that from the start security was tighter than a diving bell. "Work at night," Moss had told him. "Work the weekends, work at home, but don't spread a trail. Know what I mean?"

I do now, Roger could have said, because facts were that one Mr. George Bandy took him out for a drink, probing for particulars when even he hadn't the slightest idea of the general . . . "Of course, I've been briefed by Adrian Riggs . . ." and that, too, was horseshit.

Facts were that Johnny Haas was brought up for a security breach that six months ago would not have caused a head to turn.

And, finally, spreading the light blue print-out sheet for one more look at the figures, there was this: Ed Allen had spent three days trying to magnify Roger's original forecast to a longitudinal strip that ran right through the heart of south Brazil.

The night for Roger had taken on surreal dimensions. Only the faintest dribble of voices came floating through the hallway now. There was the shrill cascade of a woman's laugh and the distant call of a man's reply. Once Roger paused and, glancing out the window, saw a blinking red light fixed on the summit of a blackened mountain. The lab seemed supernaturally still.

Yet it was Allen's frantic trail that Roger found the most haunting element of all, for he was following the ghost of himself. All along the way he saw bits and pieces of his own work, some of which had been fairly well mutilated by Allen.

The forecast itself was a rat's maze of wrong turns. Allen had begun by trying to find a correlation between the Brazilian rainfall estimates and Roger's North American estimates. Even Roger would have conceded that this was the only valid approach given the time, but from there Allen had bungled it. It was even clear where he went to pieces.

In the end, Allen took the easy way out. He reduced his conclusion to a statistical base which covered his ass no matter how much rain fell on the slopes of Brazil. He must have been under a great deal of pressure.

AS THE lab's unofficial watcher, Billy was the first, and perhaps the only one to notice Roger's subtle change of

113

pace. There was still the jolly Roger, willing to help, good for a laugh, but Billy no longer believed that the man was simply riding on the high of a promised bonus. Quite the contrary, Billy told himself, Roger was using good cheer for cover. Beyond this theory, the Kidd had no answers. But if you wanted to take a wild guess, then maybe Dennerstein was up to something? Say, feeling out the political climate?

First stop for Roger, Billy noted, was Susan Meyers. Roger bought this happy, fat librarian lunch in the cafeteria. Nothing to it, of course, just social chit chat, but why would Roger take the head librarian of Carrage to lunch? Certainly Susan could not do much for him in her official capacity. The girl didn't even have a pass to the classified areas. (If she had, then things may have been serious.) No, the Kidd decided, Roger was not after Susan's library. He wanted her because she was supposed to have been dating Stephen Ganns, who was the Chateau go-between with the clout to help push Rog out East. Ah, so Dennerstein was really out for promotion after all.

Roger's second stop confirmed this theory. Three days into the new week, and Billy saw Dennerstein sharing a bearclaw with Trevor Johnsen. Johnsen was a pudgy Carrage runner, a messenger boy, really, who spent most of his time shuttling between the lab and the Chateau. Officially this balding, grumpy man had no real rank, but Trevor was sharp, and he had his ear to the walls. If Roger was heading East there was a good chance that Johnsen would know.

Then came the curve. Last day of the week, and Roger had lunch with Robert Hawkins. Hawk—everyone called him that because he looked like a bird—was a tall skinny kid with coke bottle glasses and shoulder-length hair. True, Hawk was no dummy, no back climber, but beyond

114

his own door he knew nothing. He worked in the retrieval section. He gathered and digitized the raw data from the outlying stations. Yes, it was an important job, but what use could a retriever from the South American desk be to Roger Dennerstein? . . .

What use indeed, Roger might have said with satisfaction, because he had never felt more the fox than now. While Susan had been some help, and Johnsen got him started on the timetable, only Hawk proved to be pure gold.

"Been much happening in Brazil?" Roger eventually had come round to asking.

"Funny that you mention it," Hawk had said, or at least something like that, because, yes, there had been odd things going on down there. First, by way of local news, there had been Ed Allen, who only last week had pestered Hawk for anything at all from that general area. Then down came Trevor with a rush order from the Chateau.

"Oh, yeah?" Roger had been casually snapping the teeth off his plastic fork. "What was that?"

"Secret," Hawk had smiled. "Crap to my mind, but there you are."

"No matter," Roger had returned, because, after all, their lunch had only been an informal chance meeting. "But it is curious," Roger had probed. "I mean it does make you wonder."

And then came the bombshell. "I don't see why it should make anyone wonder," Hawk had said. His protruding eyes had never seemed more so. "I mean the Minister of Agriculture gets shot to death and what do you expect? Business as usual?"

"Uh?" The fork snapped in two, the slivers popping in the air.

"Sure. Daniel Miguez, he was the Minister of Agriculture, and when you went to market in Brazil, Miguez was the man to know."

FOR THE sake of objectivity Roger went no further than constructing his timetable. He gathered details of the Miguez murder from back issues of newspapers but he forced himself to draw no conclusions. The implications of the murder were too complex. It could have gone anywhere. So Roger put it all aside. Miguez was killed, machine gunned on a lonely stretch of road. Nothing more needed to be said.

Roger worked on his timetable at odd hours; when he had the house to himself, in the lab before the others arrived. He made all of his notes on a yellow legal pad. Of course, he told no one, not even Julie. Eventually he came to realize that the notes, the clippings from the newspapers, the copy he had made of Allen's work, all of it: these things were to be a kind of indictment against Carrage. He had no idea what the charges were. Each night he locked the material in his safe at the lab.

THERE WAS a café in Boston where the first line crew sometimes met for informal meetings. The food in the tiny, sawdust bistro was terrible—limp salad and stiff spaghetti—but George, who was supposed to know, said the wine was good, and here the men could be alone.

Like so many traditions within the Chateau, these meetings simply came to be. It might have been George who began it all. "The slaves need to conspire against their master," he said, sounding more like Jameson. At any rate, the others were in accord, except that Hank Doris did not see himself as the slave and Sax as the master. He was too naive.

For discussions there was no agenda, and no notes were

taken. Fellow Carrage employees did not need such formalities, and besides, if there were no records there could be no possibility of subsequent blackmail. Usually the meetings were called by Bandy, sometimes to deal with a crisis, other times simply to touch base, and still others, out of lack of anything better to do. Today, however, Mike Gaddis had drawn them together, not so much for a tangible problem but rather for what he termed as a "little chill in the climate."

By climate, Mike meant the fifth floor in general, and specifically Howard Sax.

"The chief is just feeling the season," said Doris. There was tomato paste on his chin. The whites of his eyes were like dirty concrete.

"It's not the season," countered Gaddis. "It's the heat. Why do you think he's in Washington now."

"Maybe he's got a girl." Jameson smiled, only half joking.

Doris frowned. He didn't like that kind of talk, not about Mr. Sax, not about the man who had once invited him to dinner and usually called him Hank. "The chief always gets nervous at the beginning of the buying season."

But Gaddis had worked with Sax long enough to know that the man was not suffering from any pre-season blues. Whatever was eating Sax was serious. "I've seen it before," Gaddis insisted. "Remember the flap on the Russian wheat deal. Ever since the wheat deal there have been guys just itching to bust us."

"Oh, that was Nixon's fault," said Doris, and his hand went slapping through the air. "Nixon all the way."

Jameson merely rolled his eyes. Yes, he could have told them now, Nixon had bungled the Russian deal, but there had been other factors involved. "Uh, how about that the

Russians had inside help," he finally said as a tag to his own thought.

"Meaning?" Doris was angry.

"Meaning"—Jameson smiled—"that the Russians aren't smart enough to have pulled off that deal without the help of the Carrage—oh-how-we-love-it-grain-company." His fork clattered to his plate. "Look, gentlemen, the Russians come to town and walk away with our wheat at bargain prices. Now the American consumer is rightfully upset because the price of bread goes out the top. Okay, but I personally know people in Washington who have wondered more than once how the grain brokers like us came out of that deal looking so fat. Know what I mean? Something wasn't kosher. The Howard Saxes put that deal together with the Russians for profit, not out of any sense of national duty."

"Well, that's just a load of crap," Doris said, and ripped a hunk of bread from the loaf.

"Sure it is, Hank." Jameson grinned. "I just made it all up, just like I made up that *Times* article that said that Carrage was contributing to inflation with massive imports."

"Bobby's right," Gaddis said. He was picking at the straw casing on the wine bottle. "Right now the exchange is like Wall Street was fifty years ago. There's big wins and big losses. The cops have given us a lot of rope, but the times they are a-changing. I think the CEA and Washington in general are getting pissed off at us. I think the axe is going to fall. Maybe it's fallen already. Maybe people in Washington are already starting to light a fire under Sax. Maybe he's feeling the heat."

"So that's why we're all getting cold feet," Jameson snickered.

Through all of this George Bandy remained silent. Occasionally he nodded. Once or twice he smiled, even laughed, saying, "Oh, I think that's taking it a bit far," or, "Well, of course, one can't honestly support that . . ." Now, however, in the wake of Bobby's too subtle turn of phrase and for other reasons not clearly understood by any, all eyes were on him.

"Yes," he said absently. "I have been aware that Sax has been a little distraught—"

"A little distraught!" Gaddis might have just been goosed.

"Uh, if we take a look at the sequence of events," Bandy continued. "Yes, I think the sequence warrants some mention here. Uh, am I right about this? First Sax cancels the last two Thursday meetings. Then there was the word about cutting down on overall buying. Conservative, wouldn't you say? Then there were those late night meetings with Agro-bus people. Why the Agro-bus people if he's cutting down the overall buying?"

"It's got something to do with the frigging forecast. The Dennerstein forecast," Doris grumbled.

But Bandy ignored him. "And three times this month he's run off to Washington at the oddest times. And finally—"

"And finally what?" Gaddis prompted.

And finally there was the money, but George would not talk about the money. You had to keep something for yourself, and besides he hardly knew what to make of the money. It may have been the most disturbing element of all.

George found out about the money on a fluke. He had been in accounting, not really nosing around, but at least it was something to do. Casey Sloan, who was always sucking up to somebody, brought him a cup of coffee out of the machine. "So, how's the figures?" Bandy asked, just for something to say.

"Funny that you mention it," said Sloan. "I can't seem to make heads or tails of this." He laid out the accounting sheets on his desk.

Bandy could have hardly cared less. He was standing at the window. There was a girl eating lunch on the grass, some number from the typing pool. Wonder if she would like to finish in the executive dining room?

"I think I've missed something," Sloan continued.

"Missed something?" Bandy loved a girl with firm thighs.

"Well, take a look for yourself," and Sloan held the sheet up to Bandy's nose.

"Interesting," Bandy murmured. "Very interesting." However, the figures were interesting not so much for what they revealed but for what they seemed to hide.

Bandy had never been a figures man. But then what were figures men if not just glorified clerks? So Bandy never cared for figures. His strength was buying and selling, but he had been around long enough to spot what even Sloan missed.

Howard Sax was hiding money. How much, Bandy could not accurately tell. However, it was no great sum, which made it all the more curious. Let's face it, George had argued to himself, if Sax was planning to run off to an island with company funds he would not be playing around with the amount he'd stashed away. No, Howard lived in style. If he wanted to go native he would never settle for a palm thatched hut with a driftwood door. Sax would buy the whole damn island. So, then, what was he doing with seventy-five-thousand-odd dollars? . . .

Alone in his office, leaning on the desk or pressing his

fingers against the panes of leaded glass, no firm answers came to George Bandy. And if George spent time pacing the royal blue rug with its gold Carrage crest, or gazing out into the tangle of oaks and sycamores, so too did Howard Sax. But Sax, Bandy knew, was not wasting his time about what his staff was up to. Sax was, as Mike had put it, either sweating out the heat, or else the man was distinctly up to something. But if so, what?

CHAPTER 8

IN THE beginning of Lyle Severson's career there had been the Germans, and with the Germans there had been the clarity of duality. There had been right and there had been wrong, and no one ever dreamed that the two would meet.

When the war broke out Lyle had been in his last year at Harvard. The fashion had been polemics, but Lyle had been less the campus wit and more the humanist. He attended, but did not give, small dinner parties in the boys' chambers. He remembered best the minor details, the mufflers and overcoats hanging in the closet, the chops and brandy laid on the white tablecloth, and clever sneers of thin, superior lips.

Occasionally campus talk became caustic, and feelings were injured. The lads had been known to sulk for weeks, passing one another on the shady Cambridge avenues, glancing up and then frowning. But when the chips were down it was all for one and one for all. Or as the joke went, "we're all the same bones, oh, yes."

Even today Lyle could not divorce himself from old

loyalty, which was why, despite their differences, he could not hunt Allen Cassidy without remorse. And it was certainly a hunt, made all the more distasteful because the ferret was Josey Swann.

Formally the hunt had begun with Josey's tip. "Money," Swann had written in the nasty code of a one-time pad. "Cassidy may have money. Can you verify?" So Lyle began to hunt, and like any he had been through, during any era, after any quarry, the hunt was a tortuous paper chase.

For security reasons Lyle worked alone. First he sorted through the meager records of operational funds. Then he moved on to the less traveled roads of purchase slips. He found money from sources unknown, paid to sources untouchable. There was money coming in dirty and going out clean, and money that came in clean and went out dirty. But nowhere was there a stash for Allen Cassidy.

By two in the morning he felt the pages attacking him. The edges seemed to slash at his fingers. The tiny columns of figures taunted him. They may have been trying to blind him. His eyes became webbed with veins, but still, the scent of the fox kept him working until the first clue came to light.

A house had been purchased. With what money, Lyle could not tell, but authorizing the deal was none other than Dancing Allen Cassidy. Now, the old bones began to rattle. The noise set Severson's teeth on edge. He felt more alone than he had in years. He might not have gone on, but the fox was Allen, and Allen was family, and one must keep family under one's wing. So Lyle, slumped at his desk, dry in the mouth, drew the final pages together until he had it. Step by cunning step all the facts were truly there. Allen Cassidy had built himself a private little safehouse, not twenty miles from Langley, Virginia.

Dear God, Allen. Why?

"Why the safe-house?" was precisely the question which Lyle Severson put to Swann the next day. They met in a park. Both men were tired, Lyle from the hunt, Josey from an all night flight in from Brazil. Lyle sat on a stone bench. His shoes, English wingtips, were studded with beads of dew. Josey was pacing. He was agitated. He was grinding the heel of his boot into the sod. Given the chance, he would grind Allen Cassidy just as viciously. Lyle was quite sure of that. "But I won't have any vengeance," Severson was saying. "I won't have it. You'll play my way, or not at all," and the old man's breath hung in the air.

"Sure." Josey actually smiled.

"It's not that I don't understand," Severson said. His eyebrows became all the bushier whenever he tried to be honest. "I realize very well that John Donne was a friend of yours. However, Allen is a friend of mine. Whatever he's involved in now, I mustn't forget that he's a friend. Where would we be if we allowed ourselves to forget our loyalties?"

We would be, thought Swann, exactly where we are, in the shrine of the cult of the CIA.

"Allen was my protégé. I was the one who originally had him recruited."

"Dancing Allen," Josey snickered. "Isn't that what they used to call him?"

"Some did, yes." Lyle was wary of the animal character of Josey Swann. "He was very good on the open market, Allen was. Give him chicken feed, and he'd come back with gold. He got on very well with the French. I had the British, and Allen had the French. This was during the cold war, you understand."

"I never understood that it was over," Swann shot back.

125

"The height of it, I mean. We traded, Cassidy and I. We traded intelligence with the allies. It was a long, dark tunnel, I can assure you."

Josey shrugged, because what did Father Lyle know about tunnels, real tunnels, like the ones they had in Nam. Those were tunnels for you, black mud, deeper and deeper. Hardly anyone came out of those tunnels. "Look, just get on with it."

Severson swallowed. He might have been swallowing his pride, because the ones like Swann were actually dangerous, and had to be played accordingly. He had once told Josey to get a haircut, and Swann told him to fuck off, just like that, fuck off. "All right, you said that Allen seems to have gotten some money."

"I didn't say that. Mescal said that," Josey returned.

"It would have been easier if you had gotten this Mescal fellow to elaborate."

"Couldn't," Josey said. He was picking his teeth. "I told you, I had to kill him."

"Yes, all right, then. The fact, however, is that I'm beginning to believe in the money."

"Oh, yeah?" Swann at his rudest.

"I mean how else could he have funded the safe-house?"

"And why?" Josey suddenly asked. "And what for, and where did he get the fucking money?" Josey's head dropped and his eyes lowered. He might have been snarling, at least his teeth were showing, remarkably white for such a shabby beast, Lyle thought.

"If you're going to look around," Lyle began again on a softer note, "I should think you'll want to take someone along to help out with the locks and safe. I've got someone in mind."

"No. I've got my own man."

126

"As you wish," Lyle said. "But you will remember what I said. No matter how intriguing the catch turns out to be, no matter how tempting it may seem to take another step, you will check with me first, won't you?"

"Said I would." Josey might have just had his feelings hurt, except that they both knew he had no feelings.

"And you do feel all right about breaking in? I mean, if you don't think it's safe, I could always go back to the records."

"No," Swann replied. "It's time to have an inside look. Anyway, I've been through this sort of run before. I know what I'm doing. I'm cool." But Swann's smile had already frozen to a bleak grin. His eyes were glazed like plugs of dull glass. He mumbled something, turned on the soggy grass so that his raincoat swished at his knees, and skulked off through the row of hedges.

THAT NIGHT when the streets went dead and the neat lawns frosted over, Josey Swann became operational, although he was not operational in any sense that Lyle Severson would have approved of. Even in his more tranquil moments Swann was a silent killer. He didn't have an ounce of the schoolboy in him.

But now, stretched out in the back of a Volkswagen van, Josey Swann seemed more the burned out doper than operational Company stringer. He lay on a pile of Indian cushions passing a joint with Tommy Vito. The walls of the van had been paneled with pine. There was a Rolling Stones poster taped to the roof, and a tape of Linda Ronstadt murmuring softly through the speakers.

Swann was cutting lazy spirals in the blackness with the glowing red tip of the joint. The tiny, hot coal left streaks of an after-image. Swann took a final hit and singed his fingers. Vito laughed. He was also too stoned to care about very much, but Swann told him, "We've got to get going, man."

"Is that right?" Vito's face was rubberized.

"Yeah." Josey was up on his knees. He was struggling into his leather coat. There was a small automatic in the pocket, although in the night he was better with his hands.

"Don't feel like working tonight," Vito said, reaching for his tools, sliding open the door of his van. He had opened locks for Swann before. He had climbed through windows and cracked safes, but he had never been able to open Josey himself.

Cassidy's alleged safe-house was a two story brownstone, set back from the street by a low garden wall. The two men walked casually up the path, and while Josey watched the blacked-out windows and checked the street for dangerous traffic, Vito went to work on the door. "Banhum, nothing special," he mumbled, and then the door swung open. "Anybody home?"

They moved gently at first, swinging their flashlights from the walls to the floor. The corridors smelled of dust and cigarettes. The furniture was bad Regency imitation. The carpet was frayed. The stairs were split and sagging. In the dining room they found the greasy remains of a poor man's meal, a few plates smeared with egg. There was a cigar butt jammed in the coffee cup. "Who smokes these?" Vito smiled. "Cheap shit?" He handed the butt to Swann.

They were prowling nicely now, two bad boys in the night. Vito was going through the drawers. Josey was bent over the ashes in the fireplace. Against the wall there was a heavy, dark cabinet. Vito picked at the lock, but found nothing inside. So he pulled a promising strip of Rococo veneer away, splinters flew off as he ripped, but, again,

128

there were no secrets. Under the cushions of an over-stuffed sofa Josey found a flattened beer can, undoubtedly the nervous work of someone like himself. When there was nothing to do, you tended to crush things.

Josey left Vito to knock around in the small parlor off the kitchen, and he climbed the narrow stairway to the upper floor. Here the house had truly gone to seed. His flashlight streaked across hanging strips of flowered wall-paper, the water-stained ceiling, and the warped, bare floor. He searched a bedroom and found another gray mattress, sagging on the floor. Sheets and blankets were balled in the corner. A beer can held the door ajar. At the end of the hall there was another door. Josey pushed it slowly, crack by crack it opened. He had a feeling about this one. And yes, there was a light. The light came seep-ing from beneath a door at the far end of the room. He heard the slosh of water. I've caught them with their pants down, he thought.

Swann moved to the door. He waited for the count of ten, then his leg snapped out. The door jamb split away, a woman screamed. Swann saw only the briefest glimpse of her body thrashing in the tub before he turned out the bathroom light and grabbed her.

She was flailing at him, and his hands kept slipping from her arms and neck. Then he had her by the hair, a good sized clump. For a while she fought furiously, then went limp. They wrapped the girl in a bedsheet and sat her in a straight-backed wooden chair. Swann slouched against the plaster wall. Vito was perched on the dresser. He had thrown a towel over the lamp to cut the glare. He had been told not to speak, not to give away either his own identity or Josey's.

Swann was calmer now. He was casually dragging on his cigarette. "We're family," he told the girl. "We're distant cousins of Allen's. Whatever you tell us isn't going to hurt anyone. Unless, of course, you lie."

"There's nothing to say," the girl said. She had long, black hair and a very round face. She looked thirty, but may have been older.

"Housekeeper, uh? You done this kind of work before?" The smoke was drifting up from Josey's mouth.

She tossed her hair from her eyes. The thick, wet strands slapped her back. "Yeah. Allen gives me all kinds of different jobs. He took me off the desk a few years back, so now I help him out sometimes."

"What do you do when you're not running Cassidy's safe-house?" In a different place, at a different time, this might have been a proposition.

"I do all kinds of things," she answered softly. "Allen keeps me busy. Look, I'm just a Company career girl. Ask Allen, ask anybody." Then she said her name was Mary Knapp, which Swann imagined was only one of many names.

"Okay, Mary, I want you to tell me a story. I want you to start at the beginning and move through step by step. Do you know what I mean?"

The tears had returned to her eyes again, but her mouth was still rigid. "There's nothing to say. I'm the housekeeper, that's all. I don't know anything. I don't know what Allen uses this place for. I just watch it."

He's going to hit her now, Vito thought. Damn it, Josey, please don't hit her.

But Swann merely sank to the balls of his feet. He was still not through negotiating. "This is how it's going to be, Mary. Either you be straight with me, or I'm going to really have to work you over. You know what I'm talking about."

"Allen hired me six weeks ago," she said suddenly.

"Like I said, I've done work for him before. There were all kinds of jobs. You know how it is. They put you behind a desk and you can rot there. So Allen pulled me out and put me to work. This house was just one of his jobs. He calls me and tells me he needs someone to watch a house for him."

"What do you do?"

"Nothing, I just watch the house. I'm here three nights a week, unless there's a meeting."

"Tell me about the meetings." Josey's eyes were steady now. He had found the groove.

"I never see any faces. They stay downstairs, and I'm up here by the window."

"You work the signals, right?"

"Yeah."

"What are they?"

She sighed, wavered actually, so Josey hit her again with the same question. "Okay," she said. "There's a light in the attic. If everything's cool then the light stays off. If not, I switch it on. You can see the light from the street through a little window. They also gave me a kerosene lamp, just in case."

"Just in case," Josey muttered. He had risen to his feet and started pacing again. "Does this house have tapes?"

"Of course, what do you think?" The girl was shivering. The sheet around her was soaked to her skin. Her thighs and her nipples were visible now, but Swann didn't seem to care.

"And you run the tapes, right?"

She hugged her body and the sheet ballooned out. "Yeah, I run them."

"From here?"

"Yeah."

"Where?"

She pointed to a closet door beside the bed, and Vito slid off the dresser to see. The controls were set into a low console. Vito said it was a cheap and simple arrangement. "The downstairs is miked, and the whole thing is run from up here," he added. "There's nothing on the machine now."

"Where do the tapes go?" Josey asked the girl.

"Allen takes them."

"Why don't you tell me more about the meetings?"

The girl was very knotted. "All I heard were the voices."

"What were they saying?"

She shrugged. "I don't remember, I just played the tapes."

Josey took a threatening step, then stopped and turned to the wall. Now he was picking at the plaster. "I'm thinking that Allen keeps the tapes here." He glanced back at her. "That's what I'm thinking, Mary. Now I could be wrong, but if I'm not, if we find those tapes . . ."

"Okay, the tapes might be in the safe behind the mirror. I don't know the combination."

Vito was already lifting the heavy glass off the hooks. "Probably came with the house," he said, running his hands over the cold metal. "I could open this in my sleep," and then his fingers were spinning the tumblers, his ear to the black safe door. Then he had it. "Here's the catch, brother." He reached in and withdrew a large brown envelope. "That's it. There aren't any tapes."

Josey turned to the girl. "But you didn't know there weren't going to be any tapes, did you?"

She looked away.

Inside the envelope there were photographs, hastily

blurred portraits in black and white. "Who is that?" Vito asked.

Josey laid the pictures on a card table. There were two profiles and a fairly good straight-on shot. The photographer must have taken the shots on the run with a telephoto lens. "How about it?" Swann said to the girl. "You know who this guy is?"

She shook her head. "I've never seen him before."

Vito was studying the pictures under the spray of his flashlight. "Funny looking guy, isn't he?"

But Josey was watching the girl. "Tell me about the meeting," he said. "Who was there?"

"Allen and another guy."

"What did they talk about?"

"I don't know. They talked in vague terms. The other guy was putting together some sort of deal for Allen on the West Coast. They talked about money."

"And what was the other guy's name, Mary?"

She pressed her palms to her forehead. "Look, I don't remember a name."

But Swann had a feeling about this one.

"I think you do."

"Okay, it was the name of an animal. Allen called him something like Bear or Wolf. Maybe it was Mr. Wolf, okay?"

And Swann leaned into her. "Was it Zebra? Did you hear the name Zebra?"

The girl was crying out of control when she finally told Swann the truth.

SWANN AND Severson met on the grounds of the Arlington National Cemetery. The day was cold and clear. Josey wore his knee length, black leather coat, and narrow,

133

high-heeled boots. Severson first saw him from a distance. He was standing beneath an evergreen, and the mid-morning light cut even darker slashes in his face.

"You may want to put your blinders on," Josey told him. One eye was nearly shut to the glittering light through the leaves. "I'm going in with a little bit of stick."

Severson winced. "Why? What did you find?"

"Cassidy may be out to make another hit."

Severson drew his sleeve across his mouth. "How do you know?"

"I know," Josey told him. "Cassidy is using a guy named Bobby Zebra to set it up. I don't know who the target is, but I may have seen a photograph of him."

Severson blinked into a row of marble slabs that ran layer after layer over the hills of grass. "I know Bobby Zebra. He's not Company. He's freelance."

Josey began chewing on the end of a toothpick. "Well, that makes sense, doesn't it? Cassidy's running this show with a hodge-podge of freelancers."

"We don't know that it's Allen's show, and I'd rather you didn't keep accusing him so indiscriminately." Just then Severson had a clerk's fussiness about his fingertips and cuffs. He pursed his lips and then moistened them. In the distance they saw a woman leading a small boy by the hand through the gravestones. They were plodding uncertainly over the grass. "Anyway," Lyle continued, "you don't know that Allen is setting up a hit. Zebra does other work as well, routine surveillance, that sort of thing."

Josey spat the toothpick out. "You can find reasons for not doing anything, Lyle. I'm going to talk to Zebra, and that's that."

"I know how you people *talk.*" Severson's ears were red from the cold. "And I don't want any trouble."

Josey ignored him. He was squinting into the teeth of

gravestones and the light that shattered off them. Beyond the first rows stood the boy and his mother. The child was crying. The breeze whipped his voice away, but they could see him bent over, rubbing his eyes. His mother held him close to her body.

BOBBY ZEBRA was a corpulent man with a happy front to a very grim business. He did publicity for the would-be stars, threw parties for the Washington undercrust and occasionally did spot-work for congressmen. Josey hated him, but Zebra didn't know it, or if he did, wouldn't let on. He smiled for Swann, and pounded his desk. "Or should I applaud," Zebra winked. "Not every day I get a war hero coming into this office."

Josey was silent. Don't get too chummy with the ones you're about to sweat, he had learned.

"Cut any good throats lately?" Zebra laughed. The walls of his office were covered with photographs, mostly of clients who had never made it.

"What's the word then, Bobby?"

"Ah, now, Josey, don't tell me you're looking for work, not you."

Swann was playing with a paperweight, feeling the mass of the polished rock slab. He liked heavy objects—sometimes they were all that struck him as real. "No, man, I'm not looking for work."

Zebra pulled at the fat that hung from his chin. "Word is, Josey boy, that you're outside the pale. I think they said that you are unreliable."

Josey rose from his chair and walked to the window. He could have written his name in the dust on the pane, or the name of Johnny Donne? "It's true, you know," he said to the street four stories below. "I'm unreliable, never know what I'll do." The traffic was snarling, horns wailing. He saw two kids cadging quarters from old men and women. "Do you know how many people saw me come up to your office, Bobby?"

"Uh?" Zebra was sucking on a cigarette. The filter was soggy from his spit.

"Take a guess, Bobby. How many people do you think know that I'm here right now?" Swann was watching him.

"What are you talking about, Josey?" A storm of perspiration broke out on Zebra's face. He could only glance back at Swann from the corners of his eyes.

"I'll tell you, Bobby, no one saw me come here, not one single *witness.*" Josey ambled back to the chair and laid his automatic on the desk. "You going to talk to me, Bobby?"

"Sure, Josey, but what? Uh? I haven't been fucking with you."

"Lots of ways to fuck with me, Bobby. Word is that I'm crazy, is that right? Well, the other word is that Allen Cassidy is about to have a pigeon hit. Little joker, dark hair, glasses. I saw the snaps and I know you've been working with Cassidy."

"Oh, Josey, come on. It's just a little deal I got cooking." Zebra's face looked wet, naked. "All right, so I put something together for Allen Cassidy, but I don't know who the target is. I didn't use one of my scouts, I used one of Cassidy's people. That's why the pictures came out so bad. All I did was supply the man and the schedule."

"Who's the man?"

"Oh, Josey, come on."

Swann's open hand cracked across the fat man's face. Josey might never have hit him, he was so composed an instant later. There was blood seeping from Zebra's lips. "All right, the man is Shepp. Ernie Shepp," Zebra

136

managed. "I put the deal together with Shepp as the pitcher."

"When does he go?"

"Monday, Monday at twelve noon. Continental to Los Angeles. I can't remember the flight number."

"Who's running interference?" Josey might have been reading from a list of questions, he felt that detached, and foolish, too. You always felt foolish playing the role that they cast you into.

"No one, it's a solo job."

"Yeah?"

"I'm telling you how it is. What else do you want from me?"

Josey scooped up the pistol and dropped it back into his pocket. "Nothing. I don't want nothing from you at all."

"And I won't go crying to Shepp either, Josey. I swear I won't."

"Oh, I know that, Bobby." Josey turned to the door. "Oh, one more thing. If they ever ask you if I'm crazy, you'll set them straight on that point, won't you? You tell them I'm cool, okay? I'm real cool," and then he screwed up his mouth like a comic and left.

DOCTORS HAD told Swann that his periods of nausea were the result of too much dope. But Josey knew that this was not true. Dope had nothing to do with it. It was the war that made him sick, and now all of it was turning over inside him.

He sat in a small café. The cheap, red wine was making the nausea all the worse. He hadn't had enough to numb his skin and the taste was caked to his mouth, but still, Josey was ready for war, ready as he had ever been. "I leave Monday," he told Severson. "Monday at noon."

"For Los Angeles?" Severson asked. He wasn't sure of any of it.

"Yeah, nice place. Ever been there, Lyle?" He actually hated the place, but, then, he hated all the cities.

"Yes," Severson answered absently. "But who would they want to hit there?"

"The guy in the picture. What does it matter? We'll know soon enough."

"And there's Ernie Shepp." Severson's voice was low. "Do you know him?"

"Never met him, but I know who he is."

Severson began to spin his glass by the stem. Soft light from the lantern above broke on the rim. "I still think we should bring in the others, Josey. What if you lose him? What if—"

"What if the world blows up? I don't *want* anyone else along. I wouldn't get on with anyone else. Besides, I got you running the desk, don't I, Lyle?"

"I worry about you, Josey, I honestly do."

Swann was gulping down wine, and he nearly coughed it back up with laughter. "Can't imagine why, Lyle. Do I look that bad?"

Severson merely shook his head. "You will stay in touch with me, won't you?"

Josey belted down the last dregs. "Hey, have I ever let you down?" His teeth were bared. It was supposed to have been a smile, but Josey had forgotten exactly which role he should have been playing. Whether the stupid killer-grunt with his brains in his neck, which was the Josey that Severson believed in, or something more enigmatic, closer to the truth . . . Swann couldn't remember. He often forgot who he was.

CHAPTER 9

SOMETHING HAD changed. Billy hardly knew what, yet something had definitely happened to Dennerstein. Maybe a death in the family, he thought. Maybe his wife had left him. It had to have been something of that magnitude, except Billy was sure that Roger had looked all right when he arrived in the morning. He had strolled in at the usual hour, tossed an empty coffee cup into the trash, and then . . . and then what? Billy only remembered that Roger ran from the lab.

Twenty minutes later Billy found him in the bathroom. Roger was standing in front of the mirror. He was staring blankly at his own white face. "Are you okay?" the Kidd asked. "Rog, are you okay? Are you sick?"

Roger blinked, and turned slowly. "Everything is . . . fine . . . I'm okay."

"Are you sure? Roger?"

Roger wiped his sleeve across his mouth. "I'm all *right,* just leave me alone."

Replaying the morning in his mind, Billy was sure that

whatever happened to Roger occurred in the briefest space of time. Somebody said something to him? He saw something? All that Billy could recall was Roger entering, then tossing the cup, then . . . what?

Billy finally had it at the stroke of noon. Roger had entered the lab smiling, thumbed through the morning temperature reports, and then he had gone over to his safe. He had been looking for something. He had rifled through the tape canisters. Papers had spilled on the floor. Then he slowly rose, shut the safe, and looked about the room.

That was it, Billy decided. Roger must have seen something in his safe, something he had forgotten about, or something he thought was there and was not. It could have been any one of a thousand things, thought Billy, because you never knew with Roger.

ONLY, THEY knew now, Roger told himself. Whoever broke into the safe and stole the notes, knew everything. His timetable listing the dates from the start of the forecast to his meeting with Bandy, his copy of Allen's Brazilian projection, the newspaper clippings of the minister's death —all of it was gone.

For the first few hours of the day, Roger lived on the hope that his was not the only safe that had been violated. But by noon others had gone to their safes, and no cry of thief went up. So he had to face it. Last night some Carrage official with no small degree of power had come into the lab and withdrawn his papers.

But why? And how did they know? And more to the point, what would they do with him now?

No answers came. Only time ticked on, and Roger wasted the day marking meaningless figures on a plastic projection grid.

At five o'clock he was the first one out of the lab.

Rushing through the hall, skirting the desks in the typing pool, he felt that everyone's eyes were watching him. But there was no hand on his shoulder, no voice calling after his small, agitated body, "Dennerstein! Dennerstein!"

He took the freeway's fast lane, and drove flat out in the hope that raw speed would give him some relief, but he could not outrun his fear. Still, he finally decided, what was the worst they could do to him? They could fire me, he told himself. They could hand me the walking papers for stealing Allen's tape, but that was about all. And so to hell with them.

Yet, as the days passed, Roger's perspective on events became more and more oblique. He lost all sense of proportion. Innocuous events took on profoundly sinister meanings.

There was the incident with the telephone. Every time he used the phone he heard those faint and distant clicks, like two sticks clacking together on the further shore of a dead calm lake.

"Don't be silly," Julie told him. "There's nothing wrong with the telephone." They had been in the garden. Saturday, and Roger was helping out with the plants. Some of Julie's white flowers had grown immense, while the thorns of the roses were sharp and concealed.

"It's just that I haven't ever noticed it before."

"Noticed what?" She held up a lump of black soil.

"The telephone. Those little noises in the background." Roger was crouched, digging and tearing at the weeds.

"Well, if it bothers you, honey, then why don't you call the phone company?" She began slapping down the earth, smoothing it out with the palm of her hand.

"Yeah, well, maybe I will," and he wrenched at the trunk of a gnarled hibiscus, but the ugly dead wood was too strong for him.

The next incident, not to be ignored even by Julie, was the robbery. One Friday night they returned from dinner to find the television, the stereo, and a handful of cash had been taken from their home. The thieves had entered through a broken window. Drawers had been left open, clothing piled on the floor. The police, when they finally arrived, called the case "routine." Apparently there had been a rash of such crimes in the neighborhood, except that cops always said that. A report was filed, the insurance company notified, and the incident would have been neatly forgotten, had there not have been one disturbing question left unanswered. Why, Roger kept asking himself, had his filing cabinet in the study been so thoroughly searched?

In contrast to these events, the days at the lab passed peacefully enough. For a time Roger had indeed expected to see some stern little note waiting for him on his desk in the morning. "Mr. Moss would like to see you," it would have read, but there was none.

His production wasted to nothing. Hours were spent prowling about. One morning there had been those beautiful photographs of the magnificent swirling clouds above the Caribbean. Someone had scrawled "closed circulation" across the corner of the glossies, but Roger was too blown out even to correct the error. Another day brought Ed Allen to the forefront with an elaborate breakdown of North African wind cycles. Only, Roger could not be persuaded to help with the project. So he shut his eyes and saw the wild gusts tearing at the shrub, spraying thick sheets of sand hundreds of feet into the air.

Quite possibly the tedium of the days would have finally buried whatever menace Roger had sensed, but this was not to be. . . .

A cold day, fog had slithered down the face of the

surrounding hills, and the world was watery and gray. But trust Billy's eyes to pierce even the darkest corners.

"You know what they say about ghosts on the horizon, Rog." The Kidd was twisting his car key into the lock.

"Uh?" Roger flattened his hands on the hood of Billy's Triumph. This had been a chance meeting. The two had simply driven into the parking lot simultaneously.

"I said there's a guy out there by the trees."

Roger strained to see. "It's probably the gardener."

"In a suit?" Billy was padding his pockets. He may have just lost something.

"So, what's the point?" Roger was still gazing at the first row of trees. "He's just standing there."

"I'd lock my car if I were you, Rog. You never can tell. Guy might be waiting until we go inside and then he'll move through the lot car by car. It happened to me once at a movie. Guy took my tape-deck."

Twice that morning Roger saw the figure moving along the tree line. Yet as he stood at the window of the lab and gazed across three hundred yards of fog enshrouded ground, Roger had no real idea exactly who the man was. Watching that figure was like watching some sort of metal, shimmering and changing under the water as you looked down from the jetty. When he returned home that evening he was shaken.

It was Thursday, and Roger always took Julie out for lasagna. He wanted to tell her not tonight, but she was already dressed when he walked in the door. She dubbed these dinners her "mid-week break," as if Julie slaved around the house six days a week.

The food, not the atmosphere, kept them returning to the downtown hole in the wall. On some nights Roger was even afraid of the neighborhood, what with the weeping concrete walls, spray painted with the angry cryptograms of teenage gangs. But Julie, he thought, as they walked past the boarded windows and dismal warehouse doors, Julie was not afraid of anything, except perhaps loneliness.

Once inside, sitting at their usual table with its greasy checked cloth, the trash littered streets outside had never looked more threatening. Around them sat the regular crowd. There were three or four families, fat from starch, poor but seemingly happy. A few solitary men in baggy suits and no ties dined slowly, their sad eyes fixed on the edges of their plates. In the corner two girls watched them and giggled.

Dinner took an awkward hour. Julie made small talk. There were friends of hers who had been having problems with their husbands, and others with no men at all. Through it all Roger nodded, "Too bad," or "I never got that impression." Sometimes he even had to say, "Of course I feel the same way."

There was an odd sense of finality when their meal was finished. Roger paid the bill, helped Julie on with her coat and struggled into his. Then the shabby glass door banged shut behind him, and they were alone.

There were no street lamps here. Telephone wires criss-crossed above in the gloom. At the end of the block Roger saw a ragged woman reeling out of a doorway. Then he heard the slap of a leather sole on the pavement behind him.

"I think there's someone following us," he whispered. He glanced quickly over his shoulder, and, yes, there was a patchy figure of a man closing in. "Just keep walking," he said.

"He was giving you funny looks," Julie said. "I saw him." Her hand was clutching his. The perspiration cemented them together.

Now the man was only a step behind. He was tall, and

144

wore a thick leather coat. Roger had an urge to run, or maybe scream out. Then he felt the big hand on his arm, and heard the voice in his ear. "Keep moving. I've got a gun, I'll use it."

Julie gasped, and was told to shut up. The man had taken both of their arms, so that now they made an awkward trio, Roger and Julie stumbling along, the gunman behind, shoving them forward down the sidewalk.

Roger was only aware of fractured impressions. First, there was a thought to jab his elbow back, and then up with the old arm to the throat. But he might as well defend himself with the beak of his nose for all the chance that he would have had with this monster. And then he actually envisioned himself flopping on the pavement, Julie screaming above him.

Up ahead, a figure emerged from the alley and began to shuffle toward them. Hope rose, but the oncoming figure was only a drunk. His head was down and his hands were plunged deep in the pockets of his raincoat. Still, maybe he could somehow signal . . . how? So he walked on and kept his eyes fixed to the pavement.

Now the drunk was passing them by. There goes our chance, and Roger watched the bit of blue canvas shoe enter the edge of his vision as the shaky figure staggered past. For no reason, Roger glanced up, and suddenly there was the swooping ghost of something instantly materializing, reaching out for the gunman's head. There was a deafening crack. Roger felt the heat of the flash on the back of his neck. The gunman jerked, he was thrown back, tumbling into the street where he kicked, and went limp. One side of his face was black and pouring blood. And now the drunk was yelling at them, wrenching them forward, pulling Roger and Julie down the street.

145

SWANN WAS not yet so far gone that he could not appreciate his own consummate speed and precision. No doubt about it, he could kill well. Not that he himself entirely understood how he achieved the perfection. He had always been somewhat detached from those dream moves, and afterward he could be as horrified as the next man at what he had done. But this hysterical woman and her pencil-neck hubby, this end of things was already proving to be too much.

"Who is he?" Julie was crying. "Roger, who is he?"

"Swann," Josey sighed in his sanest voice, but the name only plunged him deeper into the fit. "Here, give her some of this," and Josey pulled a bottle of cheap gin from beneath the seat of his car.

"Thank you," Roger mumbled. He was as frightened of this Neanderthal as Julie, but you couldn't let on to it, he told himself. He took a slug of the killer's . . . savior's . . . gin, and nearly spit it up.

Josey laughed. "Pretty rank, isn't it?" He wanted to know the twit's name.

"Dennerstein. My name is Roger Dennerstein."

"What?"

"Dennerstein. D-e-n-n—"

"And that's your wife?"

"Yes, Julie is my wife."

She sobbed a bit louder at the sound of her name.

"Yeah," Josey breathed. "Well, tell her to stop the crying. It gets on my nerves."

"Honey," Roger said. "It's okay now. Honey?"

"Tell her I'm family. I'm not going to hurt you. I'm family," Josey ranted. "Tell her I'm your cousin." They were driving past dark, blank factory walls. There were men huddled on a blackened stoop, passing cigarettes and bottles.

"Where are we going?" Roger finally asked. He had one arm around Julie and the other clamped to his side.

"Home," Josey announced. "We're going back to your place."

"But how do you know where . . . ?"

"Ah, well, we're cousins, aren't we, cousin?" Josey licked his lips and grinned. Very feral, he thought of his act.

"I see," Roger said. On top of everything else, he thought, this man is out of his mind.

"Here," Josey laughed. "How about some of that back?" and he snatched the bottle from Roger's knees. "It's actually good when you learn to get past the bite." His mouth was full of the stuff, and he had to kick it down. "But then everything can be good when you get past the bite, isn't that so, cousin?"

JOSEY AND Roger, oil and water, each man fixed in his own: they faced each other across Julie's rustic living room. She stood at the bar, and mixed drinks, but had no real grasp on reality one way or another. The killer had asked for more gin.

"You've got to tell me who you're with, cousin." Josey was rattling the ice in his glass.

"With?" Roger's nostrils pinched.

"How you're involved." Then raising his eyes, hardly able to keep the smirk off his face, "Why somebody just tried to kill you. See where I'm headed?"

For the most part, Roger spoke slowly and coherently. He was mostly afraid now for Julie. At times, particularly when he described his own involvement, he sensed her breaking down. She began to cry when he mentioned stealing Allen's tapes.

As inquisitor, Swann imagined that he was playing it a

147

little too rough. He should have been more the Father Lyle, or even Dancing Allen with his surgeon's smile, but this clown weatherman brought out the worst in him. I'm no sympathetic spy, he thought, never will be. Once when the girl began to cry he even told her to shut her mouth. At real details, however, Roger's story lagged. He sat with one arm around Julie and pulled at his hair. Swann sat across the room, chain smoking and drinking. Sometimes his cigarette ash fell on the floor. "Weatherman," he murmured, toying with the word. "Weatherman, weatherman."

"It's what I do," Roger said, and he might even have been challenging.

"I'm sure," Josey smiled. He was entranced with the grime under his nails. Then he glanced up. "Why Miguez, cousin? Why did Carrage knock Danny Miguez?"

"Uh?"

"Why would the Carrage Grain Company want to kill Miguez?"

"I didn't say they did," Roger protested.

"But you were thinking it."

Roger shrugged, trying to show the killer that he wasn't the simple weatherman that he thought he was.

"Can't prove it, can you?" Swann's fingers were prancing on the table. "This guy George Bandy, or this guy Howard Sax, you think they're in on something ugly, don't you?"

"Not Bandy," said Roger, remembering the head of the wolf above the bar.

"Still, you want to bust them, eh? You think Carrage might have set up Miguez for the fall, right?"

"It crossed my mind," said Roger sourly. He wasn't going to be shoved in a corner, not with Julie shivering in his arms.

148

Josey strained and his mouth stretched into a toothy grin. "Well, I think you might be right, cousin. Can't be sure, but I think you may have been close. Too close?" He glanced at the woman, then back to Roger. "Ever heard of a guy named Cassidy? Dancing Allen Cassidy? About fifty, tall, thin, pretty boy? He smiles like a riverboat gambler."

Roger shook his head with a noisy breath.

"Never seen him? Never heard of him?"

"No," Roger said, and he was glad. He didn't want to know the killer's friends.

Julie was crying again, but softly, so that neither man noticed.

Then it was Josey's sigh that broke. "How about this one, cousin. Do you know if your Carrage-fucking Grain Company has any tie with the CIA?"

Roger's jaw went, literally, slack.

"Central Intelligence Agency."

"Oh, God!"

"Come on now, cousin, who did you think I was? The white knight?" He drew a cigarette from his raincoat pocket and began to pack it down on the end of his thumb. "Or maybe you thought that I hadn't come to save you at all," he laughed. Then the tap-tap of the cigarette on his dirty, cracked nail was the only sound in that maddening room.

THE EVENING might have skidded to a halt much earlier, but Josey still had plans for the clown weatherman. The wife was packed off to bed. Roger gave her Valium to help her sleep, and Josey took a couple too . . . you don't turn down free dope. He would have kept them all stoned if he could have, especially the woman. Keep them quiet and keep them stoned, he had always believed. It was the only way to handle the foolish ones.

"She won't do anything dumb, will she, cousin?" Josey lay on his back on the couch. There was no ashtray in reach, so he made neat piles of ashes on the driftwood table: more of the weatherman's rustic.

"What do you mean?"

"Dumb. Like call the police, something like that?"

"Oh, no, she's all right, really." Although Roger was thinking that maybe the trick was standing up to the brute.

"Yeah, well you keep an eye on her, cousin. We can't have her blowing it just yet. There's too much at stake. Know what I mean?" He damn near winked, restrained himself.

Roger nodded, which started his hand shaking and then his coffee was splattering into the rug. "But what are we going to do?"

"Get out of here. First thing tomorrow, we get out of here."

"To where?"

"Someplace safe, cousin. We'll go rent a house or something."

"Why?"

"Why do you think? You're on the hit parade. What? You think it's over? Cousin, it hasn't even begun."

"But when will it be over?"

"When's it going to rain, weatherman?" Swann had rolled on his side. Now he was moving his eyes across the room, from wall to wall, to coils of ferns, to a thin, crystal bowl brimmed with round, crisp fruit. Here is where these people live, he vaguely thought, so civilized, so white. Then, very consciously breaking the stillness, he spoke. "Weather, weather," he muttered. "I could use a little rain."

Roger reached for the thread of the killer's thought, because the silence was unbearable. "That's the whole point," he said. "There's going to be a drought."

"Where?"

"Asia, North America, maybe other places."

"No rain, uh?"

Roger knew that the killer was baiting him, but what could you do? So he played it straight. "Yes, maybe not a complete drought, but there will be minimal precipitation."

"What about Brazil? Is Brazil going to have a drought?" Swann twisted so that he could study the weatherman's face.

"I don't know. It's a new science. It's hard to predict on that small a level."

"I hate science," Josey sighed. "All those equations. They never add up to real life."

"But the statistics—"

"Yeah? What about them?"

Roger wasn't sure he could explain it to the killer, but he suddenly felt that he ought to try. "You take the statistics and use them to build a model as a base for the computers. The method I use was developed after the Second World War. What you do is you plug the model into the computer and then extend it through time. I'm making it simple, you understand. There's a bit more to it than that. Because, well, Lorenze of MIT found that small errors in the computed forecast grow with time. It's the property of nonlinear equations on which the models are based. So, without certain steps you end up with random weather patterns. But basically you make this statistical graph between cause and effect, or actually present effect and later effect. See the difference? Anyway, it all comes out as a formula; variations from long-term averages tend to occur as spatially coherent patches in the sea. There're other examples. Certain high altitude temperature patterns that can be measured now can also be associated with weather conditions that won't appear for several months. Do you understand?"

Swann sat up and ground out his cigarette. "Are there a lot of others that use your technique?"

"No, like I said, it's a new field. A large part of the community doesn't believe in it. I can show them results but they chalk it up to luck. The government doesn't go in for it either."

"But Carrage supports it?"

"Yes," Roger said. He was beginning to see that this killer was not as dull as he seemed. "They believe in me."

"Why?"

"Well, they've seen results."

"Yeah?"

"Yes, I once did a forecast on North American frost cycles, and I came up with an early frost in Canada. It cut the wheat crop. Carrage made a lot of money going short on wheat. They . . ."

"Going short? What's that?"

"When you sell early. You see, Carrage bought a lot on the first planting. Then the frost hit, ruined about three percent of the crop, the prices shot up, and Carrage made a bundle."

"What's a bundle, cousin? Give me a figure."

"I don't know. A lot."

"What? Thousands? Hundreds of thousands? What?"

"Hundreds of thousands."

"And this forecast you just did, is there a way to turn that into big money?"

"Yes, I suppose so," Roger said. Then his head began to slowly bob. "Yes, of course, they could make lots of money. Obviously if there's a shortage of one particular commodity then the prices rise. It would just be a question of getting enough of the market, and if they could go all the way, if they could corner the market, why, then, they could name their own price. The figures would be astronomical, well into the millions."

Swann was not impressed. He had thrown himself back down to the cushions. "Lots of ways this can go." He was speaking to the ceiling. "There are all kinds of possibilities. Commodities, they're more important than money."

"I don't follow."

"Leverage, cousin. People got to eat. When people starve the government isn't safe. Did you know that? Even the Russians and Chinese get the axe when the people starve. Moscow, they've got to keep the people happy. The stick only goes so far and for so long. See what I'm getting at?"

Roger rubbed his sleeve across his eyes.

"Not really, but—"

"You want to get the Russians over a barrel. Okay, they got oil, but what about wheat? We've been had on the wheat deals, but maybe the Company has got the idea now of how to turn the tables on those wheat deals. Maybe they're going to use the pressure of a drought to do it."

"But Carrage doesn't care about politics."

"Company, cousin, the CIA . . . *they* still care about the politics."

"I see . . ." The room was suddenly full of schemes.

"No, you don't see, weatherman. You don't see anything right now. You have no idea how weird it can get. Everything the Company does cuts both ways. That's why it's so good that you caught up with me. Yeah, with me, you stand a chance of making it." Josey's smile was terrible. He might have been leering at the little man. "See, cousin, there's a lot of crazy people in the CIA, lots of really fucked up minds. You know what I'm talking about? I know some real basket cases, I can assure you."

While you, Roger thought, are the epitome of sanity, and he turned his head away.

CHAPTER 10

LYLE SEVERSON sat in the darkness. The room was filled with his dead wife's furniture. There was her nest of Quartetto tables, there her Sheraton secretaire bookcase, here her long glass of etched crystal brimmed with whiskey and soda, and topped with a twist of lemon—just as Stewart Menzies used to take it. And along with Lyle's dead wife, Stewart was also here, still looking gaunt and avuncular, still the perennial British spy from the MI-5. Stewart often came back haunting, if not in spirit, then at least in the mind of Lyle Severson.

Lyle sat in the wing chair, the one with the lace on the arms. All afternoon he had read by the light of the great bay windows, and now that dusk had fallen, the reaches of the room were washed in indigo shadows. He would have reached above his head and switched on that lovely Tiffany lamp, but sometimes the ghosts could be so shy. Not that they had been shy lately, drifting in and out at all hours of the night. Pesty buggers. But it was the years, Lyle told himself. I'm getting old, and the ghosts, bolder.

Although they still might become frightened by the light.

Tonight a whole tribe of old ghosts had come, tipped their hats and then marched through Lyle's mind. First there had been Jenny, and whenever Lyle thought of her he thought of their wedding in London. It had been November, the heat of the war, and cold as hell. Miles Sitcombe, the Cambridge chip off the Menzies block, had been best man. He had come to the wedding in tweeds, smelling of his hip flask and brier. "They say that marriage makes the strongest bond," he had joked.

"Don't be an ass," Lyle had retorted. "Jenny is not a spy," which, of course, had also been something of a pun in the trade.

"Pity," Miles had snorted. "I could have used you both."

And, finally, tonight there had been Michael Forest, the Welsh rake who only drank claret and muscatel, said it sharpened the sense, although perhaps he was alluding to Yeats. But, still, you could believe that Michael had the keenest sense of past and future, for in the end, hadn't he proved himself the cleverest one of all? "When the Germans are buried," he had whispered to the privy circles, "we'll still not give it up, you know. When the Germans are buried we'll be spying on the Russians." And then even more profoundly chilling, "Also, perhaps, ourselves."

And isn't that the bloody truth? Because what else am I doing now, Lyle thought, than spying on my own child, the wayward Allen Cassidy.

All afternoon, Lyle had been burrowing into the life of Allen Cassidy. Initially, perhaps to get some new perspective on the man, Lyle had looked at the distant past. But even at Harvard, Allen had been dancing. Lyle remembered, and the records bore this out to some extent, that

Allen had not so much been the joiner as the organizer. Somewhere, buried beneath the piles of papers at Lyle's feet, was a handwritten letter addressed to the dean. The letter had been an apology for some minor campus infringement, but couched in the bland atonement, Lyle perceived the more typical Cassidy defense. "Tradition," the young Allen had begun, "must extend itself to the present so that its adherents do not become stultified."

What else had been justified with that very same axiom? Vietnam? The records were fairly concise on this point. Allen had been a hawk, not the first, not the last, but in his time, he had been as staunch a supporter of the war as any of them. (No wonder Swann hated the man.) "We discussed," Allen had written to the Deputy Director of Plans, "the subject of pacification. I think it can be safely said that the term is now entirely obsolete. The most that we can hope for is a decade or two of control. However, I am not opposed to throwing in our weight to achieve just such an end. I shall wait in my office for your reply."

And the reply came, and they gave Dancing Allen the money he needed, although, of course, in the end even money was not enough. When the war began to turn sour, Allen changed sides. "Hopelessness," read a wry little note to Richard Helms, "is not lost ground or rising body count. Hopelessness is the failure to discuss our options with the enemy." By enemy, Allen had not meant the Vietcong, nor even the Chinese. By the end of Johnson's term, Allen was ready to go to the Russians.

So then was mutability Allen's shield? Certainly the man was awfully good when the game came down to musical chairs. Again, the record bore accounts. The flap in Chile was a prime example. President Ford wanted some heads for the spike. (To get the liberal vote, one was to understand.) However, when the chin music of Kissinger's Forty Committee stopped playing, Allen was not one of those left standing without a seat. Some said that he should have been caught. After all, there had not been many closer to Herold Geneen than Dancing Allen, but, as always, Allen managed to dance out the door just as the roof fell in.

Another brief memo, this time an "eyes only" report to Noel Polly at the Washington Desk, gave one the impression that Allen was able to move even before the music began. "Regarding the President's 'Enemy List' which I believe we discussed at Jan Henshaw's," wrote Allen, "I can only say that I'm afraid we are looking at a tempest in the teapot. President Nixon's position appears untenable. I fear the worst." This note was significant in that it was written a good six months before the Watergate scandal.

All right then, Allen was as mutable as Proteus, as two-faced as Janus, but given the tradition, could one blame him?

At tradition, the records stopped cold. The pages that Lyle had read were peppered with only prim vignettes of the gentleman spy. There was one yellowed snapshot of the lads posing on the steps of Old Foggy Bottom, which had been the first home of the Dulles CIA. There was a hardy commendation from Wild Bill Donovan, the mother and father of the OSS. Jerry Shapp, who held up the British end of things, threw in his three cheers for young Allen, and there was an invitation to a dance at the Polish Embassy. Heaven knows why that had been included in the file, unless it was for the joke, scrawled at the bottom of the buff card in Cassidy's own hand, "No one without shoes will be admitted."

There were other glimpses of those jocular days of American espionage. There was a notice of Cassidy as head of the Company racquet club. There was Cassidy dining night after glittering night on embassy row. He was Anglophile for the British and continental for the French. To everyone else he was stone Ivy League. But nowhere did the record contain the essential tradition from which Cassidy had come.

Yet, now at last, Lyle had begun to understand. Allen had tradition, not perhaps as Lyle knew it, but there was tradition nonetheless. Everything else about the young Cassidy as contained in the records was dross. Snip off the buttons of his Brooks Brothers suit, snatch his school tie away, and what had you?

You had, thought Lyle, the quintessential Allen Cassidy, and that, of course, was a spy. Allen owed his allegiance to the craft. There was nothing more to it. The man was a spy, and that explained the amazing duplicity with which he had built his very own network.

The records only hinted at the network. Had Lyle not been looking he might never have found it, which was not to imply that he had found it now. Oh, no, I only have hints, he told himself. But even so, one could safely say that Allen had found himself a laundry.

According to records, Allen had visited a privately owned West Coast firm, remained two days at the Holiday Inn and then returned to Langley with thirteen hundred dollars. The money, records maintained, was only a token payment. The fundamental objective was, "to determine the feasibility of the Mercurial Institute's role as a deceptive channel for funds that, unless passed through an independent organization, would compromise Company operations."

Were the records to have ended with this single West Coast visit, Lyle would have passed the incident off as routine. But Cassidy returned to the Mercurial Institute, not once, but three times more. Each trip was logged in a domestic operative carry file. Each explanation was the same. The sums of money, although faithfully deposited in the Missions-Programs floater account, never exceeded seventeen hundred dollars. Had Cassidy been looking for a way to collect large sums of money, clean cash at that, he would not have been able to come up with a better way. The entire operation, if indeed it was what Lyle suspected, bore the neat, classic stamp of the famous Dancing Allen tradecraft.

Here then was Allen's money. The cover was complete. Lyle still had no positive proof, but now at least he knew that all things were possible. Cassidy could have actually funded a project that officially did not exist. He could have murdered Daniel Miguez and even Swann's latest ward, the weatherman from the Carrage Grain Company.

Swann had called the previous night. He had used the exchange they had set up for crash calls. For the most part he spoke of the weatherman, then the Carrage Grain Company. No, Lyle had no idea how either Dennerstein or Carrage were tied into Allen Cassidy. "But you'll check the records, won't you?"

"I won't find anything," Lyle had said. "Not directly, at any rate. I think you'll do better at your end."

"I don't have any end. All I got is some twit weatherman and his sob-sob wife." As an aside, Swann mentioned that he had killed Ernie Shepp.

But tonight, as intrusive as Swann could be, Lyle was still able to keep him from his thoughts. This was not Josey's moment. It was Allen's and the room was alive with secrets. Here was this thread of money with no visible source. There were Swann's weatherman and grain company with no firm connection, and here again was Allen himself, this time dancing to a strain of music that no one else could hear.

Lyle would have slept now, if only he could have slept. He was often up in the nights. There was no one to talk to. He hated the television, and his eyes began to hurt if he read too long. They hurt him now, but worse than his eyes were the joints of his ankles and wrists. The joints were throbbing. The drink had not helped. He would have had another, except that tonight he would need his wits about him. You're an old fox, Lyle, he could have told himself, and then, in the same breath sagged, because he was not a fox at all. Might have been years ago, but now you're just an old three-legged, milky-eyed, stump-toothed dog. And tonight mind that you keep your tail between your legs. No one should wag his tail over the remains of Dancing Allen, and that was what it would come to in the end. Throw young Allen to Josey Swann, and the Swann will tear him to shreds.

SWANN SAT on the porch that he and the weatherman had rented two days before. It was a good house, a real safe-house. It lay on a hill surrounded by trees. To the north were the great mountains, and on clear days one could see the fingers of snow that ran down the face of the summit and filled the higher crags. Above, the sky was netted with stars. Below Swann heard the rush of water in a rocky bed. All around him the country was still and powerful.

But Josey Swann hated the country, all those flies, and down the road there were horses, and in the morning the wind carried the stench of their offal . . . sweet smell of Nam. He also hated the circumstances, cooped up like he was with the weatherman and his wife. "Make the best of it," Lyle had said when he called a few minutes ago. "It

161

couldn't be as bad as all that."

Actually, it wasn't that bad, but Swann was wary of the hospitality that the weatherman kept trying to fob on him. Made you wonder what the little fellow was up to. Maybe he looked upon Swann as certain families look upon exchange students, brought into the home to satisfy some curiosity and middle-class guilt? Or maybe the weatherman was just scared of Swann, and the extended amenities were nothing more than bits of meat thrown to the lion to keep him content? Either way life with the weatherman was weird. Josey ate the meals that they served him. He drank the gin and beer. He threw himself all over the furniture. But the little man always did his best to accept Swann. He asked nothing at all from him, and so Swann figured it was a fair exchange. The weatherman gave Swann a certain comfort, and Swann gave the weatherman a rough time.

Now Swann heard one of them stirring inside the house. He saw a light switch on, and heard the screen door bang. The planks of the porch began squeaking. Swann turned, and what do you know, there was the weatherman now, dawdling at the railing. "I heard the telephone ring," he said. "Was that—?"

"Yeah." Josey reached for a beer and began to drink.

"Did he say anything, you know, interesting?"

Josey rubbed his thumb on the arm of the weathered deck chair, and then because it hardly mattered, "Yeah. He thinks he found out where Cassidy had his money laundered."

"Laundered?"

"Fed into a legal business so that the source of funds can't be traced. You do remember Richard and his merry men, don't you?"

"Oh."

162

"I'm going to check it out tomorrow," Swann continued. "It's close, just over the hill."

"What kind of business is it?"

"Don't know, so it will be a surprise. You like surprises? Want to come along?"

Roger ignored him and faced the night beyond the railing. "I've been thinking," he said. Below him the scrub was a black sea. The branches of trees stood out against the sky. "I've been thinking that if we could maybe find out what Howard Sax saw in my forecast, then maybe we could prove something."

Josey was creasing the beer can with his thumb. "I'm listening, cousin."

"I mean, maybe Sax is working with the CIA. What if he turned my forecast over to the CIA and then the CIA decided that for some reason they had to kill Daniel Miguez because . . . Well, I haven't figured that part out yet, but you see what I'm getting at? Maybe the CIA read my forecast, and they realized that there would be a drought, and then the Russians would want to buy a lot of wheat, and maybe somehow Daniel Miguez found out about it, and that's why they had him killed. Then it would account for why they wanted to, you know, with me too."

Swann ran his tongue along the edge of the can. "Figured it all out, have you?"

"Well, I've been thinking, you know. I've been thinking that maybe I could go back and take a look at my forecast. Maybe there's a clue, or something. Never can tell."

Josey could have laughed. "Jesus, cousin, you really have an odd way of seeing things."

"You've got to admit that I may be onto something." He had never been bolder with Swann than now.

"Yeah, well, I follow you."

"So if I could go over my forecast one night."

"Well, go ahead." Josey seemed more interested in the sharpening edge of the can. He was idly turning the thing into a weapon.

"Yes, but I need a computer." Roger's fingers were wrapped around the post of the railing.

"Oh, well, that presents a problem, doesn't it? You can't go back to your Carrage lab, can you?"

"No, but I can use the computer at UCLA. I've got a pass. I can even get in at night. No one knows me there. It would be perfectly safe."

Josey pulled at his beer until the can was dry. Then he heaved it over the railing. A moment later it clattered in the rocks. "I don't know, man. We wouldn't want anything to happen to you, would we?"

"But at the university I'd be safe. I could go out after dark. I've got a key and a pass to the lab. Anyway, it's got to be done. You don't believe that Sax has a real connection here, but I know him, or at least I know what he's like. He's capable of anything."

"Okay, cousin, I'll think about it." Swann rocked back on his chair to reach for another beer. "Want one?" and he tossed a can to Roger.

"I can help, you know. It's my life, after all, that's under the gun, and I want to help." Roger pried off the top of the can, drank. "You know, I'm not precisely what you think I am."

Now Swann truly smiled. "I can see that, cousin." He was watching the weatherman, and sure enough, you had to hand it to the little guy. He tried.

"I don't like Carrage," Roger was saying.

"So why didn't you quit?" Josey pulled off the top of his own beer and the spray went flying over the railing.

"I've thought about it. I supposed I was eventually

164

going to as soon as something better came along."

Josey threw the pop-top over his shoulder. He liked quitters. They were nearly as good as the losers. "So what did you do before Carrage?"

"I worked at the UN."

"The what?"

"The United Nations." Roger said it proudly.

"Shit! What were you doing there?"

Roger was halfway through his beer and growing a bit reckless. "I forecast the weather. I was damn good."

"Well, I'm sure you were. But what did you really do?"

"I worked with underdeveloped nations. I helped their agricultural departments with planting and fishing schedules. Sometimes they might plant too early or too late, and not benefit from the rainfall. It was the same with fish. If you bring in the catch at the wrong time you may miss the larger harvests. A lot of fish are very sensitive to sea temperature. I did well with the fish."

"I hate fish." Josey was tipping back in his chair and the planks creaked. "I only like fish on Fridays, and even then there's the bones and all. Messy stuff."

Roger began a smile, but then you never knew exactly where Swann was coming from, so he quickly drenched that smile with more beer.

"But what I can't understand, cousin, is why you did it?"

"Did what?"

"Worked with the fish at the UN."

"I liked it. I got to travel, and I like helping people."

"Where did they send you?"

"India."

"Oh, yeah, India," Josey held a finger to his eye. "Got on well with the wogs, did you?"

Roger sank to his haunches. His lips were numbing and

165

his head was light. Had he not known better he might have believed that Swann was some kind of friend.

And perhaps, in his own special fashion, Josey was, or at least he wanted to know the weatherman's secret. "I asked if you liked them, cousin."

"Liked who?"

"The Indians."

"Yes, of course, I liked them. I mean, you can get close to people if you're around them enough."

Ah, Josey thought, a true believer. "Now I see."

"See what?" Roger was swaying a bit on his heels.

"I see your secret, cousin."

The night had grown very thick between them. Somewhere beyond the first line of trees a bird was calling. "Your secret," Josey said softly, "is that you're a bleeder. You're out to save it . . . the world."

Roger tore at the cardboard container and ripped out a final beer. "Is that what you call it? A bleeder?" He sipped and then handed the can to Swann.

"Bleeder, bleeding heart. I've got nothing against it, cousin." They were actually sharing the beer. First one drank, then the other. "It's just a fact, and that's your secret."

"All right, so I'm a bleeder." Roger laughed. "Well, then what's *your* secret?"

"My secret?" Josey was abruptly sly. "My secret, cousin? Oh, you don't want to know that." A deepening blue was now soaking one edge of the sky. The moon oozed through a low bank of clouds. In the far distance lay the black shapes of mountains.

"But I do," Roger said. "I want to know." He hiccupped.

Josey's lips stretched into a mangy smile. His hair was spiked against the indigo twilight. "Cousin, I think maybe

166

you already know part of it," he said. Below, the water tumbled into the creek.

Roger glanced up. "All right, I think that maybe you're not as bad as you act."

Josey began to shake with laughter. He clamped his hand to his heart. Then he shook his head and heaved the empty beer can into the darkness. They heard it crash through the underbrush, and a bird, frightened by the clamor, broke from the leaves and wheeled off above them.

But he didn't deny it, Roger noted.

CHAPTER 11

THE MERCURIAL Institute was as bad as they came. "Institute of Personal Expression," read the warped, plastic sign, and beneath that, in burned-out neon, "Girls! Girls! Girls!" The building was green and fading. It lay in Hollywood's grimmest quarter. Sunlight glanced off the grimy shop windows. Blank torsos and the faceless heads of manikins were draped with wigs and black lingerie. Chicano graffiti, like fierce hieroglyphics, had been sprayed on the brick walls. Women leaned from windows and shrieked. Children threw garbage. A red silhouette of a naked girl had been painted above the Institute's door. Through the glass, Swann saw a live one. She was slouched on the velveteen sofa, speaking to someone that he could not see.

Langley tradecraft had an exact routine for diving in cold when you didn't know the depth. But the Langley method took time, a good week of spotting even before the agent walked through the doors. Then, for the splash, they gave you cover. On a job like this, Josey Swann imagined he should have had at least four seasoned runners to back him. Two would be stationary, parked in a van across the street, working the bugs that had been wired to the agent's lapel. Then two more afloat as needed. All of them would go critically operational, which meant that they would have been armed.

But Swann was too jaded, too stupid, said some, too crazy, said others, to follow any bullshit Langley tradecraft. Besides, Old Father Lyle hadn't the resources for a proper run of it. So, instead, Swann put his faith in his own ingenuity, which meant that he would crash the gates first and then ask questions.

He entered with his best shambler's grin, both hands crammed into his pockets. He hung at the door, browsed, and then shuffled in.

The girl on the couch sat up. She wore blue jeans cut to the crotch and a halter top. She puffed a red curl of hair from her mouth and slid into her easiest smile. "What do you say, honey?"

"I'm interested in Personal Expression," Swann said, although all he saw now were his own staring eyes, staring back from a gold painted mirror.

"Well, you've come to the right place." The girl was twisting the ends of purple tassels that fringed an oil portrait of a nude which had been thumbtacked to the wall. "Our standard introductory course is twenty-five dollars and it lasts one incredible hour."

There was more painted gold on the brass chandelier that had been fitted with tiny, red bulbs. "I wasn't really interested in that sort of expression," Swann returned. "What I want," and he paused to flick a string of glass baubles hanging from the door. "What I really want, love, is to have a little chat with the owner. Is he in?"

170

"It's a she, and the answer is no." The girl crossed her legs and scowled.

"Well, then maybe you might know where I can find her." Swann was squeezing the baubles between his fingers.

"Look, I don't know what you want, but you'd better get out of here." The girl's face had grown taut. Her makeup was cracking. Her arms were folded across her breasts.

A deep voice called from an adjoining room, "Sheila?" Swann whirled as the curtain of colored beads exploded and a heavy man in tight black pants and a bright red undershirt stepped through the passage. He planted himself on the thick blue shag. "What do you want, pal?" He had one hand on his hip, the other bunched in a fist. There were tracks of sloppy tattoos running up his massive arms.

"The owner," Swann said. He had seen this sort of bouncer before. They were street fighting trash with strength but no speed. Swann began tapping his fingers on his thigh.

"Well, the owner's not here."

The girl on the couch began picking at the stiff strands of her hair. "I told him, Solly. I just told him that."

"Is that your name? Solly? Uh? Are you Solly?"

The man hunched forward. Already he had begun to shy from the fight. Maybe he knew about Josey Swann.

"Well, listen, Solly. I've got to find out who the owner is. You understand?"

"Why?" Solly looked over his shoulder where a naked girl had just stuck her head through the curtain and then vanished.

"I've got some business."

"What sort of business?"

"Private." Swann's fingers were still tapping his thigh.

"All right," Solly finally said, and nodded toward the sheet of beads. Josey followed. The corridor was drab, with a tiled floor and dull, yellow walls. They walked single file until they reached a black door. Solly knocked twice and then called out, "Mandy, there's a guy out here to see you. It's business. He says it's important."

"Find out what he wants." A woman's husky voice.

"He says it's private."

The door pulled back and a fat, squat woman stood before them. She had blond, lacquered hair, and wore elastic stretch pants, a turtleneck sweater and high, black boots. Her eyes were dark. "What is it?"

"Talk?" Josey asked, and the woman twisted on her boot heels to let him into her office.

A girl in panties and bra lay on a mess of acetate pillows. She was reading a paperback book: *The Nigger of The Narcissus and Other Stories.* She looked up when Swann entered, but then lowered her eyes back to Conrad. Solly squatted by her side and hooked his finger in the waistband of her panties.

"I haven't got all the time in the world," Mandy said. She lowered herself into the big leather chair behind her desk.

Swann sat across from her. "I want to talk to you about some money."

Solly had been stroking the young girl's thighs and breasts. Once she half-heartedly tried to shake him off, but it must not have been worth it. Maybe Conrad was more compelling. Now, however, Solly tensed. He had forgotten the hand that lay on the girl's rump.

"What money?" Mandy would not be thrown. She merely settled back and laced her hands behind her head. Her hair was like a helmet.

172

"Oh, perhaps some money that a friend of mine picked up"—Swann actually smiled—"say three times in the last few months."

Then Solly came at him, but Swann had seen it coming. He had seen the woman nod and clench her jaws, so he met the attack with a snapping kick to Solly's groin. The man screamed, and a knife dropped to the floor. Josey fell on him, and shoved his knee into Solly's chin. He flattened Solly's arm on the rug. Solly was trying to twist free, so Josey hit him with an elbow. Then, slowly, he dragged the knife blade down the length of Solly's wrist. Blood marked the path. "Stop it!" Mandy was up from her chair, leaning over her desk. "Damn you, stop it!"

Josey rolled off the man. Solly doubled up and moaned. The young girl bent over him. She tried to staunch the bleeding with a bit of his torn undershirt. There was a good deal of blood on the carpet. "Get him out of here," Mandy shouted, and the girl helped Solly to his feet. Now he stood, bent, his bleeding arm pressed in the folds of his stomach. "I'll kill you, man, I'll kill you."

Josey shook his head.

"Go on, Solly, get out of here," Mandy told him, and the girl led him from the room. Swann locked the door behind them and slipped back into his chair. "You're a prick," Mandy spat. "You know that? You're a real butch prick, aren't you?"

Swann cocked his head and sighed. "The pick-ups were made by a man named Allen Cassidy." Swann's lips were stiff. "You know him?"

"Not by that name." Mandy wiped her eye with her thumb and smeared mascara over her face. "He didn't give me a name like that."

"Doesn't matter. I don't care about him. I want to know where the money came from."

173

Mandy's nails dug through her hair and into her scalp. "Because, if you don't tell, it's going to get rougher. You can see that."

"You're one of them, aren't you?" The woman drummed her fingers on the desk. Her nails were also bright red.

Josey still had the knife in his hands. He was turning the point into the wood. "One of them?"

"Oh, hell, you know. The CIA." She pulled at a lock of washed-out hair.

Swann, still twisting away at the desk with the knife, gave nothing away, not that he cared much for cover now. He hadn't any. He was the killer, plain and simple, angry and loose, so it didn't matter much who he worked for, did it? "Yeah," he said. "We're all spies together. Been at the game long, Mandy?"

"Long enough." She grinned. "Long enough to know when I'm covered." Her smile sagged to a deep frown. "You're a . . . friend of Allen's, huh? Well, anyway, Allen came here three times and picked up twenty-five thousand a clip."

The knife slipped and went skidding across the desk. "We know that," Josey almost gloated. "I want to know where the money comes from."

"It doesn't come just like that. We were bought. Your Mr. Cassidy was the broker, only his commission was seventy-five thousand."

"So who was the buyer?"

"I don't know, some syndicate, or something. The name won't give you anything."

"Well, let's try."

Mandy rolled her eyes and shook her head. "I'm feeling hotter every second. See, I just want to be on the good guys' side, know what I mean? I won't be trouble, and I

174

don't want trouble. Like, are you the good guy or is Allen?"

"I am," Josey said. "Allen is the bad guy."

"I hope to God you're right."

"Well, if I'm not, it won't make any difference to you, because it's my side that's going to come down heavy."

Mandy pulled at her fingers and cracked the joints. Her eyelids had fallen. She could not look at Swann now, as the confession began, at first as a trickle while the secrets strained through years of inhibitions. She had first met Allen Cassidy in Paris. "Oh God, has it been that long?" In those days Allen had been the embassy resident, and he ran a neat little network under the nose of Charlie de Gaulle. Not that Charlie would have cared, she said. Allen's string of agents were the price the French paid to keep the Russians out of their sector of NATO. It seemed that Allen had the best counterintelligence force in Europe. Pretty boys, Mandy called them, and her voice was already loosening with the memory. The East Germans were scared to death of Allen Cassidy, she said proudly. The contrite confessor had become the braggart.

"Allen was always very good to me. A gentleman, he's always been a real gentleman." Which was not to say that Mandy was a lady, not at least when Allen first picked her up. She called herself a street lamp hooker, and that was a pun as well. At the time she was supporting a thirty-five dollar a day habit, hanging on lampposts, turning tricks with any takers. Then along came Allen with his little bag of Golden Triangle smack. "It was so pure that I nearly lost my head. Literally, I nearly died." When she came around again, Allen made her an offer. The smack would keep on coming right into her lovely little veins if she would work for him. Allen a pimp? Of course not. What he had in mind was purely patriotic.

"So I said, 'What's the job, darling?' And he said, 'Same job as you've always had.' So then I said, 'What's the catch?' And he said, 'All you have to do is bed down with the boys that I tell you to bed down with . . . and get them to talk about themselves.' Honest to God, that's how I became a spy."

To this day Mandy swore that the first three johns were Allen's own people. They were out to test her, she said, but in the end, she obviously passed with flying colors, because in no time she was sleeping with everyone from the French to the Poles, to the Germans to the Russians.

How was she used specifically? Swann asked. "I went both ways," she said, but did not mean sexually. Sometimes the johns were just poor fools, a French cabinet officer or someone like that. Then her job had been simply to dig up what dirt she could get so that Allen could go in later with the torch. When Allen burned his pigeons, he was blackmailing them. Other times, however, Mandy claimed that she slept with bonafide Russian spies. Those were the worst jobs. One of them once tied her to the bed and lashed her with his belt. He wasn't normally an S. and M. john. He just didn't like Americans. For that Allen had the man's kneecaps shattered with a length of pipe, and Mandy was sent to the Riviera for a rest.

When Cassidy was called back to Langley headquarters, Mandy was picked up on the rebound by his replacement. Who was that? Swann wanted to know. But Mandy said enough was enough. "You haven't paid for the full ride, honey." She was getting cocky.

She stayed on in the service for another three years, and by the end of that period she was straight. "I took the cure at a clinic in Switzerland. Then I came back to the states." Why? "Homesick," she said.

"For anything in particular?" Swann was needling the

arm of his chair with the knife, needling her as well.

"Yeah. I missed American plumbing."

Back in the states she took up where she had left off in Paris. She was what was then called "clean and up and coming," which meant that she had her own apartment, and took calls rather than walked the streets. "But I didn't start at the top. You never do." Once, maybe twice a week she turned a trick for Allen, or one of Allen's friends. It was nothing heavy, mostly babysitting with horny defectors who missed their wives. Home, at that time, was New York, but the Company work usually took her to Washington or Virginia. She worked New York for another five years, and then gave it up. All of it, she insisted, even her relationship with Allen and friends was over by that time.

"What did you do then?" Swann asked. He had grown still. He was afraid to shake the narrative, for fear it might crumble.

"I lived a normal life," she said, and that was that.

New scene now. It's Los Angeles, and Mandy is years older. Somewhere along the way she must have picked up a husband because she was calling herself Mrs. Furthermore, she made a brief reference to leaving somebody for something. Swann did not press the point. All that really mattered was that she was in L.A., and Allen entered the picture again. "I had a massage parlor," she said. Mandy's Place, it was called, and regardless of what the cops said, business was ninety percent straight and above the boards. Guys came in, paid a ten spot, and for thirty minutes a little oriental girl would dance up and down on their spines. There were, however, special girls for special clients.

"Which was roughly where Allen Cassidy fit in?" Swann asked.

"Not roughly, darling, exactly."

177

Vietnam, that was what was happening, and Sweet Dancing Allen was playing six sides against the middle. Mandy had no idea what Allen did. She didn't want to know, but every few weeks she would be sent a man to loll in her honey traps. Naturally, she wasn't doing the bump and grind herself. Oh, no. By this time she had trained the other girls to take the bruises and collect the catch when Cassidy asked.

"What sorts were you servicing?" Swann wondered.

"All sorts," she said. There was everything from hawks to doves, from farm boys to five-star generals. It was Cassidy's belief that a man gave up secrets best under two conditions—pleasure or pain. My girls knew how to give both," said Mandy, "which then got them to talking. Like I said, Cassidy sent me all kinds . . ." Once she even held the hand of a personal aide of Nguyen Cao Ky. "The poor dear was having nightmares that the Americans would pull out and leave him and his sweet little deal in the lurch. I think Allen wanted to know if Ky was going to pull a fast one, but I couldn't get that john to talk. He cried all night and called me 'Lotus' or something. I think that was the name of a VC whore that he fell in love with and then had to shoot. They were weird times."

Mandy's Place lasted three years. In that period she figured she had made enough to retire, so she sold it. "But retirement was the pits." She laughed. "I couldn't take the pace." So eighteen months earlier she bought this place and, true to form, who should come strolling in the door but Dancing Allen Cassidy, looking just as young and dapper as ever.

"When was this?" Swann wanted to know.

"Three months ago," said Mandy, "and that, honey, was when all this laundry business began."

First time around, Allen did not say much about anything. Social visit, that was all it was, Mandy insisted. Glad to see you're back in business, that sort of thing. Allen did not make the approach for another month.

Second time back, Allen was not looking too well. He was dragging his nerves all over the floor. Sure, he tried to put on a show, but Mandy knew when Allen was straining on the boards. "After all, we'd been through a lot together." Anyway, the job was this . . . Mandy had a cash and carry business. Who writes checks to the Institute of Personal Expression? So Mandy had the cash, and Allen needed cash. Could Mandy convert some of Allen's checks to cash? Sure she could, but as always, there was a catch. The job was not to be a straight conversion. The exchange would run like this. A friend of Allen's, a very trusted friend, one was to understand, would feed a little money into the business. Mandy could skim off a bit for herself and then turn around and give the bulk to Allen, all in unmarked bills.

On paper the operation seemed simple enough, but there was more to laundering money than Mandy had imagined. No, she would not give actual details. It was one thing to blow your friends, and quite another to blow yourself. "I was a bank," she said. "Money came in and money went out. If anyone were to check my books they wouldn't find a blessed thing. All I knew was that there was a friend of Allen's that had some money that he couldn't give directly to Allen. He had to account for the money somewhere, so he spent it on a business failure: the Institute of Personal Expression." She gave Swann her best whiskey smile.

"So Allen's friend is a partner?"

"Silent partner, honey, and it's by no means half and half."

Swann's elbow dropped on the desk and his cheek

leaned into his palm. This is where she begins to run down, he thought, so he stuck her again with the goad. "Did I tell you that Allen is heading for a fall? Did I tell you that he's in trouble?"

"Oh, I can see that there's trouble. I can see that, because you're here, and I know your type."

Swann could believe that she did. "Yeah, but I'm still the good guy."

She threw back her head and laughed, although she might have been offering her throat to Josey's knife. He could have slit it, too, it was inviting.

"Ah, give us a break, honey," she winked. "I'm a good girl."

"And a good girl looks after herself, is that it?" Which was clearly Josey's first concrete proposition.

The old pro went coy. "Of course, darling, it's been that way since day one. Look after myself, that's what Daddy always told this little girl. But now I'm clean. I've run everything clean. I'm clean. Allen's clean—"

"And who else is clean, Mandy?"

"You really want to take me all the way, don't you?" She began nibbling on the end of a pen.

"If I don't, someone else will, so who else is clean?"

"Are you *sure* you're on the side of the good guys?" Was she?

Josey reached across the desk and took her by the wrist. "You're clean, Allen's clean, and—"

"Howard Sax," she whispered. "Damn you, but he's not with the Company. He's something else altogether, and for the life of me, I don't know what."

THE DARK lake was about a mile up the road from the safe-house. On the way to the lake one passed a grove of white birches and a field of gray, tangled scrub. There was no shore on the side of the lake where Swann and Denner-stein stood. There was only the sheer drop from a sand-stone cliff. Clumps of weeds and dry grass were quivering now, for the wind had come up and the air was cold. The sun had set, twilight was down, and the water looked very black.

Like certain aspects of Josey Swann? No. Too pat, too easy. Roger would not have compared Swann to that lake even as a joke. But still, the lake did have a certain mystery. "They said it's very deep."

"Who?" Josey had told the weatherman not to talk to strangers.

"The guy done the road. He said the lake was volcanic. Once two boys were drowned and they never found the bodies." Roger was scratching at the bark of a scraggy tree. He had been told about the drowning early that morning, and even now his first impression had not dissolved. Somewhere, buried in the silt were the bones of two boys that had been picked clean by the crabs.

"What man down the road?" Swann asked.

"Just some guy, the one who owns the horses."

Josey's coat billowed in a sudden gust. "Don't talk to him again, okay?"

Roger dropped his eyes and kicked at a tuft of bush. "All right. I won't." The serious Josey Swann may have been the worst Josey Swann of them all.

But Swann was already softening. "It's just that you've got to learn these things, cousin. You've got to learn to play it cool. When you go out hunting, I don't want you blowing anything."

"But I'm just going to UCLA," Roger said. "I wouldn't talk to anyone, even if I saw somebody that I knew, which is not going to happen because I don't know anybody that would be in the lab at night."

Swann squinted into a streak of light that shimmered on the face of the water. He wasn't sure about sending the weatherman out. He was concerned about the risk, and he was concerned about the catch. He didn't know if the two were commensurate. What could the weatherman possibly find?

"Look, Josey, this isn't something I would do if I thought there was any real danger." Roger was speaking to Swann's ragged profile.

"You wouldn't know danger if it hit you in the face," Swann told him.

"That's not exactly true," Roger returned. "I know about you, don't I?" and he smiled. "Anyway, there's Julie, isn't there? I mean I've got to think of her, don't I?"

Josey did not respond. Something in the way that shred of light glinted on the water may have stunned him, or perhaps the sheet of black water was trying to pull him in. All you had to do was jump, he thought. Then he spoke. "You like her, don't you?"

"Julie? Of course, she's my wife. I love her."

"Yeah," Swann conceded. "She's pretty."

The two men had sunk down on their haunches. They were speaking out to the expanse of the lake. "What about you?" Roger asked. "Are you married?" He really should have known better.

"Married?" Swann frowned. Roger had not seen him so vulnerable. "No," he said. "I live with myself. Alone."

182

CHAPTER 12

THIS WAS a night for slumming. Cassidy's shabbier side was brought to the forefront, while the more modest tones of Gentleman Allen were briefly attenuated. Yet, tough Allen in his lean and angry forties was precisely the face that the boy would respect. Be all faces for all people, said the secret code of Dancing Allen. So now that Allen Cassidy was sweating Tommy Vito, he came on mean as a cobra, and more deadly.

Vito sat in a straight-back chair that might have been provided for just such a scene as this. All he needed was the gooseneck lamp, or was the naked bulb more the item? The room itself, however, could have used some improvement, for the room was Vito's own, a boy's room with posters on the wall and psychedelic overtones. In the corner was a twisted, gleaming water pipe. The bed was unmade. Stacks of records were piled on the floor. A sign on the wall read, "No Exit," and you could believe it. On the wine crate coffee table lay a Smith and Wesson snub-nosed revolver, but the weapon, Cassidy's own, was merely for ambiance. Real muscle was supplied by a man named Rocky—truth, that was his real name, Allen had felt the need to explain. Rocky was nothing more than big. He hit people, and generally, only those who did not hit him back. He was proud of the fact that he had never killed a man except in self-defense. Something to do with his religion, Cassidy had been told. He was an Arab of some sort, and he had a face smooth as wax.

But Rocky's religion aside, Vito seemed scared to death of the man, which was just the effect that Cassidy had hoped to achieve. Fear, he had guessed, was all he would need to break this long-haired brat, this hippy locksmith that had overstepped himself with a private job. "And it was a private job, wasn't it, Tommy?" Allen sat on the edge of the unmade bed. Rocky stood at his side, ready to hit Vito again. Vito's eye was already swelling shut, and the nasty cut above would leave a scar.

"Yeah, okay, so I did a little job."

"But for whom, Tommy?" Perhaps I should be buffing my nails, Cassidy thought, except even Vito would think that corny.

"I told you, Lyle Severson."

"Yes, Lyle." Allen sighed. "But I knew that, didn't I, Tommy?" Cassidy picked at the crease in his trousers. "Obviously, Tommy, I didn't come to inquire about what I already knew." Then Cassidy nodded, and there was a crack as the Arab slapped Vito across the face. "Oh, God, don't cry," Allen said. "We're merely playing here, Tommy."

The boy began shaking his head. His lips were trembling. There were tears smeared on his cheeks. "He'll kill me—"

"No one's going to kill you, Tommy . . . Rocky, bring him a glass of water, will you?" Allen leaned forward and

184

placed his elbows on his knees. "Now let's try to tell it from the beginning, shall we?"

The Arab called from the kitchen. "There's no clean glasses, Mr. Cassidy."

Allen rolled his eyes and smiled. "Oh, for heaven's sake, then wash one out." And back to Tommy, "Impossible, those people are still impossible. All that oil money, and they still act like a bunch of nomads. Now, where were we? Yes, the beginning, Tommy boy. Let us start from scratch, shall we?"

"Lyle . . . says to me . . . he says he's . . . got a job . . ."

The Arab handed the glass to Cassidy. "Oh, thank you, Rocky. Now, drink this, Tommy. The adrenalin makes one thirsty, doesn't it?"

The boy began sucking at the water. His lips were numb and a stream went dribbling down his chin. When he finished he handed the glass back to Allen, who placed it on the floor. "Yes, now Lyle calls you, Tommy. Then what?"

"He says he's got a job."

"How does he describe it?"

"Safe-house, said it was a milk run."

"And so you didn't know that you'd find my housekeeper and that she would eventually blow the whistle, did you?"

Vito shook his head. "He said it was a milk run, so I went in."

"Uh now, Tommy, take it a bit slower. I *love* details."

"All right, I got there about midnight, and I waited in my van for about two hours. I had to wait, see, until that other guy showed."

"Yes, your partner in crime, Tommy. This nameless, faceless figure that you do not remember."

"Well, I'd never seen him before. He was one of Severson's people."

"All right. So you waited until this other fellow showed. Now that makes it about two in the morning, correct?"

"I don't know exactly if it was two hours. I was stoned. I smoked a couple of joints before I went in."

"Do you always do that, Tommy?"

"Yeah, sometimes."

"Dangerous, isn't it?"

"Oh, come on." Vito wrinkled up his nose.

"All right, Tommy, so you waited in your van *about* two hours."

"Yeah, and when that other guy came, I made the break."

"How, Tommy?"

"Through the front door, what else?"

"Weren't you worried about alarms?"

Vito threw up his hands. "Jesus," he sighed, a sure sign of recovery. He was growing sarcastic again. "What do you think? I checked. I scanned the casings electronically."

"All right, then, what next?"

"Then I'm in—"

"We are in, Tommy. You had Lyle's man with you, our nameless and faceless friend."

"Okay, we're in. Then we searched the place and eventually Lyle's man found the girl."

"Mary, poor Mary Knapp," Cassidy added.

"Yeah, Mary."

"And you roughed her up a bit."

"Not me," Vito protested. "I didn't do it. Lyle's man did it. You know I don't go in for that kind of stuff."

"Of course, I know, Tommy. You're just a locksmith,

eh?" Cassidy's tongue swished across his lower lip.

"Okay," Vito continued. "Then we found out where the safe was, and it wasn't much of a safe. Like, the tumblers are all gone. You should get them replaced. Then I got out my camera and photographed everything in sight, just like Lyle wanted."

Cassidy glanced at the Arab and then back to the boy. "Tell me, Tommy, what sort of camera did you use?"

"Uh, it was a Langley special, sub-miniature."

"What about the light?"

"It had a built-in flash."

Cassidy raised his eyebrows. "Flash? You weren't concerned about the flash?"

"Drew the shades."

"What was the setting?"

"Look, I don't remember everything, you know." The boy was perspiring.

Cassidy pulled his shoulders forward and slowly shook his head. "Tommy boy, no one can say that you didn't make a try at it. You truly did your best, but I'm afraid to tell you that I know you're lying. Oh, yes. Son, I've been at this a very long time, and I know when a man lies. So this is how it's going to be. Either you tell me the way it actually happened, or I'm going to let our Rocky, as they say, have his way with you. I'm serious about this, Tommy. I want to know who Lyle's man was. I know you have the name burning, right there, right now. It's burning, isn't it? So, who was it? Come on, boy. Who? Right now, right there, you're thinking of it now. Who? Damn you, *who?*"

Vito dropped his head, but his eyes stayed fixed on Cassidy's. His mouth went tight and firm. "Josey Swann. It was Josey Swann, all the way."

187

So it was Josey Swann, the serviceable villain. Father Lyle could not have been keeping any worse company. Allen had once seen Swann perform at the night course at Langley. Some remiss instructor had thrown him in with a group of Company freshmen and a dozen more trainees on the first time out. Swann was awesome, stalking through the underbrush with his knife and bit of piano wire. He nearly killed one boy, and a girl broke down in tears and resigned from the Company then and there. "I didn't think it was going to be like this," she had cried.

Well, dear, Allen could have told her now, I didn't think it was going to be like this either.

But you had to deal with whatever came out of the woodwork, and since the problem was mad Josey Swann, Allen would need professional clout.

The clout was Ralph Cowie, known romantically in the trade as the Hungarian Hammer. Cassidy dropped Rocky off at his swinging single apartment, then he placed a call to Cowie from a gas station pay phone.

He had known Cowie from the days in Europe. Word had it that Cowie was queer, or at least he went both ways. Beyond that, Allen knew first hand that the man was a sadist, but, unfortunately, he was also afraid of Josey Swann.

They met in a circular bar high above the city. Cassidy had not been expecting Harv Stepskey, but Cowie explained, "We're working together. That's the way I want it. You buy me, and you get Harvey, here, free."

Cassidy nodded and shook Stepskey's hand, a moist, large, pink one. Two of a kind, Cowie and Stepskey, tall, beefy men with big heads and small eyes. Cowie had lost some hair since Cassidy had last seen him. Now he kept the flimsy strands combed forward and to the side. Stepskey's hair was razor cut, not a black strand out of place.

Each wore a sports jacket, expensive, garish. Their shirts were open to their navels.

Cassidy had brought photographs. The shot of Dennerstein was only passable, but Swann's, taken from the Langley record, was really quite remarkable. The vacant glare of the eyes, the shy, skeletal smile; a portrait to be remembered.

"And this one, I know," Cowie said, and he tapped one thick finger on Josey's face. "This guy, I know."

"Sure." Cassidy grinned.

"It's Swann. It's Josey Swann."

"Hey, you didn't tell me it was going to be Swann. Over the phone, you didn't say nothing about that."

Cassidy shrugged. "Well—"

"Well nothing." From where they sat there was a long and frightening view of the lights over Washington. "You said it was going to be pigeon hunting. All right, so this guy Dennerstein's a pigeon, but I know Swann, and he's no fucking pigeon."

"Would you keep your voice down, please?" Cassidy said.

And even Stepskey put in, "Come on, Ralph, it's no big deal. This guy, he's no big deal."

"Not you, too, Harv, because you don't know this guy, Josey Swann."

"Ralph," Cassidy said. "There's nothing he's got that you don't have." He said it with a straight face.

Cowie was actually pouting, and had one finger raised, as if for permission to speak. Stepskey reached out and gently took his hand. "Listen to me," he said. "We can *take* this guy, I know it."

Cowie remembered Vietnam. He had flown a chopper, not for the army, of course, but as Langley's special operations man. Up there, in the eye of your own storm, the

189

blades of the chopper whipping at the shiny jungle leaves, it had been an easy war. But Cowie remembered the ones like Swann, the ones that fought at ground floor, killed at point blank, lived in the mud like the scum that they were. "And now this bastard's loose," he finally muttered from the edge of memory.

"But, Ralph," Stepskey was shaking Cowie's wrist, trying to shake him from his daydream. "Come *on,* Ralphie boy."

"No, Harv." Cowie's face was flushed. The view of the dark, purple city may have been all that he wanted to see. "You don't know him, Harv. This Swann is weird. He's a creep, you know? I remember once I was talking to him, just like I'd be talking to you, or Allen here, or anybody. I said something like, 'How are you doing?' Swann looks at me with his real weird eyes and says, 'Me? I'm just eating this orange, bit by bit, piece by piece, seed by seed.' And he gets all huffy looking, like I should fuck off of his earth . . . He says things like that, real strange things. He'll start talking about something dumb and obvious as if it's real important, a big deal . . ."

"Look, if you don't want the job," Cassidy tested.

"I didn't say that I didn't want the job," Cowie said. "I'm just saying that Swann is weird, okay? I mean, he could be sitting here at this table in this bar and you could ask him something like, 'What do you think of the view, Josey?' He just might pick up this glass and say, 'Imagine yourself trapped inside this ice cube.' You know what I'm saying?"

"You don't have to speak to him," Cassidy said. "You may not have to even kill him. I'll let you know all that later." He was growing impatient. His own ice was melting and the scotch was growing paler. "The first, and foremost, target is this Dennerstein . . ."

"Yeah, well, if Swann is watching over Dennerstein—"

"Oh, come on, Ralph," Stepskey cut in.

Cowie began fiddling with the red plastic swizzle stick. He looked genuinely sad. "Swann's good too. I've seen that for myself. I've seen him train. He's real good, real smooth. That guy can move up on you and you'd never know what hit you."

"All right," Cassidy said sternly. "You either want the job, or you don't. You can't just take Dennerstein. It's both or nothing." It was his trump card, played and waiting.

"*Yeah,*" Cowie said. "I'll take it. Me and Harv here can do it. I just wanted to tell you about the way it is with Swann. It's the speed he's got. He's not that strong, but he's fast."

Beyond the panes of smoked gray glass the city was turning bluer. The carpet of lights was broken here and there by darker furrows of blacked-out streets and fields. "It was something Swann said to me. He said to me, 'You want to know how I do it?' See, I had asked him how he did it, how he got the speed. And he says to me, 'Metamorphosis, Ralph, metamorphosis.' I never understood what he meant by *that.* It bothered me, I tell you."

Cassidy had torn off the corners of his cocktail napkin. He was rolling the soggy wads of paper. "You can do it, Ralph. I'm completely confident that you can do it. Furthermore, I'm glad of your reservations. You seem to have examined the odds fairly well." This was more Cassidy jive, but at least he believed he had said it with a certain style.

"And so what if he's got the speed?" Stepskey reassured him. "We've. got the power, Ralph."

191

But Cowie was glum. Both hands lay still on the table. "Where do we find them?" he asked, and his eyes slowly lifted to Cassidy.

"I told you, Ralph, I'm going to have to let you know on that score. I've got a little deal to make with an old friend that knows. So, there're still arrangements to be made on my end. You understand?"

"Your end." Cowie frowned, turned back to the window.

"It won't be long, Ralph," Cassidy said. "I just have to make this deal." He had begun to slowly spin his glass. Deals, he thought, deals will be the death of me. "With any luck, Ralph, I'll have it set up very nicely in just a few days."

But Cowie was shaking his head again. "Metamorphosis," he said to himself. "I didn't even know what it meant. I had to look it up in the Webster's." He was staring down to the wavering lights, and the other men were silent.

CHAPTER 13

THERE WERE moments in the days that passed when Roger saw another Josey Swann. Of course there was still that ghoul with double incisors and a blank, limpid stare, but now and again Roger saw the traces of another Josey, a human Josey, a Josey that sometimes peeked out from behind the habitual rancor. God knows, Swann wasn't the clubbable sort. He wasn't just a wayward kid at heart, fallen in with the wrong bunch. No, Josey was hard core. Roger would see him wake in the morning to his bottle of gin and then tramp down the dusty road, virtually cursing the sun for shining. But there *was* something else in Josey's eyes, something in the way he wet his lips, in the way he stared into the still, muddy waters of the dark lake. There were moments when Roger sensed that Josey, despite all that tough talking stuff, was immeasurably sad after all.

They sat on the bluff above the dark lake. The sun was falling, twilight was inching across the rolling hills of scrub. Long shadows fell from the distant mountains. The birds had stopped crying. "They always do," Swann said.

"What does?" Roger asked. He was idly plowing the soil into tiny furrows.

"The birds," Swann said. "They always stop singing just as the sun sets, because that's when the world stops spinning for the briefest second . . . the whole world stops . . ." He was nearly swallowing the words.

"Uh, do you really believe that, Josey?"

"It's a legend, cousin. There's lots of legends."

"I see." Roger smiled. He was watching Josey's profile, which was silhouetted against the darkening sky. He had noticed before that Swann could be strangely reflective at times. He saw importances in odd places.

At the edge of the mountains a misshapen moon was throbbing at them, although the sky was not yet black. I've been thinking," Roger finally said. He might have been dreaming, his voice was so distant.

"Yeah, cousin . . ."

"I've been thinking about this whole problem here. Right now all we know is that Howard Sax gave Cassidy some money, right?"

"We don't know what for, cousin. In fact, we don't even know if that's the truth."

"But that woman said—"

"You've got to get motives before it all fits together. That's what Father Lyle says, get the bottom motive." Swann began tossing pebbles into the water.

"Well, that's exactly what I've been thinking about. We still don't really know the relationship between Sax and Cassidy. But tonight if I find something on the computers, then what do we do?"

"We play it by ear," Josey said. The setting sun was glowing in the strands of his hair.

"Yeah, but I've been thinking that if we can get enough

on Sax one way or another, then we can get a case together. Maybe we can take it to the District Attorney's office in Boston. Or maybe it would fall under the Washington jurisdiction. I'm not too sure about that, but I could check up on it tonight. UCLA has a law library—"

"Cousin," Swann's cheek was lumped sarcastically. "Cousin, I don't think you fully understand the ramifications here."

"Ramifications?" Josey was full of surprises this evening.

"You see, what we have here is Company business," Josey said.

"Of course," Roger said quickly. He had been working out the problem for days.

"No, that's Company as in CIA. You don't take the CIA to court."

"Why not?"

"Because they'll kill you, Rog."

Rog. Swann had never used the name before. "Yeah, well, they're trying to do that now."

"Cousin, take my word for it. You don't take the CIA to court."

Roger blinked into the wind. "Well, let me worry about that."

Josey flung a flat, smooth pebble, and it went skipping off the water's surface. "I should tell you about the CIA, cousin. Everything you've heard about them is true. They're a rotten bunch."

"So why did you work for them?"

Josey smiled. "They kept me fed. Scraps is all, but out back, just a little ways down the road they have this Company diner. That's where they feed us. Wonderful little place, plenty of warm beer and cold beans. On Saturday nights there's the special, on Sundays, deep fried chicken. And they show you cartoons, Loony-Toons, circa 1930. Eating that chicken from a greasy bucket, wiping that grease on your shirts, washing it down with warm, flat beer, all together now, laughing. Ah, we had some good times. Only they messed us up a little. See, those cartoons were changed around. The duck had all the lines. You understand me, cousin? You know what I'm talking about. The duck had all the lines."

The lake below them was now fully black. Perhaps it had no bottom at all. "No," Roger said, "I don't understand."

"The CIA is mad, cousin. You'll read about this tradition of pranksters. All the old boys are just pranksters at heart, that's what they'll tell you. Well, don't you believe it. They're not playing tricks. When this is all over you should go back to India. I'm serious, go back to India and feed the people with a basket of bread and the head of a fish. You're a bleeder, cousin, but at least you're honest."

Yes, Roger thought, I'm a bleeder, but you, Josey Swann, you have been bled dry. I think that's your secret.

ODD TO be thinking about Josey now, or perhaps it wasn't so odd in that Roger often found himself dreaming when the numbers began to snarl, the equations pile up and then tumble back down under the weight of unknowns.

Had he been in the Carrage lab, armed with his own computer, he might have been able to make some sense of it. But this university digital toy was impossible. Although you really shouldn't blame the computer, because the computer was only as good as the program, and that was the knot of his problem now. Roger had no workable program. In fact, he didn't really know what he was trying to solve.

The evening had been consumed with random stabs for

linking factors. He had begun by retracing the salient features to Brazilian agricultural production. But somehow the Russians got into the act. He wasn't sure exactly when, but with the Russians came wheat, and with wheat came the vagaries of a circumpolar vortex. For a while the computer had been smoking with activity. He had felt so close to something, so near the verge of something important.

Suppose, he had asked himself, the Russian drought of '72 was somehow connected with the sub-Saharan drought? There was Mali, Mauritania and even the Upper Volta. (If he had only had a grid of the Upper Volta.) Could they have all been connected? If so, why wouldn't there be a link between the Russian drought and the Australian drought? The computer was skeptical. It gave twelve percent, no more. But still, the possibility was intriguing because link the Russians with the Australians and one could easily find a bridge to the "Seca," the drought that occasionally struck northeast Brazil.

But Brazil would not budge, not so much as an inch. Roger threw in a more compromising program, but even then there were no takers among the statistical groupings that the computer kicked back. It could have been the machine's fault. Roger had known some embittered digitals, and these UCLA models were so overworked that they often grew cranky. Once he had even worked with an IBM that had tried to attack him. The thing shredded his tapes, blew out a unit and the only way he managed to stop it was to rip out its plug. That had been a mean one.

Roger sat in a swivel chair with coasters on the legs. During the heat of the search he had been whirling all over the linoleum, pushing off from his work bench, skidding past the computer banks, tearing out print-outs and spinning back to the desk. But now he only gently rocked.

197

There was an old guard limping through the hall. Now and again he stopped and peered in, or tested the lock on the double glass doors. Poor fellow had hardly known what to make of Roger and his laminated pass to the lab . . . those science fellows were a funny lot.

Roger even sometimes saw himself as funny, funny as in strange, not as in ha ha. Once he had developed a theory that weather trends could be detected by animal migration patterns. Not an original theory, but Roger took the subject one step further. Too far, some said. Armadillos had been Roger's niche. He had constructed an entire base on the migration of the North American armadillo. It seemed that the armadillo extended its range as far north as Nebraska, but had lately been beating a retreat southwest again. They were sensitive animals, Roger argued. But the computers only laughed at him and his armadillo theory, just as they had been laughing all evening at the Russian link to Brazilian drought.

All right, then to hell with the droughts. He would go back to the forecast and start again. Roger stretched, swore, and swept a pile of useless papers to the floor. Begin with an entirely new approach, he told himself. Forget about the damn weather. Look to the money. What else would Sax have been doing in Brazil if not attempting to make more money?

Initially, Roger came up with coffee. All Brazil was running on coffee. They were wired on the stuff. Their bladders were bulging with it. But coffee did not quite fit. He ran the obvious program through looking for a link between the conditions of his forecast that would possibly affect the supply of coffee, but nothing set lights to flashing, bells to ringing.

Then it began to happen. It started, not with figures and equations, but ironically enough with a vision, his real strangeness. He saw Howard Sax and Allen Cassidy together in a small Chateau library. The shine on the parquet floor was enough to sell you on anything. But Sax would have had his pitch well prepared. There had been statistics to recite, odds and marketing trends to explain. And above all else stood this enormous sum of money.

Slowly, carefully, Roger went backward and forward. He plotted the averages. He drew material from the records. As he knew there would be, he found a temporary upwelling of the el Nino current off the coast of Peru. In the coming months this change in the current would result in a collapse of the anchovy fishery. He ran a check through the computer to verify, and, yes, the el Nino current, coupled with low precipitation, was a critical factor.

But a critical factor of what?

The answer came in the next few frantic minutes: soybeans. The price of soybeans was about to go out of sight.

Strange that the Carrage analysis had picked up soybeans when Roger had not. But then maybe it wasn't so strange. Chateau analysts were trained to look for the money, and when the anchovy fishery sagged, and the drought hit, that's all there would be with soybeans—money. Furthermore, Roger had always been a wheat and rice man. When they actually went down starving, it was for wheat and rice. But now, he realized, it was more complex than that. There were all those countries dependent on soybean meal for their beef. There were Russia and Japan, Britain and France. The list went on and on. They would be at each other's throats for the beans, and therein lay the Howard Sax touch. What with the drought, the Brazilian market would be critical. Corner that market and Carrage could name their price. Of course, in the ensuing shuffle for beans, those on the edge of starvation would go off the deep end. Who had enough for charity when their own larders were empty? But Carrage would not have cared about the darker side of a forthcoming drought. They were pushing for famine prices.

Odd, really, how detached one could be now that the pieces fit so neatly together. Roger still sat rocking on the swivel chair. He chewed on the rim of a styrofoam cup. He felt neither happy nor sad, tired nor hungry. Here I sit, he vaguely thought, the perfect scientist, devout, circumspect, even, at times, blasé.

SWANN, HOWEVER, had not known lately what to make of the weatherman. The little guy had a way about him. There was no denying he could worm his way beneath your skin. And tonight, particularly, Josey could not keep the weatherman in focus. But then Josey was drunk, flat out drunk. He lay squashed in the deck chair, dangling that wonderful bottle of gin from his fingers. There were those black swells of mountains in the sky, and above, those wicked clumps of stars, surreal. While inside the house was the weatherman's wife.

What about the weatherman's wife?

Possibly, Josey hated her. He had seen her kind before. She was a fox, with eyes that could be as sly as his own. But they were sly in a different way from his. They didn't go for the throat. They teased your cock.

He had watched her in the morning, picking up the dregs of their breakfast, then pirouetting with an armful of dishes, and leaving you with that last, snappy vision of her pert little ass. Whores in Saigon had used the same move. They had known how to catch the American man, and the weatherman's wife was as good as any general's whore. So, then, what was she doing with the weatherman?

She wasn't a bleeder. She wasn't the sort that changed bedpans for lepers. So, then, what was *her* secret?

And now, watching her cross the deck, slide her hand on the railing and move toward him, he knew. She had no secrets. The weatherman probably picked her up on the rebound. She wasn't a bleeder—she was a sucker.

"I've made some coffee, Josey." Her blue jeans had been hemmed high on the thigh. Her red checkered shirt was tied by the tails across her belly. This is how the suckers dress for war, he thought, and scowled.

"I don't like coffee," he told her.

"Well, come inside. I want to talk to you." Her hair went swishing in front of her eyes. Swann grunted and rose. "You can't stay out here, it's too cold. If you don't like coffee, I'll make you something else."

What was this? The woman pushing him around? Ah, but of course he knew . . . she's on the make, and here I go, padding after her because she is . . . Before the night was up, he thought he might kill her, if only he hadn't been so drunk . . .

"Sit here," she commanded, and pushed him down to the sofa. "I'm lonely, and I'm worried about Roger."

Ah, thought Swann, the loyal traitor. "Don't worry about the weatherman. He's all right."

"I don't like it when you call him that," and floated down beside him and crossed her legs.

"Well, that's what he is, isn't he?" Swann was hunched over with his hands between his knees. Clamping them like that was the only way he could keep himself from crushing her throat.

"You're a bastard, you know that?" Look how the flesh on her thighs swelled.

Josey frowned. He wouldn't be cute with the weatherman's wife.

"After *all* he's tried to do for you. Do you know that he likes you? He actually likes you."

Swann squinted and looked about the room. "There's no harm in that. I like him."

"You don't like anybody," and stretched out her leg for its firmest pose. "Because you never give anyone a chance."

"I've learned better."

"Well, you're missing something," and softer, she spoke his name. "Josey . . . Josey. How tough are you, Josey Swann?"

Not very, he should have told her, to encourage her, but he didn't really care, which was about par for his course with most women. Still, he let her lean over and kiss him.

"I think I'm going to find out, Josey, I think I'm about to find out just how tough you are—"

He took hold of her hair and pulled her head back. "Just because I kill people, honey, doesn't mean I'm a man," and he laughed and let her fall on top of him.

She was picking at the buttons of his shirt, fastening her mouth to his chest. When she finally had him naked to the waist, she slipped off her own clothes and pressed his face into her breasts. They were smothering him. "So you're Josey Swann." She began to moan, "Josey . . . Josey . . ."

But I'm dead, he wanted to tell her, although she probably already knew. She had to work his hands for him, run them along her legs. Her lips were sucking at his ribs as if to draw his blood out. If she were to gnaw through his flesh and reach his heart, would the cold seal her lips?

For a long time they lay side by side, barely alive, he thought—he was rough stone, she was sleek marble. Finally he gave her a hump or two, just to prove that he still had it in him. She cried out, faking it, and now he even hated her voice. Other than that he felt nothing.

202

When it was over Josey fell on his back and smoked. Julie also lay still. She had one pale arm draped across his chest, probably thinking, well, that's done. While Josey was grateful that at least she did not pretend that he had given her anything more than a half-hearted fuck. Thank God she didn't try to kiss him again.

Instead she rose impersonally and ran a brush through her hair. "What's the time?" she asked. He told her, and she nodded. "I'd better get dressed. He could be back soon."

"Have you done this before?"

"Once, but don't think that I'm not in love with Roger, because I am."

"So? So why did you do it?" Swann asked, although he thought he probably knew the answer to that one. He had had women before who thought that because he acted tough he would also fuck tough. Wanted a real brute, did you? Well, all you got was a corpse.

"I did it," she said, "because I felt sorry for you." The words came out in a monotone, and the statement was a lie. She may have felt sorry for him now, but before she had wanted to take in his imagined brutality, his strength. And I was a damn fool, she thought, while her brush snagged in a clump of hair.

"Sorry for me?" Swann laughed.

Julie shrugged. "We all make mistakes. Anyway, at the time, I thought it might have done you some good. What's that they say? Even the stars need love?"

Oh lord, thought Josey.

CHAPTER 14

FROM THE start Roger sensed the truth. Not from Josey, Josey was unreadable. He gave nothing away, but when Roger returned from his night with the computers, he sensed the truth in Julie's eyes.

There was really nothing to say. You could only tell her it hurt a bit, and would truly be grateful if everyone concerned would let the matter drop. Ask me no secrets and I'll tell you no lies. Roger had never been a jealous guy. He knew what his wife did to men. Besides, there would never be any chance of Julie running off with Josey Swann. One day she might leave him for another, but never for a man like Josey. He would crush her inside of a week.

Julie, however, had left. Going to her mother's, she said. "Do you understand, darling?"

Oh yes, Roger understood. He understood that she was leaving him with her mess. She was leaving until the smoke cleared. She was leaving because she could not bear to face them both in the same room. He understood.

Had Josey been around he might have been able to stop

her. He had all those arguments about how people were trying to kill them, and how easy it would be for them to find her at her mother's. Josey, Roger decided, had a way with women, with everyone for that matter. But Swann was gone. There were his balled up sheets on the foot of the couch where he had slept, there his pile of cigarette butts. (The spit out ends of his days, he had once rather dramatically called them.) But Josey, himself, had left.

For their goodby, Roger and Julie stood on the gravel by her little red suitcase. On this still morning the trees around them were steaming in the light and moisture. "I love you, Roger. I want you to know that. Nothing has changed, do you understand?"

There had been real tears in his eyes and his throat was raw. He could only nod his head.

"I'll call you when I get to mom's," she said, and then kissed him. After the engine fired, the wheels kicked and skidded over the gravel, the silence was absolute. Roger kicked at the gravel, looked up to the swirling cover of gray and then tramped back to the house. There was half a pot of last night's coffee on the stove. He struck a match and lit the burner. There were dishes in the sink, some smeared with fat, others encrusted with the remains of Josey's half eaten eggs. When the coffee was boiling he turned off the gas, poured himself a cup, and sat down at the rickety wooden table.

He took two sips, scalded his tongue and then heard Swann pounding slowly up the steps. "Where's your wife?" Josey demanded, and the screen door banged behind him. He looked hungry and mean. His eyes were bloodshot, and his cheeks were hollow. This was no contrite sinner come back to be forgiven. But then he did not feel proud to have fucked the weatherman's wife, either. He felt dirtier than ever.

"She's gone, Josey." Roger sat staring at the brown mug of coffee.

"Gone where?"

"She went to her mother's. I couldn't stop her. I tried, but she wouldn't listen."

You could have hit her, Josey thought. "Well, it doesn't matter now anyway."

"Because of what I found out last night?"

Josey nodded and tossed a cigarette in his mouth. "I've had enough of it here."

Roger had his hands cupped around the mug for warmth. "So now what, Josey? Where do we stand, where do we stand with any of it?"

"It's over, cousin. Neither of us has any more secrets to share. From here on out it becomes a family affair, and you're not family."

"Are you?" Roger was growing angry.

"Oh, yeah. We're all just brothers back at Langley, and now that I've solved the case, I've got to go back and tell father." Swann was banging about in the kitchen, talking above the clatter of pans. When he returned to the table he was chewing on the end of a cold hot dog.

"But we can't let it go like this," Roger said. His fingers were tighter than ever around the mug. "We've got more than enough to bring formal charges against Carrage. There are senators right now who have just been waiting for an excuse to investigate Carrage. This is something I've got to do. If you can't help me, then I'll do it alone."

"Cousin," Swann sighed. His eyes were drooping with fatigue. "Cousin, who are you trying to kid?"

"What do you mean?"

"I told you, it's a family affair now. You keep your mouth shut, and no one's going to hurt you. You're in the clear. I'll get back to Washington tonight, and I'll see to

207

it, cousin. It's the least I can do. No one will be coming after you anymore. I'll make sure of that. So the war is over. The war . . . it's over . . . right?" Swann tore off a piece of his hot dog and bolted it down.

"But you won't do anything," Roger accused.

"Sure, I will, cousin. I'm going to ram it home to Allen Cassidy."

"That's not what I mean. You don't know what will happen if Carrage drives up the price of soybeans. You don't know what will happen if no one is allowed to prepare for the drought. You've never seen it."

"Seen what?"

"My God. Starvation. What else?"

Josey held up the remains of his chewed hot dog. "There's lots of ways to starve, cousin."

"Will you cut that shit out. Jesus! When are you going to learn?"

"It would appear that I'll never learn," Swann said.

"But, damn it, we've got the facts. We can point to witnesses. I know people in Washington will listen to us. God, why can't you trust me?"

Josey tugged at his ear. "I do trust you, cousin. I trust you as much as I've ever trusted anyone."

"Oh, go to hell."

Josey breathed deeply, and leaned forward on the table. He laced his hands before him, and laid his head on them. Then he slowly raised his eyes again. "Roger," he said, "I want you to know that I'm sorry about your wife. Sometimes I do things. I don't even know why, they just happen. It's like with my hands, I can't always control them. But I want you to know that you're okay. You're a bleeder, but at least you're good at it. In fact you're the most accomplished bleeder that I've ever known. You can even bleed for the likes of me, and that's a feat. Because look at me, cousin. I'm twenty-seven years old, and don't you think that I know just how fucked up I am? That's why I'm grateful to you. You've been pulling for me. You've been on my side from the start, but listen to me now, cousin. Listen, I'm only going to fuck you over in the end. I can't help it. There's just no such thing as a good guy spy. That's a fact."

Swann turned away.

For a moment Roger only looked at him. "Oh, go to hell," he finally said, and went out through the rusty screen door. His steps on the stairs rattled the windows.

Swann sat and nibbled at the shredded end of his pale hot dog. He saw the small figure of the weatherman through the ragged gap in the curtains. The guy was tramping up the road. He'll probably sit at the edge of the lake, Swann thought. He'll sit there and brood until he gets fed up, and then he'll come puffing back . . .

Ten minutes later Josey heard the footsteps falling on the creaking wood stairs. The screen door squealed. Swann turned and called out. "Cousin—" And at that same instant he knew. He started up, kicked back his chair. Framed in the doorway was Ralph Cowie with his heavy, blue revolver in his hands.

"Down, Josey. Just get on down." Cowie crouched by the wall. He held the revolver straight out, classic firing position. "Now, just take it easy, Josey. Just get down and take it easy. I didn't come for you, so just sit down and stay cool." Cowie was sweating.

His eyes were fixed on Josey's hands. Watch his hands, they had told him. Break your neck with his hands.

"What do you want, Ralph?" Swann sank back into the chair.

"That's a boy." Cowie was still crouched with his back against the wall.

"I said what do you want, Ralph?"

Cowie rubbed his mouth on his shoulder. "It's a job, Jose. I'm on a job."

"For the weatherman?" Swann's fingers were tapping on the table, tapping away the seconds. The sound might have been killing Cowie.

"Dennerstein. Just him. No one's after you, Josey." Cowie was in danger of shaking. Even with the weapon, he could not look into Josey's eyes.

"Yeah, well, I see it now," Josey said calmly. "But how did you find us, man?"

"Allen. Allen Cassidy set it up. That's all I know."

Swann pretended hurt professional pride. "Why didn't he give the gig to me?"

"I don't know, Josey. Allen just gave us a call."

"Who is us?" Josey was very nonchalant. He was idly spinning the weatherman's cup.

"Me and Harv," Cowie said. "Harv Stepskey. I don't think you know him. He's the one out there with Dennerstein now."

"Yeah?" Swann looked up, one professional to another.

"Yeah, Jose. We got a game plan. We worked something out here."

"I could have done better." Josey frowned.

"What are you talking about?"

"I could have done better, that's all. What? You think me and the weatherman got something going here? I'm babysitting, that's all. It's a job, just a stupid job."

"Sure, Jose. I didn't say anything. I just said that me and Harv got this thing worked out. Harv follows Dennerstein up the road. He takes care of him, then fills the guy's pockets with rocks. Then he drops him in the lake. It's clean."

Swann shrugged. He was picking off splinters from the

210

leg of the table. "I could have done it cleaner."

"I'm not saying that you couldn't have, Jose. I'm just saying that Allen thought that maybe you and Dennerstein were together, know what I mean?"

"Well, we're not, okay?"

"Yeah, okay."

"I mean I could have done it." He smiled a little. "Could have used the bread, all right?"

Now the revolver was nothing more than something to be held. "I know how it sometimes gets, Jose."

Swann got up from his chair. He shoved his hands into his pockets and dropped his head. He would have given a disgruntled kick at the floor if there had been something to kick. "I don't know, Ralph. Maybe they're right. Maybe I've lost it."

"Hey, Josey, don't get yourself down by talking like that. If you—" Cowie stopped, cut off by the sound of several gunshots echoing in from far up the road. "That will be Harv," Cowie said. "Harv's just taken care of Dennerstein."

For an instant Josey tensed, then he slowly shook his head. "At least someone's done something," he muttered.

"Look, Jose, you can come back with us. We'll get something together for you."

Now Swann stood very close to Cowie, an arm's length away. Less. "Oh, I'll come back." Josey sighed. "But it's hard, Ralph. It's hard because I'll keep seeing the weatherman in my mind, and know I could have . . . oh, the hell with it . . ."

Cowie turned and reached for Josey's shoulder. He understood. Swann was human, after all. "Hey, Josey . . ." Cowie's fingers lightly touched Swann's arm, which was all that he'd been waiting for.

He brought his knee up into Cowie's groin. The big man

211

gasped and doubled over. Swann's fist came down at the base of the skull, followed by a palm to the temple. Blood came from Cowie's mouth. Swann could not stop. He was locked into the rhythm, hitting Cowie's head against the wall until the flakes of plaster were specked with blood. Even when the man was dead he could not stop. *Hail Mary . . . pray for war.*

He rested only when the silence, and the lifelessness, intruded on him. There was still Stepskey.

He picked up the revolver and moved out the door. At the bottom of the stairs he paused and pressed himself against the weathered siding. Minutes passed. He heard the pounding footsteps on the gravel.

"Ralph . . . Ralph." Swann walked out, dropped to one knee and fired. The bullet hit Stepskey in the face and threw him back to the road.

Swann dragged the body beneath the stairs, and kicked at the dust to cover the trail of blood. Then he walked on up. The leaves were listless in the mid-morning heat. Once he skidded on loose pebbles. Sometimes his boot heels sank into the sandy soil. When the path became narrow, brambles tried to snag him. Thorns tore at the cuffs of his jeans. The light from shards of broken bottles nicked his vision. More than once he thought he would simply collapse.

He reached the edge of the dark lake. There was no sign of a struggle, no trace of blood in the grass. The water was still and brown, and no, cousin, it's not like my life, the way you said. It's just a lake where they weighted you down and threw you in.

Swann knelt in the dry mud. Funny how you never thought the weatherman would die. But it rains on everyone sooner or later, doesn't it, cousin? He tossed the revolver over the edge and the water gulped it down. Now there were tiny ripples heading for the rocks. The last thing I did for you, weatherman, was betray you and screw your wife. But we had our times together, didn't we? A finger of wind began tugging at the brush. Dry stems of gray scrub were rattling behind. Clouds were massing in the sky. Well, don't worry, the weatherman can predict any storm. Josey sniffed at the air and got to his feet. On the way back the shaggy clumps of scrub were tamer. The pebbles no longer tried to throw him. Gravity seemed to pull him back to the house, which was just as well, because he had never felt weaker.

"Cousin . . . Cousin."

CHAPTER 15

IN THE gloom of his study an entire world came flooding back to Lyle: Harvard. He would have liked to have traced the seed of Allen's skulduggery back that far. Surely, it was at the college that Allen became what he was today. They were all cunning rascals then. They had their pranks and private clubs. Nothing was above them, nothing beneath them. The world was full of humbuggery, they snickered, and so one had to learn the rules.

But Lyle could not remember any single seed which gave birth to the Allen Cassidys. They were spies, from the start they knew they would be spies, and there was nothing else to it, or if there was, Lyle could not remember. All he saw, closing his eyes, drifting back, were the trappings of a young gentleman's world. His cocktail shaker had been of beaten silver. There had been a row of shoe trees in the closet, keeping the form of his brogues, wingtips and the patent leathers, which he wore on special evenings on Mt. Auburn Street and Beacon Hill. One such evening he had spent the dregs with Allen. The two walked down to a gray stone bridge. It had rained that afternoon and the leaves shimmered with silver drops of water. The Charles River beneath them softly gurgled. "I'm afraid, sir, that I'm intoxicated," Cassidy announced.

"What's that, Allen?"

"Drunk, sir. I'm drunk."

"Well, don't go telling me any secrets then."

"I never tell secrets," Cassidy whispered. "Only lies."

In the beginning, simply because there had not been as many lies, issues were somewhat clearer. Like neckties, Lyle thought, the issues were rich and modest. Now, however, one hardly knew where one stood. Somehow in the last two days Lyle had betrayed someone. He wasn't sure whom, but perhaps it was that Josey Swann. Yes, certainly he had betrayed Swann, and so now he had come back to him. The boy wanted vengeance. Lyle knew that Swann's kind lived by the most fundamental codes.

Swann did not knock. He jimmied the window and slipped inside. He moved through the twilight, past cabinets with too many cut glass knobs, along the curtains that quivered as he floated past. Then at the door to Lyle's study, he wavered, listening, his ear to the wood. Finally he turned the brass handle and gently pushed in the dark oak.

For a moment Swann remained hidden. The shower of yellow light above Lyle's chair threw his shadow on the wall. Lyle stirred, and the old leather cracked. "Hello? Who's there? Is that you, Swann?"

"Yes," Swann murmured. "I'm here."

"Come with your shoes full of blood, no doubt." Nice turn of phrase.

Swann walked to the desk and poured himself a brandy. He had been drinking all day. There had been those tiny bottles of gin on the plane, and more in the airport bar.

In the men's room at the airport he downed reds with handfuls of water, drenching his face, leaving puddles on the floor. He looked awful, with black rings around his eyes.

The crystal decanter rattled against his glass. Brandy sloshed up the side and onto the rug.

"Question, Josey," the old man asked. "Where next?"

"Don't know."

"Where's Ralph Cowie?"

Swann sipped and then shivered with the warmth of Lyle's brandy. "I killed him. His friend Stepskey, I killed him too."

"Oh, my," Lyle said. "Did you really? Before or after they got the Dennerstein fellow?"

"Yeah, the weatherman is dead," Josey said. "That's why I killed Cowie. Lot of scores to even tonight, eh, father?"

"I had no choice, Josey. It turns out that Allen had a truly sizable catch in his net."

"So you brought him and made it official. Now the Company is in the soybean business, is that it?"

"So you know."

Josey dropped on the low divan. A Wedgwood jasper vase sat on the marquetry end table. Etched in the glaze, two nymphs dozed beneath an acorn tree. There were floor to ceiling shelves filled with books, and a plaster skull stood on the desk by Lyle's chair.

"You told Cassidy where to find us, didn't you, Lyle?" Swann's head was bowed morosely to his chest. "You told him where the safe-house was. That's how Cowie found us, right?" He was tracing the figures on the jasper vase, running his fingers over the smooth, cold glaze.

"Yes. That should be clear enough."

"But why?" Josey was genuinely asking for the answer.

"Because Allen was afraid of Dennerstein. 'The weatherman will not tow the line.' I believe Allen put it like that. We were afraid of a scandal. One never knows what a fellow like Dennerstein will try to do. Wouldn't want to read about us in the papers, would you?"

Swann sat teetering on the edge. He downed another brandy and lay back to the cushions. "You should have told me, Lyle. You should have told me what was happening."

"There wasn't anything happening. When I found out what Allen was doing I couldn't turn his offer down. He came to me, laid out the entire project, and . . . well, I saw a certain worth to it all. It's not just the money, Josey. Money is the least of it. It's the influence. We could not afford to pass the chance up." He coughed and twisted his snowy head to the side. He seemed almost embalmed in the great leather chair. "How old are you, Josey? Thirty, thirty-five?"

"Twenty-seven," Swann said.

"Well, you're too young to know. I've been having difficulty remembering myself. These nights, sitting in this old chair of mine, I've been trying to remember. It was a long, long time ago." Severson's eyelids might have turned to walnut shells. He spoke from far inside his chest. "When Allen was your age," he said, "the world seemed very different. There was the war, of course, but apart from that, things were different. When Allen was your age, Josey, life was something else altogether for those of us inside the . . . the intelligence community."

Cynicism, wrote Allen Cassidy during the days of his Harvard years, is the last refuge of the true idealist. Lyle now believed that the line was not so sophomoric. "It shows that Allen was no fool," he said. "None of us were fools." Damn right.

Lyle's hand reached out and clutched the iron branches of the lamp. "It was the business of spies," he continued, "to know their own hearts. Yes, the best spies are idealists, because it takes a commitment to some higher good to keep you going. Believe me, Cassidy, in his day, was one of the best men in the field. I don't believe anyone can honestly deny that. The man's record is simply too impressive. He had the timing. He had the feel for it. He even had, when necessary, that controlled touch of brutality. What I mean here, Josey, is that Allen is not above the violent act when the ethic of his calling demands it."

A paradox? No. "Listen carefully, Josey, because here is the key. Nights I've sat up wondering, but now I know."

Severson went on to explain how Cassidy had studied law at Harvard, and what else was law if not the contemplation of ethics? God knows truth, not man. Man has only law. However, and Cassidy learned this point early, an ideal is as important as the law. Higher than. So should the law be forsaken for an ideal? Allen said yes, and so he became a spy.

"Spies," Lyle said quietly, "have always had their own ideals. We have had to, because no law protects or even recognizes us. We may be shot, tortured, forgotten. So quite naturally we have evolved our own ideal. The best of us stick to it."

Lyle paused and closed his eyes. "Allen," he said, "joined the Company because it was the only place he could find that took the duplicity practiced but denied in the world around him and organized and *used* it in behalf of something to be proud of. The world was an imperfect structure, needing to be put right—and the rules of the game were those most respected in the outside world— win by whatever means necessary. By that standard, Allen has done no wrong. And this is not merely Allen's story.

It's all of ours. It's mine, it's yours. We're all in the same imperfect world, Josey. Do you follow?"

Swann looked at him. "But it's not the weatherman's story, Lyle. I can assure you of that."

Lyle twisted in his flannel cocoon. "Yes, there is your weatherman, isn't there? The tragic footnote to my apology. Well, there was a reason. I'll explain."

Now the old man was on a different track, and the pace was faster, the details specific. "Let's lay out our cards," Cassidy had said to him three nights ago. They had driven to the rise at the West Potomac Park, which had been a trick that Allen had learned from Lyle. Men speak better to a view. They spent an hour fencing, testing, trading secrets back and forth. Eventually the story emerged, and the story was exactly as Lyle had pegged it.

Howard Sax had known Allen from a number of deals involving South America. Sax had been worried about the grain, Allen about the politics. Their paths had crossed, but they had never actually worked together. Then one day Allen got a call from Sax. "I'm in Washington. Lunch?"

"I'm busy," Allen told him, for he had never particularly liked Sax.

"It's important," Sax importuned, and so they met at some small café where neither man was known.

Sax began cautiously enough, but when Allen took the first bite, he pulled in hard. There was going to be a drought, Sax explained. The word was, from a very reliable source, that the weather was going a bit funny this year. Allen was dubious. He did not believe in this long-range weather trick. But you don't have to believe, Sax told him. Carrage was going to lay out all the money. Lay out money for what? Cassidy wanted to know.

The story was this. Low precipitation was going to

damage U.S. production of corn, wheat and soybean, a tasty menu for any trader. However, of the three, one stood out as the real money maker. Soybeans, Sax explained, were like oil. The Russians, the Chinese, the Europeans, the Japanese; they all needed soybeans. The beans contained some of the highest protein levels of any commercial commodity. If one were running a country of people accustomed to a diet with meat in it, as say the Russians, one *had* to have soybeans to feed to the livestock.

But Allen knew a thing or two about the game. So what about the anchovies? he asked. Ah! That was the little nut which was to be their jewel. This same Dennerstein forecast pointed out that the el Nino current would soon be on the fritz. The anchovy market was about to go to hell.

At this point Cassidy was listening, albeit wondering what the catch was. The catch was: The critical source of the next year's soybean crop was going to be Brazil. However, the Brazilian Minister of Agriculture was not going to sell Carrage the beans. It seemed that Daniel Miguez had his own ideas about how to deal with soybeans. The man was a nationalist, and if he had his own way the United States could go to hell.

The future appeared grim. When the first signs of drought began to appear Miguez would realize he was, so to speak, sitting on a gold mine, that it was just a question of waiting until the bids came in.

Sax got down to business. How far, he asked, would Dancing Allen Cassidy go to ensure that the United States would not have to bid its treasure on an inflated soybean market? Far enough, Allen replied. All right, then, Sax continued, how far would Allen go not only to keep the U.S. officially out of the arena, but also to ensure that we had the goods, all of them? The answer was all the way.

221

Hence the death of Daniel Miguez. Hence the payoffs to Miguez's successor, Alvera. Hence all of it.

Lyle had begun picking at the tufts of wool on his comforter. Across the room Swann was submerged in the low divan. The light oozing through the parchment shade was not strong enough to reach the edges of the room. "So you see," Lyle finally said, "There *were* reasons. It was a simple, well-respected equation. The ends, quite literally, justified the means. John Donne, having performed his mission, was a security risk. He was killed. Dennerstein died for the same reason. Allen even wanted you dead, but I talked him out of it. Do I shock you?"

Swann pressed his wrist to his forehead. "Nothing to say," he intoned. "Nothing to say, and nothing to do."

"Haven't convinced you, have I?" Lyle wet his lips. There were white flakes at the corners of his mouth. "Haven't really convinced myself, either, I suppose." Then quickly, "Say, Josey, what's the time?"

"Midnight."

Lyle began to grin. Now his mouth was as wide as the mouth on the plaster skull. "You're young, Josey. You're young, and you're a lot brighter than you've led any of us to believe. Although you shouldn't have given me the number of your safe-house. You shouldn't have let me talk you into that one. Don't trust the old fox, Josey. Haven't you learned that by now?"

"You've got to trust your friends," said Swann.

"Oh now, Josey. Listen to me. I admire you. Truly I do. I like you even though you've come back to murder us all in our beds. I still like you. And I suppose that's why I couldn't let Cassidy kill you too. Should have though, shouldn't have I? Mistakes, we all make them. You gave me the telephone number of your safe-house and so I traced the address. And I, I let you live and now you've

222

come back to balance the books, right?"

Swann glanced away. There had been generals in Nam who had had the war figured out in terms of keeping score, counting bodies, balancing books. There had been contests held to see which unit could bring back the most ears. At the end of the month there had been all those bags of dried ears, like bad mushrooms. But Josey was too tired now to add up points. Gin and brandy had plowed him under, reds had ripped his stomach. "No, I didn't come back to even it up," he said. "Not now anyway. I'm waiting, that's all. I'm just waiting."

"For what, Josey?"

"Don't know. Maybe for rain. Know what I mean?"

"I don't follow, Josey. The weatherman, is that it?"

"Well, he was a friend of mine."

"Dennerstein? The weatherman?"

"The only one. Jesus, you didn't have to kill him. He was a little guy. What harm . . . ?"

SWANN LAY on the long divan. What with the dope and the drink, the walls had begun undulating, the floor heaving, the rugs ready to sail off into the night. Now it was nearly dawn. Soon the light would crack through the drapes. All over the house clocks were ticking. Came the distant ring of the telephone, once, twice, it stopped. The old man sleeps lighter than you thought, Josey told himself. He sat up, waiting.

Severson came padding through the corridor. The door to his study brushed open and he hobbled in. "That was Allen on the phone. He called to tell that you've kidnapped Howard Sax."

"Uh?"

"I said that Allen just called. He said that you've kidnapped Howard Sax."

"What are you talking about?" Swann was sober now.

"Allen got a call from Howard Sax. Mr. Sax said that a man had broken into his house and now had him at gun point. The gunman was not identified. In fact, we don't even know that there's only one. The point, however, is that Allen assumed it was you."

"I don't know what you're talking about."

"Of course, you don't." Lyle allowed a smile. He may have never been younger than now. His hands were jammed in the pockets of his blue flannel bathrobe. "Somebody has kidnapped Howard Sax. We're to meet Allen at Langley in twenty minutes. There will be a helicopter there to take us to Boston. Apparently Sax's abductors wish to meet with Allen and myself, but you may as well come along."

"Do you have any idea?" Swann asked.

"Frankly, no. Although if it's a Company project, then I believe that we may be in for a good deal of trouble. When I said that this operation had gone official, I was lying."

BY THE time they reached the helicopter at the field in Langley, Swann felt very close to some kind of bottom. He was cold. His famous raincoat was torn at the shoulder. He wore jeans and track shoes, and over his shirt, a dirty purple sweater.

When Cassidy arrived there was nearly a scene. He didn't want Swann along, didn't see the point of it. Lyle might have agreed, but Swann was adamant. "I'm coming," he said, and that was the end of the discussion.

Only the pilot was cheerful. He was a thin, not overly bright kid in a nylon jump suit. On the sleeve of his windbreaker was a patch in the shape of a black gorilla. Beneath the patch it read, "Vietnam."

Whole valleys were obscured in fog. They had circled high over the Boston harbor before heading inland. They had seen a gray sheet of mist over the water. The pilot became nervous. He wasn't sure that he could find the Chateau in the fog. Cassidy had begun yelling out directions of the din of the whirling blades. At one point Swann told him to shut up.

Twice the pilot lowered to the wrong spot, hovered over some desolate foggy patch of Boston hillside while the foliage was whipped by the blades and Cassidy yelled louder than ever. They rocked back up and continued.

Finally, skimming over the river of fog, Cassidy spotted the spired tips of the Carrage Chateau. The pilot brought the chopper down on a broad stretch of lawn. Trees shook furiously, hordes of leaves flew off and scattered in frantic swarms. They were met on the lawn by a guard and two Carrage employees in dark suits. Clothing was slapped against bodies, flapping wildly in the blast of the whirling blades. Somebody was shouting. "Cassidy? You Cassidy?" Swann's raincoat billowed out. There was more strained loud talking and men leaning into the words with their hands cupped to their ears.

"Yes, I'm Cassidy."

The dark suited Carrage man put out his hand. "I'm George Bandy," he shouted. "Bandy. I'm the one that took the call."

"What?" Cassidy winced as a leaf struck his face.

"Bandy. I'm the one that took the call."

"What does he know?" Severson shouted. The flurry was confusing him, the leaves spraying around them.

Bandy shook his head and motioned them forward. "Come on inside," he yelled, and still bent over, the others followed. They made their way along the flagstone path. The garden was full of mysterious scents. All around them were the filigreed and columned walls of the outer Chateau. Vines twisted in and out of the spikes of the iron fence. Moss was eating at the yellowed plaster.

They entered through the rear and moved down a long, smothering corridor. Swann took up the rear. They passed through rooms of rich, polished paneling. The skirting boards had been cut into ovals of Hesperian fruit. Here stood a vase, there a Queen Anne settee. The burgundy carpeting was lush.

Bandy led them into a long, high ceilinged office in the east wing. Large bay windows looked out to the tangled vegetation of the grounds. The lamps, mounted to the wainscot on delicate brass fixtures, were turned down low. A wag-on-the-wall clock ticked away in the corner. It also told the phases of the moon.

On a butler's table stood a silver pot and china cups. Bandy was pouring the coffee. "I don't know what the hell is going on," he said. A saucer was rattling in his hand.

"Neither do we," Cassidy said.

Severson stood by the glass. He was watching the helicopter wobble up through the trees, then bent to see it sail away. "How much do you know?" he finally asked.

Bandy spooned in his sugar, and the grains went spraying over the silver tray. "I told you, nothing. Mr. Cassidy's call was the first thing I've heard. I don't even know who you are," and he tried his best at a quick, wry smile.

"So much the better," Cassidy told him. "And perhaps you had better leave us."

"Look, I don't have authority to just let you stay. What are you, anyway?"

"They're spies." Swann from the corner. He sat on the chair with one thigh over the arm. "They work for the CIA. They're spooks, you know?"

"He's drunk," Cassidy snapped.

"At ten in the morning?" Bandy said. "What in God's name is going on here?"

"You wouldn't want to know," Cassidy said, "and as I've already suggested, you'd better leave. When the call comes in from Mr. Sax, we may need a car. Please have one ready for us."

Bandy's head dropped back. "What is this? You can't just order me around."

Severson coughed and stepped forward to the tray. "I must tell you, young man, that if you want to see Mr. Sax alive, you can help by doing what we say. This is a very difficult situation for all of us. I cannot explain how much is involved, but you will have to trust us. We intend to try and negotiate with Mr. Sax's abductors, but no one is to know what's going on."

Bandy shrugged, placed his cup and saucer back on the tray. "All right, you take it from here, but if something breaks, I want to know—"

"And the police are out," Cassidy told him.

"Sure, you've already been through all this with me." He stood by the door, his hand on the knob. He would have gotten angry if he thought it would have done any good. "I'll be in my office. Just pick up the phone and ask. They'll connect you."

Now the three were alone—Swann, Severson and Cassidy. "What do we do now, wait?" Lyle glared at the red telephone that sat on the marble-top desk.

Cassidy tossed his head to the side. "*Yes,*" he said. He turned to Swann, started to speak, but Josey's eyes seemed to beat him down. He looked back to Severson. "How much does he know?"

"Josey?" Lyle seemed surprised. "He knows everything."

Swann laughed. "I'm family, Allen. Didn't you know?"

227

"Oh, for Christsakes, Lyle. Why did you tell him?"

"He had a right to know."

And Josey, the strange imp in the corner, intoned, "I want to be a spy, I'm tired of just killing people." He was watching the back of Cassidy's neck.

"You're out of your mind," Cassidy mumbled, and his spoons went clattering against the china.

"What did you say, Allen?" Swann reared up in his chair. "I'm talking to you, Allen. What did you say?"

Severson held up a placating hand. "Josey, please, not now, please."

Then the phone was ringing, and the jangle seemed to shake the walls. "There it is," said Cassidy, and he scooped it up. "Yes . . . yes, Lyle is here. Yes, of course, we'll come. Howard, can't you . . . I see. Ask him if I can't speak . . . okay, just hang on. Howard . . . Howard?" Cassidy let the telephone slowly sink to the cradle, when he turned to face the others. "Howard says we're to get on the main highway and drive about fifteen miles. There'll be a turn in the road. We're to follow this other road up to a church. There was the usual bit about not trying to muddy the meeting."

"And they'll be at the church?" Lyle asked.

Cassidy began to button his overcoat. "He didn't say, but we'd better get going. We've only got thirty minutes."

Lyle's fingers were doddering at the sides of his trousers. "Well, he must have given you some idea . . ."

"Look," Cassidy shouted. "I don't know anything else. Howard had a gun to his head. Whoever is running this seems to know what he's doing. We had better go along."

Swann was rising from his chair, stretching, yawning. "Ah, it's a lovely little war."

THEY TOOK the car that Bandy had provided. Cassidy drove. Lyle sat by his side, and Swann lay in the back seat. They were moving through gray country. Tufts of thick fog hung in the trees. "When we meet them, then what?" Severson asked. He was watching the landscape sweep by. "Then we'll see where we stand. If Sax has been picked up by a Company man, then—" Cassidy broke off.

"Then you're both up the creek," Swann put in from the back.

"I'm too old for a real battle, Allen. You know that, don't you?" Severson was still staring out the window.

Cassidy wiped his mouth on the sleeve of his coat. "None of us wants to run against any Company interference, Lyle. We'll just have to wait and see."

The road was rising and dipping through the gray shrouded hillocks. Swann lay with his eyes closed. A cigarette burned between his lips.

The ruins of the church lay on the rise of an open, green field. The side chapels stood in a heap of crumbling stone. The vestry door was off its hinges. The roof had fallen in. Cassidy left the car at the side of the road, and the three men tramped up the hill through the knee-high carpet of fog. Now and again larger clouds brushed past, twisting and curling.

"But there's no one here," Severson complained. They had clumped around a bit, and now sat huddled on an oblong slab of cold stone.

"There will be," Cassidy said, and after a time, "Did anyone think to bring a gun?"

Swann withdrew a Walther PPK from the pocket of his raincoat. "I always bring guns," he said. "It's the least I can do—"

"But that's mine," Lyle said. "You've stolen my pistol."

229

True enough. Swann had found the thing in a drawer in Lyle's study. But now it was his. Finders keepers. Besides, we like Walthers.

"I want it back." Lyle's voice cracked.

"Leave it alone, Lyle," Cassidy told him.

Josey turned and winked at Cassidy. "If I were in your position, I'd watch every little move I made." Then, with another bit of seedy drama, he drew back the bolt of the Walther, and snapped on the safety.

They heard the car approach before they saw it. Swann stood and led the way, stepping high through the damp grass to the shelter of the church's cloister. Mold grew in the cracks where the stones had been fitted. Somewhere below the sea of fog, an engine was straining. They heard the engine die, and the car doors slam shut. The mist was growing thicker, swirling and heaving in the gusts of wind.

"Call him, Cassidy," Swann commanded. "Call him."

Cassidy glanced at Severson. Then he cupped his hands to his mouth. "Howard! Howard!" There was no reply. He called again. The breeze blew the strands of his hair back. His lips were pale.

They heard steps, but the fog had cut them off from anything else. "Go out there, Allen," Swann whispered. "Start walking out there."

"Why me?"

"Because I've got the gun and I'm telling you to."

"Oh, Jesus." Cassidy looked back once and then started forward. He moved with small, unsteady steps, held his arms near-rigid away from his body. "Howard? Howard? It's me, Allen Cassidy. Lyle Severson's here. We can talk. Whoever you are that has Howard, we're ready to talk. Come on—"

A gunshot cracked, and the blast rolled across the valley. Cassidy leapt to the grass. For a moment he thought he had been hit, but it was only his knee striking a stone. "Who *are* you?" he yelled. "What the *hell* is happening?" Followed by the high-pitched voice, cracking some under the strain. "You've come far enough. Just tell Severson to come out too. If you try anything, I'll blow your head off."

Swann began laughing. He shook his head, but could not stop laughing. "Do you . . . can't be . . . goddamit, it's the *weatherman. Cousin.*" He repeated, "Cousin!" He began stumbling forward, trotting out through the curtain of fog, shouting, "Cousin, cousin!"

And Roger Dennerstein indeed rose from the clump of bushes. There were dark stains on his knees, and his glasses had been jolted down his nose. For a moment he merely stood, undecided, the pistol still trained on Howard Sax, who sat in the grass at his feet. But Josey was bounding toward him, arms out, "Cousin! Damn you, cousin!"

When they met, Swann swept Roger off his feet and spun him around. Their heads bumped. Roger's glasses flew off. "Damn you, cousin. What the *hell* are you doing here?"

Roger tried to fight his way free, but Swann's bear hug held him fast. "Listen, Josey. Wait a minute. I'm trying to get something done here."

"Ah, damn, cousin. It's fucking good to see you. Damn! *Damn!* I like it. I *really* like it." Josey was waltzing him in the grass.

They stood on the rise in a sloppy little circle. Roger had put his revolver away. He had taken it in high dudgeon from Stepskey's body, but now he felt foolish with it.

"You are supposed to be dead," Lyle said stiffly. "You are Dennerstein, aren't you?" He wet his lips. "Yes, well, we thought you were dead."

Roger was distracted, glancing from one stone face to another. Except there was Josey, and *he* was smiling. "Nearly dead," he began . . . "The crazy guy made too much noise, I got a running start, he shot at me and missed and I managed to jump into the lake and hid out among the rocks—"

"In the lake?" Swann laughed. "Cousin, I didn't even know you could swim."

Roger glanced up at the pale wafer of a sun. He had been up all night, and now here was the sun, though white as if it had no heat at all. "I jumped into the damn lake . . . I guess they took me for dead, but I hid in the rocks, and when I got back to the house there were the bodies and you were gone. I got the gun, anyway."

Swann had his arm around the weatherman's shoulders. *"Damn* it, cousin." Then to the others, "Can you beat this? I'm talking about this weatherman here."

But Roger's mouth had begun to tighten. "This is not over." He had to belt out the words. "Josey, you've got to help me with this."

"Sure, cous, whatever you say." Swann bent close to Roger's ear. "But I'm not sure what you're after. You have this all worked out, or what?"

Roger tottered under Josey's weight. "We're going to the police, at gun point, if necessary."

Cassidy glanced at Sax. They were two of a kind, wrapped in their black coats, planted on the grass. "Swann, you'd better talk to him," Cassidy said, and Severson nodded.

"Yeah, cousin, they may have a point here. Ah, I'm not sure you're going about this the right way, see." He ran his hand through his hair, and pulled the weatherman closer. "You see, cous, there's nothing to be accomplished in taking these clowns to the cops. They're above the law, or beneath it. Remember when I told you it was a family affair?"

Roger tried to duck beneath Swann's arm. "You too?"

"Ah now, cous, I'm on your side. We've just got to play it cool, okay?"

"No, it's not okay. We can't let them go through with this. I've written it all up, on the plane out here." He patted the pocket of his powder blue parka. It was too big, and he wore it zipped to the neck. "Well, we can take this to a newspaper then. The Washington *Post* . . ."

Swann put his hand on Roger's shoulder. "Tell you what, cousin. You go back to the car and wait for me there. I'll have a word with these friends of ours. Okay? You just wait for me there. He was guiding Roger back down the hill. "Go on now, cousin."

Swann, Severson, Sax and Cassidy; they watched as the fog absorbed the descending weatherman. Then Swann stepped back and withdrew the automatic from his pocket. He raised the weapon, slid his heels along the grass and traveled his eyes from face to face.

"Josey . . ." Lyle stuttered, and raised his spotted fingers.

Swann flicked the safety off. Once again, the empty eyes. "Turn around," Swann told them. "Now get down on your knees."

"Oh, now look here . . . wait a minute, Josey." Lyle reeled back on the lawn, but got down with the others on his knees. "Josey, boy, what in the world are you doing?"

Josey was sucking in air. "What do you think I'm doing?" He nudged the back of Cassidy's neck with the muzzle of the pistol.

"Swann." Cassidy was at least controlled. "You can't do this. You know it—"

"But I can, Allen, I really can do it. I can do it and be

233

gone by tonight, and that would be the end of it. So I want you to remember this. I had my chance, but I didn't take it. Swann, the crazy killer, declines. *But . . .* no matter what the weatherman does, you keep away from him. Because if you don't, then I swear I'll come after you. I'd do it now, but . . ." He swallowed hard. "I really should just do it. I should just hit you all. That's what I should do. *Dammit.*" But instead he lowered the gun, and glanced up at the sky. When he turned back down the hill, no one made a sound.

ROGER DROVE. Swann dozed in the back seat. They had gone for an hour, passed through denser wood to the soft hills where groves of oaks and sycamores studded the landscape. The fog had lifted. Gray clouds gathered in the sky and became humped, floating mountains. Then came the dry flash of lightning, and finally the rain.

When the first drops plunked against the windshield, Roger stopped the car and walked out into a field of high grass. As the rain grew harder, ringing out on the metal and glass, Swann woke and joined his friend. Now they stood side by side. Their hair was matted and dripping. "It's not supposed to be raining," Roger said. "It's too early." He may have been confessing his very last secret. But Swann did not yet understand. "Today's what? The twentieth? Well, it shouldn't be raining this far east. It's not right."

"What, cousin?" Josey was shivering. He was also dazed by the sheet of rain.

"Maybe I was wrong," Roger muttered. "Maybe I was wrong from the start. It's possible, because of the statistics. Or maybe I used the wrong data base. That would have thrown off subsequent forecasts . . ."

"What, cousin?" Josey turned slowly on his heels and

stared up at the mysterious sky and the undulating clouds. "The forecast." Roger smiled. "I may have been wrong. Christ! Wouldn't that be something if I was wrong?"

EPILOGUE

INITIALLY, ROGER had not been wrong. February and
March were dry months. The sinking air, called subsi-
dence, prevailed over much of the North American conti-
nent. While the absolute quantity of water vapor in the air
parcels remained unchanged in descent, the relative humidity decreased and so cloud formation was inhibited.
Those clouds that did form were quickly dispersed, and
the farmers rose each morning, shaded their eyes and
looked up to a white sky.

There were dead things on the landscape, lizards
cracked and belly up. When the wind blew, the dry leaves
rattled together and tossed their hopeless seeds to the
earth. Animals gathered at water holes and nosed at the
green scum.

Then the pattern began to change. It had been Roger's
theory that the drought would be precipitated by air
masses dropping a few hundred meters a day, which
would cause a warming on account of the compression
effect. The capacity of this air to hold moisture would

decrease, and no clouds would form.

The rain, however, fell in the spring.

In all fairness, the Dennerstein forecast could not be entirely faulted. His estimate did imply a statistical margin of error. Perhaps, as some claimed, his presentation did not sufficiently reveal the possibility of error, but still, the odds had been on the side of a drought.

Billy Waterman remained the staunchest Dennerstein defender. "The forecast," he wrote in what was essentially an apology, "was not technically incorrect. Instead, what we have witnessed is the liability in statistical forecasting. The Dennerstein prediction did not materialize for the months in question because the degree of equatorial retreat was not substantial enough to inhibit the normal rain cycle. Nevertheless, the basic direction is evident."

Surprisingly, even Ed Allen was sympathetic when it was finally clear where the chips had fallen.

Initially, the bidding price of soybeans did experience some gain. Trading, however, never achieved what could even be termed "brisk." Carrage showed moderate to light profits on the whole, although this was mainly due to some quick selling in the final months of the season. To those on the inside, George Bandy came out of it all looking the best.

Some four months into the new year, the story began to break. Apparently Roger Dennerstein, although sources were not named, leaked what he knew about Carrage activities in Brazil. Washington *Post* reporters investigated and found some convincing evidence that certain Brazilian officials had, in fact, been bribed. Another unnamed source stepped forward and testified to Carrage strong-arm techniques in Brazil and other South American countries (namely Argentina).

Eventually the wheels of the Department of Justice

began to turn, the grand jury picked up the ball from the papers and ran with it. Howard Sax appeared twice on behalf of Carrage. Witnesses reported that the man appeared calm, and even at times jovial, answering questions, joking with Justice attorneys. Those close to the investigation said that Sax might very well get his hide nailed to the wall, but the outcome was less dramatic. Carrage was reprimanded and fined.

Inside circles in Washington attributed Sax's escape to intervention from the president. The CIA was involved, they claimed, and the president was out to protect his people. Perhaps, perhaps not. No concrete evidence had emerged, one way or another.

Roger's own part in the final chapter was small. He was called before the grand jury, but never given an opportunity to testify. One or two papers picked up his name as an aside, but otherwise he seemed to be ignored and forgotten.

He and Julie picked up their life and marriage, not far from where they left off. Roger took a job at UCLA, teaching three days a week, and in the lab the other two. What research he was involved in proved academic. Still, the money wasn't bad, and he enjoyed the campus—the casual deportment, the kids, and in the mornings there was the smell of green lawns glistening with dew, and the trees, some white, some gray, steaming in the stillness.

And, finally, there was Josey Swann. For a long time after, Roger did not see him. Then, unexpectedly, he turned up in the fall. Roger went to visit him alone, because he knew that Julie would not have approved. She had written Swann off for good. . . .

Roger found Swann in a small apartment. He was living alone. He had a job as a night watchman in a chemical plant. He worked long hours, and slept most of the days.

He had no friends, and it was a mean life. Nevertheless, he looked better than Roger had ever remembered.

"Yeah, well, I took the cure." Swann laughed.

Roger assumed this meant that he had stopped the drugs and cut down on the gin, which was true, but Swann's cure involved more than conventional abstinence. It began back there when he'd gone cold turkey with a gun in his hand and Messrs Severson, Cassidy and Sax in his sights. He had set his sights higher. At least further. He seemed to be looking ahead, though to what he didn't specify.

For a time, at Roger's urging, the two spent afternoons together. Mostly they went out for beers, and knocked around the city streets. It had been the Christmas season which gave Roger the excuse of shopping to hang out with his friend.

Christmas, and Josey had nobody, but then he did not seem to care, and you couldn't feel sorry for him. At that time he had still been living in something of a different world. Roger best remembered him talking abstractly but articulately, and peering into old shop windows. He always had a graceful way of walking—fluid, casual.

During those days together Roger noted with some satisfaction that Josey had become much more open about himself. Once he even spoke of the war. Roger remembered the incident distinctly. They stood on a corner in the dying light of dusk. The wind had been whipping the brightly colored plastic wreaths that hung from the street lamps for the holidays. The war, Josey had said, looking up to the flapping bits of plastic holly, was neither a moral nor a political issue. The war was biblical, he said, and not just Vietnam but all of it. All of it, he said, was biblical.

Eventually, the days with Josey Swann came to an end. He left suddenly, with hardly a word, and in the dead of winter too. He did not say where he was going, but after a number of months Roger received a postcard from Paris. The card bore a picture of the Eiffel Tower, and Roger assumed that Josey had picked up the card in an airport, or a drugstore. It looked like that sort of thing. The typically wry message read: "All's well that ends well."

There was another card, this one from the south of France. The message was uncharacteristically fragile. "Getting on," it read. "My thoughts are with you."

Finally there was the photograph sent from Sweden: Josey standing on the steps of a library, wrapped in what must have been an expensive fur coat. He looked dark, but relatively happy.

All in all, these scraps, these photographs, these fragments of Roger's memory did little to put Josey Swann into any comfortable perspective. For Roger, it seemed that the man would always remain a little out of focus. But then, ambiguity was an essential part of Josey Swann. There was no denying it, Josey was a romantic figure. He had, in Roger's own words, the way about him.